Author Note

From Runaway to Pregnant Bride completes The Fairfax Brides trilogy.

His Mail-Order Bride tells the story of the eldest sister, Charlotte, who finds happiness with Thomas Greenwood, a strong, steady farmer. *The Bride Lottery* is about the middle sister, Miranda, who ends up married to Jamie Blackburn, a part-Cheyenne bounty hunter.

From Runaway to Pregnant Bride is the story of Annabel, the youngest sister, who longs to prove her independence. Disguised as a boy, she sets out to join her sisters in the West, but robbery and bad luck see her stranded in a New Mexico mining camp.

Clay Collier, orphaned son of tricksters and thieves, grew up with poverty and neglect and now scratches out a living from the earth. Not fooled by Annabel's disguise, he gives in to the attraction between them, but his fear for her safety and welfare drive them apart.

When writing this book I worried about repeating myself because there are so many parallels in the stories of the three sisters—they all flee from their Boston home to the West and end up penniless, in forced proximity with an attractive although reticent man. I worked hard to make each character and relationship different, and I hope you'll enjoy Annabel's story.

In the final chapters the sisters face their enemy, Cousin Gareth, and learn that everything is not always as it seems. Perhaps one day I'll get to write the story of Gareth Fairfax, and give him the love and happiness he deserves.

TATIANA MARCH

From Runaway to Pregnant Bride

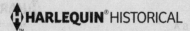
HARLEQUIN®HISTORICAL

ISBN-13: 978-0-373-29935-5

From Runaway to Pregnant Bride

Printed in U.S.A.

www.Harlequin.com

Before becoming a novelist, **Tatiana March** tried out various occupations—including being a chambermaid and an accountant. Now she loves writing Western historical romance. In the course of her research Tatiana has been detained by the United States border guards, had a skirmish with the Mexican army and stumbled upon a rattlesnake. This has not diminished her determination to create authentic settings for her stories.

Books by Tatiana March

Harlequin Historical Romance

The Fairfax Brides

His Mail-Order Bride
The Bride Lottery
From Runaway to Pregnant Bride

Harlequin Historical *Undone!* eBooks

The Virgin's Debt
Submit to the Warrior
Surrender to the Knight
The Drifter's Bride

Visit the Author Profile page at Harlequin.com.

Chapter One

Boston, Massachusetts, August 1889

Annabel Fairfax tore open the envelope the post office messenger had delivered and peeked at the document inside. A money order! A money order for two hundred dollars! Glancing around the shadowed hallway to make sure the servants were not spying on her, Annabel slipped the envelope into her skirt pocket and hurried upstairs to her bedroom.

Two hundred dollars meant freedom.

Four years ago, after their parents died in a boating accident and their greedy Cousin Gareth came to live with them, the three Fairfax sisters had become prisoners in their own home—Merlin's Leap, a gray stone mansion perched on a rocky headland just north of Boston.

Charlotte, the eldest, was the heiress, and Cousin Gareth had attempted to force her into marriage. Three months ago, Charlotte had escaped and was now living under an assumed name in Gold Crossing, Arizona Territory.

With Charlotte out of his clutches, Gareth had contrived to have her declared dead and Miranda, the middle sister, had been named as the heiress. Rather than fight Gareth's advances, Miranda also had chosen to flee from

Merlin's Leap, and was now on her way to join Charlotte in the Arizona Territory.

Cousin Gareth had set off in pursuit, leaving Annabel alone with the servants, and their laxness had allowed her to receive the money order. With Gareth gone, the household staff no longer bothered to intercept the mail, or to keep her locked up in the house, which had allowed Annabel to walk into the village and post a letter to Charlotte, alerting the eldest sister that she was officially dead and buried in a grave at Merlin's Leap.

Up in her bedroom, Annabel inspected the money order. The sender was Thomas Greenwood, the man whose mail-order bride Charlotte was pretending to be. The beneficiary was Miranda Fairfax, but Annabel was certain the local postmaster would let her cash in the document.

She grinned into the empty room. *Gold Crossing, here I come.* Not brazen enough to travel without a ticket, as her older sisters had done, she now had the funds to pay for her passage. And, with Cousin Gareth gone, she didn't even have to plot for an escape. She could simply walk out of the house, as bold as a captain on a ship.

The adventure of it! Annabel sat on the train, trying to take in everything at once—the scenery flashing by, the passengers sitting in their seats, the uniformed conductor strolling up and down the corridor.

The constant craning was making her hair unravel from beneath the flat cap she wore, and she hurried to shove the long, dark tresses out of sight. A threadbare wool coat and trousers completed her outfit. On her feet she wore leather boots, much too large, but two pairs of thick socks improved the fit.

Would she pass for a boy? Her skin was too smooth and her features too feminine, and the rough garments swamped her slender frame, but she hoped the disguise would make the journey safer for a young girl traveling alone.

In truth, she wasn't frightened, merely apprehensive. Her sisters liked to call her highly strung, but she was brave in her own way, almost as brave as Miranda, and no less determined than Charlotte. And everyone agreed she was the cleverest. It was merely that her emotions ran a bit closer to the surface, sometimes gushing out like water from a fountain.

On the bench beside her she had a canvas haversack, the kind sailors used. Annabel gave the bulky shape a pat with her hand, and in return she heard the reassuring clink of gold coins, hidden away in a secret compartment.

To start with, the postmaster had refused to let her cash in the money order, but she'd persuaded him by telling him that Miranda had suffered a mental collapse and the funds were required to pay for her care at a sanatorium.

Feeling the need to stretch her legs, Annabel slung the haversack over her shoulder and set off to visit the convenience at the far end of the car. Clumsy in her big boots, she trundled along the corridor.

The lock on the cubicle door showed red, indicating the convenience was occupied. Annabel waited, trying to look masculine. She dipped her chin, seeking to lower her voice in case someone addressed her and she would have to reply.

A minute passed, then another. Perhaps the cubicle was empty, the lock merely stuck on red. Annabel curled her fingers around the brass handle and twisted. The lock gave with a rattling sound, and the door sprang open.

Inside the cramped convenience stood a voluptuous young woman. Her gown was unlaced, the bodice folded out of the way. A plump baby suckled at her naked breast.

Fascinated at the vision of motherhood, Annabel stared. The woman stared back, a stunned expression on her face.

Without warning, the iron wheels bounced over a junction in the tracks. The woman gave a shriek of alarm. She teetered on her feet, nearly dropping the baby as she struggled to maintain her balance against the rocking of the train.

Darting into the convenience, Annabel gripped the woman by the front of her gown. "I've got you!" A few stitches ripped, but Annabel succeeded in holding the young mother upright until she had recovered her footing and could hold the baby securely to her breast.

Vaguely, Annabel noticed the train was slowing for a stop. The woman, a blonde with arched eyebrows, glowered at her rescuer. "Young man, unhand me this very instant."

Startled, Annabel released her grip. "I was only trying to——"

"Conductor!" the woman shouted. "Conductor!"

The conductor, a burly man with a moustache, sweat shining on his face, hurried over to them. By now, the woman had regained her composure and was using one hand to cover herself with the shawl she wore draped around her shoulders.

She gestured at Annabel with her chin. "This young man, this...*urchin*...forced the door on the convenience while I was inside, tending to my baby. He stared at my breasts and laid his hands on me, tearing my gown." The woman lowered her voice. "Pervert, and just a boy. What's the world coming to?"

Annabel shrank back a step. "I was only——"

"Is it true, young man?" the conductor boomed.

"I'm not..." Annabel glanced down at her clothing. *I'm not a boy.*

"Are you questioning me?" The woman's voice grew shrill. She glowered at the pair of them. "Are you suggesting that I invited this perverted young man to ogle at me and damage my gown?"

Annabel fisted her hands at her sides. Her eyes stung with the threat of tears. She'd been so proud of how well the journey was going…she'd only been trying to help…but how could she explain without giving her disguise away?

"I'm sorry," she muttered, only now remembering to lower the pitch of her voice. "I thought the convenience was vacant."

"Sorry is not good enough." The woman lifted her nose in the air and addressed the conductor. "I demand that you remove this young man from the train. He is a menace to the female passengers."

Not bothering to investigate the accusation, nor giving Annabel a chance to defend her actions, the conductor merely caught her by the scruff of her neck and shoved her along. "Let's be off with you, then."

Stiffening her legs, Annabel braced her boots against the floor to halt their progress. The conductor swore and jerked her up in the air. Annabel kicked with her feet and flailed with her fists, but the burly man dangled her at a distance and her blows failed to connect.

By now, the train had rolled to a stop. Behind them, passengers were crowding to the end of the car, waiting to alight. A man carrying a suitcase pushed past them and swung the door open. The conductor stepped forward and without ceremony flung Annabel down to the station platform.

She landed on all fours. The impact jarred her bones, nearly tearing her shoulders from their sockets. The skin on her palms scraped raw against the rough concrete surface. Gritting her teeth, blinking back tears, Annabel fought the pain. Only vaguely was she aware of the stream of passengers filing past her.

Behind her, the train doors slammed shut. Her knees and hands throbbed, but the shock of the impact was slowly fading away. Annabel lifted her head. At least her flat cap remained securely in place, protecting her disguise.

Carefully, she rolled over to a sitting position and inspected the abrasions on her palms. Through the holes in her ripped trousers, she could see her skinned knees. Around her, people bustled about, boots thudding, skirts swishing, voices calling out greetings.

As her senses sharpened, Annabel could feel the hot afternoon sun baking down on her, could smell the scents of smoke and steam from the train. Gradually it dawned on her that something was missing…*the weight that should be dangling from her shoulder.* Her haversack, with all her possessions! With her money!

Panic seized her, making her forget the aches and pains. Frantic, Annabel scrambled to her feet and rushed over to the train and climbed up the iron steps and jerked the door open. The burly conductor stood waiting inside. Annabel tried to dart past him, but he lifted one booted foot and placed it against her chest and pushed, sending her toppling back down to the platform.

"Didn't I tell you to get off?" he roared.

Sprawled on her rump, ignoring another wave of throbbing from the hard slam against the concrete platform, Annabel gave him an imploring look. "My bag… I must have dropped it when you threw me out…please…it is all I have…"

The conductor's angry scowl eased. "What kind of bag?"

"A canvas haversack. Brown. This big." She spread her hands wide.

"I'll look." He turned on his polished boots and strode out of sight into the corridor. Annabel waited. It was only a few steps back to where he had grabbed her. He'd find her haversack…unless one of the alighting passengers had taken it!

Alarmed by the idea, Annabel surveyed the platform. The crowd had thinned. She could see three disreputable-looking men—probably pickpockets—loitering against the wall of the station building. A shoeshine boy sat on a wooden box, and a woman in a gray dress was tidying up a display of fruit laid out on a trestle table.

The conductor reappeared at the door. "There's no bag."

"Please. Look again. Maybe it fell when I tried to help the lady. Maybe it is inside the convenience."

Once more, the door to the railroad car flung shut. Annabel waited, too petrified to move, too petrified to do anything but stare at the closed door, her mind frozen in denial. The engine blew its whistle. A plume of steam rose in the air. The iron wheels screeched, and the train jerked into motion.

Desperation jolted Annabel back into life. She jumped to her feet and rushed over to the edge of the platform. She tried to grip the handrail by the steps, but the train was accelerating too fast for her to attempt boarding.

"My bag! My bag! Help!" Shouting, she ran alongside the train as it pulled away, leaving the station behind. Something appeared in an open window. A bundle of brown canvas. Her bag! She could see a pair of big hands clutching it in the air, the brass buttons at the end of the conductor's sleeves glinting in the sun.

Relief poured through Annabel. She halted at the edge of the platform and watched as the conductor tossed her haversack out of the window. The bag fell onto the tracks, but the shoulder strap became tangled in the iron wheels.

With each revolution, the bag flung up into the air and smashed down to the rails again.

Aghast, Annabel stared as the sturdy fabric tore into shreds. Clothing spilled out onto the tracks. Her food parcel unraveled, sending a loaf of bread rolling along. And then there was a flash of gold as a coin spun out…and another…and another…

Behind her, Annabel could hear the clatter of running feet. A man hurried past her and jumped down to the tracks. A second man followed, and then a third. The three ruffians who had been loitering by the station wall!

Annabel held her breath, hope and fear fighting within her as she watched the men race along the tracks, jumping from sleeper to sleeper. When they reached the remains of her scattered belongings they halted and began dipping down, in a rootling motion that resembled chickens pecking at the ground.

"Thank you," Annabel shouted and waved her arms.

One of the men straightened to look at her. "How many?"

"Nineteen!" she called back.

The men resumed their search and then conferred, counting the coins in their open palms. Satisfied, they glanced back at her once more and waved a casual farewell before cutting across the tracks and running off into the fields. Annabel watched them shrink in her sights and finally vanish between the farm buildings in the distance.

"You was a fool to tell them how many."

"What?" Stifling a sob, Annabel whirled toward the voice.

It was the shoeshine boy. Around twelve, thin and pale, he had wispy brown hair and alert gray eyes. He lifted his arm and brushed a lock of hair out of his eyes. In his other hand he carried a wooden box filled with brushes and polishes.

"You was stupid to tell them how many. If you said seventeen, they might have left a couple of coins behind. Now they kept looking until they had them all."

Annabel sniffled and gave a forlorn nod, unable to fault the logic.

"Where was you going?" the boy asked.

"The Arizona Territory."

"Blimey. That's a fair piece away." Curious, he studied her. "You got any money left?"

"Three dollars and change. It's all I have left. I bought a ticket to New York City. And I bought some food." A sob broke free. "The rest of the money was in my bag."

"It was a fool thing to carry the money in your bag."

"The gold eagles were heavy. I feared my pocket would tear."

"Ain't you got a poke?"

"A poke?"

"Like this." The boy swept a glance up and down the platform to check for privacy, then pulled out a leather tube hanging on a cord around his neck. Quickly, he dropped the leather tube back inside his faded shirt.

"I only had a purse," Annabel said. "And I couldn't take it because—"

The boy snorted. "You'll not fool no one. You walk like a girl, and you were yelling like a girl, and your hair is about to tumble down from beneath your cap." He gave her another assessing look. "How old are you anyway?"

"Eighteen."

The boy grinned. "A bit skinny for eighteen, ain't you?"

"I've bound…" Color flared up to Annabel's cheeks. She made a vague gesture at her chest, to indicate where she had bound her breasts with a strip of linen cloth to flatten her feminine curves.

"What's your name?" the boy asked.

"An…drew."

The boy shook his head. "There you go again. You almost came up with a girl's name. What is it anyway? Ann? Amanda? Amy?"

"Annabel."

"Annabel. That's a fancy name. I guess you'll be gentry, the way you talk and that milky-white skin of yours."

Annabel nodded. "Papa was a sea captain. I grew up in a mansion, but I am an orphan now, and I have no money, in case you are planning to swindle me."

The boy grinned again. "Hardly worth it for three dollars and change." He jerked his head toward the station house. "Let's get out of the sun for a bit. There's another train due in an hour. I'll take you home with me. My sister likes nobs."

Chapter Two

The home where Colin took Annabel was a lean-to shack in a New York City freight yard. Twilight was falling when they got there. Annabel plodded along in her heavy boots, grateful for the evening cool that eased the sultry August heat.

A stray dog growled at them from behind a pile of empty packing crates and then scurried away again. Unfamiliar smells floated in the air—rotting vegetables, engine grease, acrid chemical odors, all against the backdrop of coal smoke.

Colin pulled the door to the shack open without knocking. "Hi, Liza," he called out. "Brought you a visitor. A lady."

Caution in her step, Annabel followed Colin inside. He'd not said much about his sister, except that she was sixteen and worked in a tavern because her full figure no longer allowed her to masquerade as a shoeshine boy.

While they'd been waiting for the train, Colin had dozed off, and once they'd boarded the express service to New York City, he'd introduced Annabel to the conductor as his apprentice, and they'd become too busy for conversation.

Normally reserved, Annabel had found a new boldness in the anonymity of her disguise as a street urchin. It seemed as if the social constraints that applied to gently bred young ladies had suddenly ceased to apply.

In the first-class car, Colin had demonstrated how to tout for business by quietly moving up and down the corridor and offering his services. Shouting was not allowed. When they got a customer, Annabel knelt between the benches. After spreading polish on the shoes or boots, she used a pair of stiff boar brushes, one in each hand, to buff the leather into a mirror shine while Colin supervised.

By the time they reached New York City, her hands, already tender from the fall, were stained with polish, and her arms ached from the effort of wielding the brushes, but she had earned her first dollar as a shoeshine boy.

There were no windows in the shack, but the low evening sunshine filtered in between the planks that formed the walls. In the muted light, Annabel saw a tall, shapely girl bent over a pot simmering on an ancient metal stove.

The girl turned around. "Pleased to make your acquaintance."

She moved forward, one hand held out. Annabel took it. The palm was work roughened and the girl's blue gown was a mended hand-me-down, but her fair hair was arranged in a neat upsweep and her clothing freshly laundered.

"The pleasure is all mine," Annabel replied.

She released the girl's hand and surveyed the cabin. Everything was painstakingly clean and tidy. A sleeping platform, decorated with a few embroidered cushions, took up half the space. On the other side, a packing crate with a cloth spread over it served as a table, with two smaller packing crates as seats.

"Is it true, what Colin said?" the girl asked. "Are you a lady?"

"Yes." Annabel felt oddly ill at ease.

"You are welcome to share everything we have, as long as you like, but I have one condition. You must correct my speech and manner. I want to learn how to behave like a lady."

"Why should that be important?" Annabel said gently. "Is it not more important to be a good person? And it is clear to me that both you and your brother are."

The girl's gray eyes met hers with a disquietingly direct gaze. "You'd be surprised. Some people…*some men*…believe that if you sound like a streetwalker, then you must be one."

Compassion brought the sting of tears to Annabel's eyes. Her sisters worried about her sentimental nature, but sometimes emotions simply welled up inside her. And now, the understanding of how she had taken for granted her privileged life, how someone might so fervently aspire to what she had received as a birthright, tore at her tender heart.

"Of course," she replied. "I'll teach you all I can."

Liza smiled. "In return, I'll teach you how to look like a boy."

"Shoeshine! Shoeshine!"

Annabel made her way down the corridor in the second-class car on the train along the Southern Pacific Railroad. Her hair was pinned out of sight beneath a bowler hat. A touch of boot black shadowed her cheeks and her upper lip. She walked with a swagger, shoulders hunched, chin thrust forward. She did not smile.

As she strode along, she studied the clothing and the footwear of the passengers, to identify the most likely customers. When she spotted a man in a neatly pressed broadcloth suit with dust on his boots, she halted at the end of the row.

"Sir," she said, holding up her wooden box. "Polish your boots for two bits."

The man, around forty, clean-shaven, contemplated her for a moment, then glanced down at his boots. Looking up again, he nodded at her and shuffled his feet forward. Annabel knelt in front of him. Swiftly, she applied a coat of polish and wielded the brushes. A final buff with a linen cloth added to the shine.

She got to her feet and put out her hand. The man dropped a quarter in her palm. Annabel studied the coin, then leveled her gaze at the client. "If a gentleman is pleased with the result, he usually gives me four bits."

The man's eyebrows went up, but he dug in his pocket again and passed her another quarter. Annabel thanked him and hurried off on her way. Bitter experience had taught her not to ask for the extra money until the initial payment was safely in her hand.

"Shoeshine. Shoeshine."

For two weeks, she had stayed with Colin and Liza in their freight yard shack, becoming skilled in her new trade. It had been a revelation to learn that if she boarded a train and introduced herself to the conductor—Andrew Fairfield, was her name—they allowed her to travel without a ticket, as long as she obeyed their rules and offered to polish their shoes for free.

By the end of the second week, she had earned enough money to buy her own brushes and polishes, and had taken an emotional farewell from Liza and Colin. One day, she hoped to reward them for their kindness, but she did not wish to raise any false hopes by telling them that she came from wealth.

"Shoeshine! Shoeshine!"

The train was slowing for a stop. Annabel used the lack of speed to cross over the coupling to the next car.

Sometimes men had their boots polished just to break the tedium of the journey, but she enjoyed the traveling, even the endless monotony of the prairie they had left behind two days ago. As the scenery changed, it pleased Annabel to think that not long ago her sisters had looked upon the same grass-covered plateau, the same rolling hills, the same high-peaked mountains.

"Shoeshine. Shoe—"

The word died on her lips as her gaze fell on a sun-tanned man in his early thirties. Dressed like a dandy, he had a lean, muscled body. He looked just like Cousin Gareth had once been, before drinking and gambling ruined him, turning him from a laughing boy who did magic tricks into a bitter, brooding man.

As she stared, spellbound, the man gestured with his hand and leaned back in his seat, stretching out his feet. Annabel edged over and sank to her knees. Her heart was beating in a wild cadence, her hands shaking so hard she struggled to unclip the lid on a tin of polish.

It's a coincidence, she told herself. *Everyone has a double.*

She spread the wax over the man's hand-tooled Montana boots and started brushing. Anyway, she reminded herself, Cousin Gareth had gone off to chase after Miranda, who'd left Merlin's Leap almost two months ago. It would make no sense for him only now to be on his way to Gold Crossing.

"There is something exceedingly familiar about you," the man said. "I get an image in my head, but it is of a girl with your features."

Annabel lowered the pitch of her voice. "Girl, huh? If I was the gun-carrying kind, I might call you out on that."

"I meant no offense."

Head bent low, Annabel moved from the right foot to

the left. Her mouth felt dry. The man had spoken with Gareth's voice. She kept silent, working as fast as she could. The train had come to a stop now, but from her kneeling position Annabel couldn't see if it was for a town, or just a water tower in the middle of nowhere.

"What is your name, young man?"

Ignoring the question, Annabel flung her brushes back into the wooden box with a clatter and straightened, omitting the final polish with a linen cloth. She put out her hand. "That'll be two bits."

The man grabbed the walking stick that had been leaning against the end of the bench. A chill ran through Annabel. It was Cousin Gareth's walking stick, with a silver handle shaped like the head of a wolf. She nearly swooned. It had to be him. Somehow, Cousin Gareth had transformed into this fit, healthy stranger, but he had not recognized her...*yet.*

The man banged the walking stick against the floor of the railroad car, making a hollow booming sound. "Your name, young man," he demanded to know.

Deepening her voice, hiding beneath her bowler hat, Annabel muttered, "Andrew Fairfield."

"Andrew?" The man frowned and shook his head, as if to clear the veil of mist inside his mind. "Andrew... Andrew... Ann..." His blue eyes widened. "Annabel! I have a memory of a girl called Annabel who looks just like you."

Panic took hold of Annabel and she bolted. Behind her, she could hear the clatter of the expensive boots as Cousin Gareth surged to his feet and set off in chase.

"Wait," he shouted. "I have questions for you."

Clutching her box, for it was her ticket for transport, Annabel hurtled along the corridor. People turned to stare at her, startled out of their books and magazines, but they were no more than a blur in her sights. She careened into a man who had risen from his seat. Barely slowing, she dodged past him. Beneath her feet she could feel the train jerking into motion and knew they were about to set off again.

Cousin Gareth was yelling something, but Annabel couldn't make out the words. With one hand, she touched the small lump of the leather poke of coins beneath her shirt. She had only twelve dollars—most of what she made shining shoes went on food—but at least her meager funds were secure.

With a final dash, Annabel burst out through the door at the rear of the car, onto the small platform at the end of the train. They were gathering speed now. What should she do? She had no way of telling if Cousin Gareth knew about Gold Crossing, had figured out Charlotte was hiding there. If Miranda had shaken him from her trail, how far into the journey had that been?

Annabel stared at the flat desert dotted with knee-high scrub. She had three days of traveling left, but she couldn't risk leading Cousin Gareth to her sisters—could not take the chance that he would follow her if she stayed on the train.

With a swing of her arm, Annabel threw her wooden box down to the side of the tracks. The ground was hurtling past now. She said a quick prayer and jumped. On the impact her legs gave and she rolled along the hard desert floor.

There was no crunch of breaking bones, only a dull ache down her side. She scrambled to her feet and dusted her cotton shirt and mended wool trousers. The train was shrinking in the distance. Cousin Gareth emerged onto the platform at the end, but by now the speed of the train was too great for him to jump down after her.

"Who am I?" he yelled. "I have no memory."

No memory? Annabel's brows drew into a puzzled frown.

"Do you know me?" Cousin Gareth shouted. The wind tossed his words around the desert, and then the train vanished into the horizon, with only a puff of steam in the air and the slight vibration of the iron rails to mark its passing.

Annabel did a quick survey of her surroundings. She could see for miles around, and the only construction was the water tower fifty yards back. She caught a flash of movement and strained her eyes. In the shade of the water tower stood a mule, with parcels loaded on its back. And beside the mule stood a big buckskin saddle horse. She caught another flash of movement. A man had vaulted into the saddle.

"Wait!" Annabel yelled and set off running.

The desert gravel that had appeared so flat was full of holes to trip her up. The sun beat down on her. The horse and mule stood still, but she dared not slow down her pace, in case the stranger wouldn't wait. By the time she reached him, her lungs were straining and perspiration ran in rivulets down her skin beneath her clothing.

It was cooler in the shade of the water tower, the air humid from spills evaporating in the heat. Annabel looked up at the man on the horse. Against the bright sunlight, he was little more than a silhouette, but she could tell he was young, perhaps in his late twenties.

He wore a fringed leather coat and faded denim pants and tall boots and a black, flat-crowned hat and a gun belt strapped around his hips. He had brown hair that curled over his collar, beard stubble several days old, and narrow eyes that measured her without a hint of warmth in them.

"What is this place?" she asked.

"It's nowhere." He had a rough, gravelly voice.

"Where is the nearest town?"

"Dona Ana. Thirty miles thataway." He pointed to the south.

"Phoenix? Which way is Phoenix?"

"Four hundred miles thataway." He pointed to the west.

"When will the next train be?"

"Don't rightly know. Same time tomorrow, I guess."

"But you must know. You came to meet the train."

The man shook his head. "I came to collect the freight a conductor had unloaded here. Could have been yesterday. The day before. A week ago. I don't know."

"Is there anything closer than Dona Ana? An army post?"

He shook his head again. "Fort Selden closed years ago. And if you want the train, Dona Ana is no good. The train goes through Las Cruces. That's another seven miles south." He raked a glance over her. "Ain't got no water?"

"No," Annabel replied, her panic escalating. The stranger was the only one who could help her, but he seemed wholly unconcerned with her plight.

The man untied a canteen hanging from his saddle and leaned down to hold it out to her. "Leave it in the mailbox."

Clutching the canteen with both hands, Annabel turned to look where he was pointing. By one of the timber posts holding up the water tank she could see a long wooden box with a chain and padlock anchoring it to the structure.

"It's a coffin!" she blurted out.

"It will be one day," the man replied. "Now it's a mailbox." He swept another glance up and down her. "Got no food?"

"No!" Desperation edged her tone.

He bent to dig in a saddlebag, handed down a small parcel. Annabel could smell the pungent odor of jerked meat.

"Got no gun?" the man asked.

She replied through a tightened throat. "No."

The man shifted his wide shoulders. "Sorry. Got no spare. Watch out for the rattlers." He wheeled the buckskin around. "Stay out of the sun."

And then he tugged at the lead rope of the pack mule and kicked his horse into a trot and headed out toward the west, not sparing her another look. A sense of utter loneliness engulfed Annabel, bringing back stark memories of the despair and confusion she'd felt after her parents died.

"Wait!" she yelled and ran after him. "Don't leave me here!"

But the man rode on without looking back.

Chapter Three

Clay Collier made it a mile before he turned around. Reining to a halt, he stepped down from the saddle to picket the pack mule next to a clump of coarse grass, and then he remounted and pointed the buckskin to retrace his steps.

As he rode back to the railroad, Clay cursed himself for a fool. He had a poor record in looking after scrawny kids, and he had no wish to add to it. He'd been minding his own business—he always did—but a man didn't live long in the West if he failed to pay attention to his surroundings.

He'd seen the kid tumble down from the train as it pulled away. And then he'd seen the man in fancy duds chasing after the kid, yelling something. The wind had tossed away the words, but most likely the kid had been caught stealing.

Clay slowed his pace as he approached the water tower. The kid was sitting on the ground, hugging his knees, head bent. When the thud of hooves alerted him, the kid bounced up to his feet and waited for the horse and rider to get closer.

Clay shook his head in dismay at the forlorn sight. As scrawny kids went, this one was scrawnier than most. The threadbare shirt hung limp over a pair of narrow shoulders. The trousers, patched at the knee, stayed up only with a leather belt drawn tight. Beneath the battered bowler hat, the kid had a white, innocent face and the biggest amber eyes Clay had ever seen on a scrawny kid.

Fourteen, he guessed, and still wet behind the ears. At fourteen, Clay himself had been a man, capable of doing a man's job.

He brought the buckskin to a halt in a cloud of dust, adjusted the brim of his hat and looked down at the kid. The hope and relief and gratitude stamped on that innocent face made something twist inside Clay. Damn that soft streak of his. Life would be simpler without it.

"Here's the choice," he told the kid. "You can stay here and wait for the train. Likely as not there'll be one tomorrow, or the day after. You have water and food and shade. You'll be fine. If coyotes bother you at night, you can hide in the coffin."

Clay paused, fought one final battle with himself and lost.

"Or you can come with me. In a month or so I'll pick up another delivery and I'll bring you back and wait with you until the train comes. If you come with me, you gotta work, mind you. Mr. Hicks, who owns the mine, hates slackers."

One more time, Clay raked an assessing glance over the slender frame hidden beneath the baggy clothing. "In a mine, the only use for scrawny kids like you is to crawl into narrow passages. If you panic about feeling trapped, don't come."

The kid said nothing, merely passed back the canteen and the parcel of jerky and waited for Clay to put them away. Then he held up both arms, as though asking for salvation. The sensitive mouth was quivering. Clay reached down a hand and kicked one foot out of a stirrup. In another second the kid would burst into tears, and he did not want to watch.

"I assume you can ride," he said.

"Only side—" Panic flared in those big amber eyes. The kid made a visible effort to pull himself together and spoke in a deeper voice. "I mean, I am used to mounting on the other side."

Clay assessed the situation, nodded his understanding and wheeled the buckskin around. Most men preferred mounting with their left foot in the stirrup. At least there was something normal about the kid.

"Climb aboard." Clay moved the bridle reins to his right hand so he could use his left to swing the kid behind him. A tiny hand slotted into his. Clay noticed the smooth skin, unused to hard work. He boosted up the kid. He was so light Clay nearly flung him all the way over the horse's back and down the other side.

"Ready?" he said when the kid had settled down.

"Ready," the kid replied.

Clay could hear a hint of weeping in the muttered word. It gave him an odd, uneasy feeling when the kid wriggled to get comfortable against him, cramming into the saddle instead of sitting behind the cantle, so that their bodies pressed close together.

He kicked the buckskin into a gallop, taking his frustration out with speed. The kid wrapped his arms around his waist and clung tight. The tension inside Clay ratcheted up another notch.

A bad idea, he told himself. It was always a bad idea to give in to the soft streak inside him. A wiser man would have learned from experience to leave scrawny kids to their fate, instead of picking them up and trying to protect them.

He'd come back for her!

Annabel clung to the taciturn stranger, tears of relief

running down her face. She'd been so afraid. She'd been sitting in the shade of the water tower, blaming herself for everything that had gone wrong.

When the money was stolen, she ought to have telegraphed Charlotte in Gold Crossing, but she'd been ashamed for her carelessness. And she knew nothing about the man to whom Charlotte was pretending to be married. Two hundred dollars might be a fortune to Thomas Greenwood, and she didn't want to add to his burden by confessing she'd lost it.

And it hadn't seemed to matter if she earned her passage as a shoeshine boy instead of buying a ticket. If anything, after two weeks of instruction from Colin and Liza, she was better equipped to take care of herself during the journey.

But it had been a mistake to run from Cousin Gareth. She should have brazened it out, pretended not to know what he was talking about. He'd appeared confused, unsure of himself. His wind-whipped cry echoed in her mind.

Who am I? I have no memory! Do you know me?

Now that she thought of it, there'd been a scar on his forehead. Cousin Gareth must have received a blow to his head and be suffering from amnesia. He'd not truly recognized her. He'd merely been fumbling in his mind for fragments of recollection. By fleeing, she had alerted him to the truth.

And now, he might come after her. He could get off in Las Cruces, less than forty miles away, and take a train coming the other way. He might even have a horse in the freight car and persuade the train to stop. He could be back before the day was out, and she'd been like a sitting duck beneath the water tower.

But the stranger had come back for her. Annabel pressed her face to the buckskin coat that covered the man's back.

She could smell leather and dust and wood smoke on him, could feel the rock-hard muscles on his belly beneath her clinging arms,

A tension sparked inside her. Never before had she felt a man's body so close to hers. Before their parents died, she'd been too young to attend social engagements, and for the past four years Cousin Gareth had kept her imprisoned at Merlin's Leap.

Despite his reticent manner, her rescuer was young and handsome, the kind of man a girl might dream about. Annabel let his features form in her mind. Curly brown hair, hollowed cheeks, straight nose, sharply angled jaw, eyes narrowed in suspicion.

His surliness reminded her of the sailors she'd met from Papa's ships, but on many occasions she'd discovered a streak of kindness beneath their gruff exterior. She hoped the stranger might be the same, however why was it that men felt compelled to hide their compassion, as if it eroded their masculinity instead of emphasizing it?

The thudding of the horse's hooves beneath them altered rhythm. They were slowing down. Annabel eased her hold around the stranger's waist and peeked past his shoulder. Ahead, the pack mule was grazing on stunted vegetation.

They came to an abrupt halt. The man twisted around in the saddle, curled one powerful arm about her and swept her down to her feet. "You'll ride the mule."

For an instant, Annabel stood still, staring up at the rugged features of her rescuer. Regret filled her at the loss of his warmth and strength and the sense of safety she'd felt huddled up against him.

"We ain't got all day," he said. "Get on the mule."

"The mule?" Jolted out of her thoughts, Annabel took a cautious step toward the animal. The mule lifted its head and bared its teeth. Parcels and bundles filled the pack saddle, leaving no room for a rider. She turned to the stranger. "Can't we ride double on the horse? I don't weigh much."

If anything, his expression grew even starker. "You cling like a flea."

"I…" Her mouth pursed at the cutting remark, but she fought back. "And you're no softer than a rock."

"Good," he said. "Then we'll both be more comfortable if you ride the mule."

He vaulted down from the saddle, went to the mule and rearranged the load to create a space for her. Turning to face her again, he studied her in that disconcerting manner he had. His gaze lingered on her features a moment longer. He started to say something, then shrugged his shoulders as if deciding it didn't matter.

"I'll boost you up," he told her. Annabel stood and waited. At Merlin's Leap, if there was no mounting block for her to use, the grooms laced their hands together to create a step.

The stranger made no effort to link his hands to form a step. He merely stood in silence, then gave a huff of frustration. Bending at the waist, he placed one hand against her midriff, the other hand beneath her rump and shoved, tossing her up like a sack of grain. The mule bucked. Annabel flung up in the air, but somehow, as if by miracle, she landed astride between the packages.

"Let's go," the man said.

In a blur, he was up on the buckskin and on his way. Alarmed at the prospect of being left behind, Annabel kicked her heels into the flanks of the mule and started bouncing along.

They rode at a steady lope through the dusty desert plateau, stopping only to let the animals rest and drink every now and then. When they came to a river crossing, they refilled their canteens. At another rest stop, the stranger retreated a few paces. Turning his back, he unbuckled his belt and set to work with the buttons on his fly.

"I've got to go, too," Annabel mumbled and darted off in the other direction.

The man glanced over his shoulder. "Mind the rattlers."

Annabel's heart was pounding while she took care of her needs behind a creosote bush. Pretending to be a boy would turn out to be a lot more complicated if she had to share close living quarters with a man, especially with a young, attractive one.

The kid had been crying. Probably had no idea the tear tracks on his dusty face gave him away. When Clay had first noticed the evidence of weeping, he'd tried to think of something reassuring to say, but words had failed him, just like they always did. He didn't like lying, and in most cases reassurances were nothing but lies, or at best over-optimistic guesses.

The kid found a rock to stand on and mounted on the mule. It seemed to be a point of pride for the kid to climb into the saddle unassisted. Clay vaulted on the buckskin, but instead of setting off he idled closer to the mule.

"What's your name, kid?"

"Andrew Fairfield."

"I'm Clay Collier. The man who owns the claim is Mr. Hicks. He can be a bad-tempered devil, but he is generally fair, and he doesn't go in for beatings."

"How many men does he employ?"

His brows went up. "How many men?" he said with a hint of mockery. "What do you think he owns, the Vulture Mining Company?"

From the blank look on the kid's face, Clay surmised the kid had never heard of the richest gold and silver deposit in the southwestern territories.

"You said it's a mine." The kid gave him a belliger-
ent scowl.

"Out here, any shovel hole in the ground is called a
mine. Where're you from, kid?"

"Bos—New York City."

"Well, kid from New York City, this mine employs me,
and now you."

The kid lifted his chin and spoke with a grave ear-
nestness. "I will work for my keep. I am grateful for the
opportunity."

"Ain't those fancy words. You must have some schooling, kid." Clay gave him an encouraging nod. "Forget what
I said about crawling into holes. Swinging a shovel and
a pickaxe is just what you need. Get some meat on your
bones."

Clay took another second to make sure the kid was
safely mounted on the mule before he sent the buckskin
into an easy trot, satisfied that the kid didn't seem quite
so scared anymore. The familiar feelings of protectiveness surged inside him, mixed with memories of grief
and guilt. He quashed the flash of regret. It would be for
only a month. Surely, he'd manage to keep the kid safe
that long, and could send him off along his way in better
shape than he'd arrived.

The sun sank behind the hills. Twilight fell. As they
gained altitude, the sagebrush gave way to pine forests.
Gradually, the scenery grew rugged, with deep ravines
cutting across outcroppings of gray rock.

Annabel concentrated on staying on the mule while her
rescuer led the animal by the rope. Her buttocks hurt from
bouncing on the pack saddle. Her stomach growled with
hunger. Dust clogged her throat. But she dared not sug-

gest that they stop for a rest, for Clay Collier might have little sympathy for weakness.

When they finally pulled to a halt, darkness blanketed the landscape. The air had turned chilly, making Annabel shiver in her thin cotton shirt and threadbare wool trousers.

Wearily, she observed her surroundings. They were in a clearing of some sort. Ahead, she could see a big, burly man looming in the light of a storm lantern he held high in the air.

Behind the man, shadows played on a solid wall of gray rock. A wooden canopy with a primitive kitchen beneath it huddled against the cliffs. To the left of the canopy, a bonfire burned, illuminating what looked like a cavernous stone overhang.

"I was worried," the big man said. "Thought you might not make it before the storm breaks."

"Pushed it hard," Clay replied. "Brought you another worker. A kid from New York City. Got off the train at the water tower and was left stranded. I'll take him back next month."

The man stepped closer, lifting the storm lantern higher. The light fell on his features. Between the brim of his hat and the thick black beard Annabel could see a hooked nose and a pair of shrewd dark eyes.

"I'm a good worker, sir." She deepened her voice. "I'll earn my keep."

The man studied her in the light of the lantern. "Polite, too," he said. "I have nothing against a kid. It's women I can't abide."

He turned his attention to Clay and questioned him about the delivery. Annabel slid down from the pack mule, alarmed by the man's blunt words. In silence, she waited while the burly mine owner went to hang the storm lantern on a hook beneath the kitchen canopy. He returned to take the mule by the rope and led the animal to the open cavern, where he began to strip away the load.

Clay had dismounted and was moving about in the darkness. Annabel could hear water sloshing and the clang of metal, perhaps a bucket being set down on the ground, and then slurping sounds as the buckskin lowered its head and drank.

In the yellow glow of the storm lantern and the flickering flames of the bonfire, the men and animals formed eerie shadows, appearing as insubstantial as ghosts as they went about their business, appearing to have forgotten all about her.

Driven by hunger pangs, Annabel edged toward the kitchen canopy. There was a table, with four log stumps as stools, a work counter with shelves above, and a sheet metal stove, similar to the one she'd learned to use while staying with Liza and Colin in their freight yard shack.

On the stove stood a cast-iron pot. Annabel touched one soot-covered side. Still warm. She leaned closer and inhaled the succulent smells. Rummaging on the table, she found a spoon and ran her fingers over the surface to make sure it was reasonably clean before she dipped the spoon into the thick stew and ate in greedy mouthfuls.

Behind her came the thud of footsteps. Annabel spun around, feeling like a child caught at the cookie jar. Clay said nothing, merely reached over to a shelf for a tin plate and filled it with a wooden ladle he took down from a peg.

He picked out a metal spoon from a box on the counter and sat down at the table to eat. "There's cold water to wash." He jerked his chin toward a wooden barrel on the ground outside the kitchen canopy. "We sleep under the rock overhang," he added. "I'll find you a blanket."

Shivering with cold, Annabel hugged her body with her arms. She could feel the humidity in the air, could hear the wind gathering force. "Mr. Hicks said something about a storm," she commented. "Will it rain?"

"Like the angels are tipping buckets over us."

Clay took another mouthful, gestured with his spoon. "Go wash your face. I'll fix you a bed." His eyes lingered on her. "Got no coat?"

Annabel shook her head. "I left it on the train."

She resisted the urge to touch the money poke hanging around her neck. Instead, she pulled out the tails of her shirt and unfastened the canvas pouch tied around her waist and swung it from her fingers. "I have my own soap."

"Your own soap, huh? Ain't you a real gent?" Clay lowered his gaze and focused on his meal.

Annabel went to the water barrel, found an enamel bowl and a ladle propped against the side and scooped water into the bowl. A mirror fragment hung on a piece of rawhide string from a nail hammered into the canopy post. In the dim light Annabel caught her reflection. Embarrassment broke through her fatigue as she noticed the tear tracks on her dusty skin and knew Clay Collier must have noticed them, too.

She scrubbed her face clean, dried her skin with the tails of her shirt. By the time she'd finished, Clay was waiting beside her with the storm lantern. He guided her to the overhang, where a blanket had been spread out on the hard-baked earth.

"You can use your boots for a pillow."

Annabel glanced around while Clay put away the lantern. Another blanket lay next to hers, and farther away Mr. Hicks was already stretched out and snoring, a hat covering his face. The fire had burned down to coals. The mule and packhorse filled the other end of the cavernous overhang.

"Will someone stand guard?" she asked.

"No need." Clay stretched out, unbuckled his gun belt

but kept his boots on. "The buckskin will hear if anything comes. Wolves don't stray this far south, and we've had no trouble from bears. Go to sleep." He rolled over, turning his back on her. A minute later, Annabel could hear the sound of his even breathing.

Chapter Four

~~~~~

Clay woke to a crack of thunder. Lightning flared, throwing the pine forest higher up on the hillside into a stark relief that made him think of fingers pointing toward the sky. An instant later, darkness closed around him again, but his mind clung to the image of a small shape sitting on the ground near the edge of the overhang.

He waited for another flare of lighting. When it came, he knew his eyes hadn't deceived him. He tossed his blanket aside and rolled to his feet, as agile as a mountain cat. Instead of strapping on his gun belt, he pushed the heavy Walker Colt into his waistband and eased over to the kid.

He dropped down to his haunches. "There's no need to be scared, kid. It's just a storm, and the ground slopes away. When the rain comes, the cavern will stay dry."

"I'm not scared." The kid's voice was dreamy. "I love thunderstorms. It is different here. At home, you can hear the fury of the ocean and smell the salt spray. The seagulls screech in warning. A storm can mean death to a sailor."

Clay listened, fascinated. Years ago, he used to carry around a book of poetry he liked to read from, but he had never heard anyone talk like that.

The kid went on, "Here the entire nature participates in

the storm, like an orchestra playing a symphony. Thunder roars. Lightning cracks. The wind wails in the trees and the cliffs echo it back, multiplying the sound."

Clay nodded in the darkness and spoke softly. "When the rain comes, it will add a drumbeat. Sometimes the water cascades down the cliffs so hard you can hear the rattle of pebbles as they roll along."

Lightning was almost constant now. He could see the kid's face, in quick snatches as the darkness broke. The delicate features drew his eyes. He liked looking at the kid, although he struggled to understand why. Maybe it reminded him of Lee and Billy, the other two kids he had tried to rescue in the past. Those memories were painful, but he found that looking at the kid gave him pleasure.

"I shouldn't really like storms," the kid said. "A storm took my parents. They drowned when their boat capsized. My father was a seaman."

Clay nodded. His eyes searched the darkness, waiting for another flare of lightning, waiting for another glimpse of the kid. "I know what you mean," he said quietly. "Sometimes a man can like something without understanding why."

The storm passed overnight, and Annabel awoke to a bright dawn. With caution, she surveyed the cavern. The men were gone, their bedrolls and blankets neatly folded on a natural rock shelf by the entrance. At the opposite end, where the animals had sheltered, the stone roof sloped down, and in the far corner she could see a stack of equipment partly covered by an oilcloth tarpaulin.

Satisfied no one was watching, Annabel scrambled to her feet. The aches and pains from the tumble from the train made her wince. She patted her bowler hat, to make sure it remained securely in place, then ran her fingers beneath the brim, to tuck back out of sight any strands of hair that might have escaped. Next, she stamped her feet into the big boots, folded away her blanket and walked over to stack it with the others.

Voices came from the kitchen. Taking a deep breath, Annabel emerged out into the sunshine and set off along the path. The ground steamed in the morning heat, but the air felt cool and fresh after the storm. Mixed in with the scents of mud and wet leaves she detected the tempting aroma of coffee.

Under the timber canopy, Mr. Hicks was bustling by the stove and Clay was seated at the table, eating breakfast. His head was bent, his attention on the food. Annabel slowed her pace to study him. He was wearing a hat, but she could see curly brown hair peeking out beneath the brim, and lean, stubble-covered cheeks. His wide mouth pursed as he chewed each mouthful.

He must have heard her footsteps, for he looked up. Their eyes met, and her breath caught with the sudden jolt. She'd seen handsome men on the train—men who cared about their looks were more likely to have their shoes or boots polished—but none of them had affected her in the same way as Clay did.

A recollection flooded her mind of how it had felt to ride double with him, her body pressed against his. She'd worried about being stranded in the mining camp because it would postpone her reunion with her sisters, but now she welcomed the delay, for it would allow her an opportunity to get to know her rescuer.

"Good morning, gentlemen," she called out from a distance.

"Ain't that polite," Mr. Hicks replied. "You got breeding, kid."

Pausing to wash at the water barrel, Annabel inspected

her appearance in the mirror fragment, not out of vanity but to make sure her disguise remained undisturbed. She continued into the kitchen and settled on one of the log stumps.

Mr. Hicks clattered a tin mug onto the table, poured in the thickest and blackest coffee Annabel had ever seen. He pushed the mug in front of her. "What do they call you, kid? Andy?"

Annabel took a sip of the bitter brew and shook her head. There was safety in the familiar. "My friends call me Scrappy."

"Scrappy, huh?" Clay reached over and pinched his forefinger and thumb over the slender muscle on her upper arm. "We'll soon fix that. Get some meat on your bones."

When he withdrew his touch, the edge of his thumb brushed against the side of her bound breast. Annabel flushed. A strange tingle skittered along her skin, and she covered up her agitation by adjusting her weight on the log stump seat.

Mr. Hicks banged the pots and pans at the stove, came over to set a plate of ham and beans in front of her and settled at the table. She thanked him and ate in silence, observing the men, listening as they discussed the mining.

Mr. Hicks was more bark than bite, she decided, and Clay was one of those people who held his emotions tightly bottled up inside. Last night, during the storm, she had sensed a melancholy in him, but in the daylight he presented a front as closed and forbidding as the cliffs that soared behind the kitchen canopy.

When Clay got up to rinse his plate in the bucket that stood on the floor in the corner, Annabel took the opportunity to speak. "If you tell me what you like to eat and where everything is, I can help in the kitchen. I am accustomed to a stove like that."

"Tomorrow," Clay said. "Today I have another job for you."

He gestured for her to follow. Annabel leaped to her feet and hurried after him, clumsy in her big boots. Clay paused to collect a sledgehammer from the low end of the cavern, and then he led her to the other side of the clearing where four huge timber spokes jutted out from a central hub, like a horizontal wheel set into a circular stone pit. Annabel could see two large rocks hanging on iron chains from the spokes.

Clay halted by the edge of the stone pit and studied the smaller rocks that filled the bottom. He picked up one, discarded it, selected another and straightened with the stone in his hand. "Do you know anything about mining, kid?"

"I thought it is done with pans in creeks."

"That's placer mining. We're lode mining." He gestured at the rocks covering the base of the stone pit. "That's the ore. We dig it up in the mine and bring it here. This device is called an *arrastre*. The mule gets harnessed to one of the spokes and turns the *arrastre* around. The big rocks chained to the spokes crush the ore. That frees up the gold to be separated with water, just like in placer mining."

He smiled at her. The low morning sun caught his eyes beneath the brim of his hat. Annabel felt a sudden tug in her chest. *Green.* His eyes were green, like the ocean by Merlin's Leap. Oceans were mostly blue, Papa had told her, but the Atlantic by the Eastern Seaboard was usually green.

"Today," Clay continued in a solemn tone, "the mule is tired from carrying you, so you'll have to do his job for him."

"I couldn't…" Annabel stared at the *arrastre*, imagined herself harnessed to one of the spokes. She frowned at Clay. "You're making fun of me."

"Not at all. But you'll crush the ore one piece at a time."

He carried the small rock he had selected a few yards away and placed it on a big flat stone that stood inside a timber circle. He hefted up the sledgehammer and smashed it down on the piece of ore, breaking it into fragments. With a few more blows, Clay ground the fragments into rubble and swept them down to the ground within the timber circle.

"Watch your eyes, in case any stone chips fly up," he instructed. "And try to make sure the pulverized ore stays inside the fence, so we don't lose any gold."

He handed the sledgehammer to her. The weight made her drop it.

Clay grinned. "You are meant to hit the ore, not your toes."

He fetched another small rock from the *arrastre*, placed it on the stone slab. Annabel heaved up the sledgehammer and smashed it down. The piece of ore glanced off and landed on the ground outside the timber circle.

"Let's try again." Clay bent down, replaced the ore on the slab.

Annabel swung the hammer. Again. Again. Every blow jarred her arms and shoulders, but the rock resisted her efforts.

"Like this." Clay took the sledgehammer from her.

At the fleeting touch of their hands, Annabel could feel the strength in him, could feel the roughness of his palm against the back of her fingers. Acutely aware of his nearness, almost as if he was touching her even when he wasn't, she watched Clay lift the sledgehammer with one hand, then casually swing it down again. The rock crumbled into rubble, and he swept the remains down into the timber circle.

"Try a smaller rock," he suggested.

This time Annabel chose a piece of ore the size of a grapefruit. She swung the sledgehammer. The rock merely bounced up and down. She turned to Clay. "I understand the task. You can go now." She gestured at the *arrastre*. "It is not as if I am in danger of damaging the equipment. I think I can work without supervision."

Clay contemplated her, shifted his shoulders and walked off. Annabel waited while he spoke to Mr. Hicks and then vanished out of sight behind a dried-up oak that leaned against the cliffs, presumably hiding the entrance to the mine.

The instant he was out of sight, Annabel attacked the piece of ore, using the physical task as a means to ease the mental agitation that had taken hold of her. She searched her mind for a suitable sea shanty from the repertoire Papa had taught her and her sisters and sang as she pounded, determination in every blow. A rock would not get the better of her. Not as long as there was a spark of life left in her.

Clay stepped into the harness and jerked the ore-filled cart into motion. The *arrastre* was already full from the labors of Mr. Hicks the day before, so he left the cart at the mouth of the mine tunnel and returned inside to collect the storm lanterns that eased the darkness and made the seam of gold glitter in the rock face.

Curious to see how the kid was getting on, Clay mopped his sweaty brow with his shirtsleeve, adjusted the brim of his hat and stepped out into the sunlight. As he sauntered toward the *arrastre*, he could hear the steady pounding and a grim, breathless voice singing some kind of a tune.

He never kissed his girl goodbye...pang
He left her and he told her why...pang
She drank and boozed his pay away...pang

With her greedy eye on his next payday...pang
She'd robbed him blind and left him broke...pang
He'd had enough, gave her the hove...pang

Clay halted, mesmerized by the sight. The kid was
flinging the big hammer high, nearly leaping into the air
to increase the arc of his swing, and then he brought the
hammer down, his whole body driving the motion.

Clay's gaze fell on the rounded posterior. With each
blow, the kid bent over, and the baggy pants pulled tight
over his rear end. Clay felt his gut clench. Aghast, he closed
his eyes. What the hell was wrong with him?

Gritting his teeth, he marched over, fighting the confusion and panic that surged within him. "That's enough."
His tone was brusque. "You are scaring every living creature for miles around with that hollering."

The kid whirled around and smiled at him. "It's a sea
shanty. Sailors sing them to accompany their work. I told
you, my father was a seaman."

There was such warmth in the kid's smile, such joy of
life, Clay felt his breath catch. Proud as a peacock, the
kid pointed at the pulverized ore inside the timber circle.
"See? I told you I'd earn my keep."

Clay peered down. He'd crushed that quantity of ore
in ten minutes.

"Good," he said. "That's enough for today. Go help in
the kitchen."

As he reached to take the hammer from the kid, his
eyes refused to lift from the kid's radiant features. Sweat
beaded on the smooth skin and the innocent face shone red
from the effort, but the sense of achievement emanating
from the kid was almost thick enough to put into a bottle.

The hammer, slick with sweat, slipped from Clay's
clasp. He waved the kid on his way, then wiped his hands

on the front of his shirt and bent to pick up the hammer from the ground. His attention fell on the dark smears his hands had left on his shirt. He lifted the hammer, studied the handle, spotted a trace of blood.

"Kid," he roared. "Come back here."

The kid edged back, hands hidden behind his back.

"What did you do?" Clay asked, gently now. "Did you cut your skin on a sharp stone?"

"No."

He made a beckoning motion. "Kid… Scrappy… let's take a look." When the kid refused to obey, Clay inserted a touch of steel into his tone. "Put out your hands."

The soft mouth pursed in mutiny, but the kid put out his hands, palms up. On each hand, a line of blisters marred the delicate skin.

"You fool," Clay said, but not without kindness. "You'll be no good to anyone if you injure yourself. Haven't you heard of gloves?"

"I tried them. They were too big." The narrow shoulders rose and fell in a careless shrug. "It's nothing. Because I'm small and young, I'm used to having to work extra hard to prove myself."

"Let's patch you up." Clay led the kid into the kitchen. Mr. Hicks had gone to inspect the ore in the mine tunnel, leaving dinner bubbling on the stove.

Clay poured hot water into a bowl and located a jar of ointment and bandages on the shelf. Every time a cotton shirt wore out, it was torn into strips, in preparedness for the accidents and mishaps that were inevitable in mining.

He settled the kid on a log stump. Finding it awkward to bend to the task, Clay sat down himself and perched the kid on his knee. One at a time, he washed the kid's hands in warm water.

The kid had small, fine bones. Clay rubbed ointment

on the damaged skin, his fingers sliding gently over the blisters, and then he wrapped a bandage around each hand and secured it with a knot.

He tried to ignore the sudden pounding of his heart. The kid smelled unlike any other scrawny kid he'd ever known, fresh and clean, like a spring meadow. Clay felt his body quicken. Appalled, he realized that holding the kid was stirring up the masculine needs he'd learned to ignore. Roughly, he pushed the kid off his knee.

"That should do." His voice came out strained. "Leave the dressings on for a couple of hours, until the blisters stop weeping. Then take them off. It's better to let the air to the skin." He jolted up to his feet. "I'll go and check on the horse and mule."

Not pausing to wait for a reply, Clay hurried down the path that led to a small meadow where the animals stood grazing. Out of sight, he leaned his back against the rough trunk of a pine and inhaled deep breaths, the unwanted waves of lust and protectiveness surging through him.

In the orphanage he'd seen it—boys desperate for the comfort of love formed a bond with another boy, treating each other like a sweetheart. He didn't condemn the practice, each man to his own, but he'd always dreamed of girls, had even paid for the company of a few, but perhaps in the face of loneliness a man could change his preferences? Could he? Could he?

Chapter Five

Annabel watched Clay walk away and felt a pang of regret. Why had he suddenly turned so morose? Why was he so unfriendly? While she'd been sitting on his knee, his attention on her hands, she'd taken the opportunity to study his face. She'd seen concern in his eyes, concern and protectiveness, but he'd covered them up with a brusque, efficient manner, as if resenting his kindness.

How could anyone keep such a tight rein on his emotions? Her own feelings ran close to the surface, impossible to hide. A moment ago, sitting on Clay's lap, cocooned in the heat of his body and his fingers gently sliding over her palms, the physical proximity had made her tremble with strange new yearnings.

She longed for his company, his companionship. She'd never been to a dance, had never had a chance to learn about flirting, test her powers of attraction on a man, and now those feminine instincts were surging inside her with a force she found difficult to control.

Annabel sighed in frustration. Of course, Clay thought she was a boy. *A scrawny kid.* She'd be a fool to endanger her disguise by acting on those new and untested feminine impulses that were suddenly buffeting her, as if she were a boat adrift in the ocean.

A few minutes later, Mr. Hicks banged a wooden spoon against a saucepan lid to announce the midday meal, and Clay strode back up the slope. He must be angry at her for some reason, Annabel decided, for he avoided looking at her while the three of them sat down to steaming plates and ate in silence.

Clay finished first. He dropped the spoon with a clatter on his empty plate and got up without a word and marched off to his task of hacking ore at the mine. A few minutes later, Annabel could hear the dull reverberations in the mountainside.

She remained seated at the table, idly spooning the thick stew of stringy meat and tough, tasteless vegetables. Mr. Hicks was leaning back on his log stump, tamping tobacco into his pipe. Annabel speeded up her eating. A gentleman would wait for her to finish her meal, but it was clear to her that the big, burly, bearded Mr. Hicks was no gentleman.

"Where are you from, Mr. Hicks?"

He took the unlit pipe from his mouth. "In the West, you don't ask a man such questions, kid."

Annabel lowered her gaze, chewed and swallowed another unpalatable mouthful. She heard the rasp of a match, heard puffing sounds and smelled the smoke. It was not the usual smell of tobacco, but the pleasant scent of fragrant herbs.

"I'm from Kansas," Mr. Hicks said, contradicting his command not to pry. "My ma was from a good family, but my pa was a good-for-nothing wastrel. She ran off with him and lived to regret it."

Annabel had no idea how to reply to such a blunt revelation, so she kept eating. Sometimes silence worked better as a prompt than bombarding someone with questions.

"Kid, sometimes you might think I'm two different people," Mr. Hicks went on. "When the mood strikes, I can talk like my ma, all educated, with fancy turns of phrase. At other times, I hit the bottle and curse like a trooper.

"You'll find men like that all around the West. They might be a college professor, or a duke's son, but they all try to sound like a cowboy, for a man feels more comfortable if he blends in with his surroundings. It's no good being a tiger in the desert, or a camel in the jungle."

"How long have you known Clay?"

"Clay?" Mr. Hicks puffed on his pipe. "Five years ago he rode up on a flea-bit pony to my claim in northern Californy. I was just about to pack up and leave that worthless ditch in the mud. There was something stark about Clay, but he was a good, strong lad, so I let him tag along.

"For a while, we worked for a big outfit in Nevada. Clay seemed to have some kind of a death wish. When there was blasting to be done, he volunteered for the job. When a mine tunnel was unsound, he chose to work there. Then he settled down, became more sensible. I never figured out what had been eating him up. He never talks much about his past. All I knew is that he grew up in an orphanage."

Empathy tugged at Annabel. He was an orphan, too! She recalled the grief, the emptiness, the terrible sense of being alone after Mama and Papa died. At what age had Clay lost his parents? Or could it be that he'd never known them, had been abandoned at birth. She longed to find out more, but Mr. Hicks had already declared he'd shared the sum of his knowledge, so she chose another line of questioning.

"How long have you been at this claim?"

"Since April. If we want to stay on when the winter comes, we'll have to build a cabin, or at least a wall to enclose the front of the cavern. Winters are fierce this high up in the mountains."

"Is there much gold in the mine?"

"Some. Might be more, but we ain't found it yet."

"Are there other claims nearby? Is the area rich with strikes?"

"This here country is called the Mimbres Mountains, after an Apache tribe with the same name. There're still a few Indians around, but they haven't bothered us none." Mr. Hicks paused to inspect his pipe. "There was a big strike in Hillsboro some years back. That's ten miles north of here. They have a town there, with stores and everything."

"Why don't you get your provisions there?"

"Don't get on with the storekeepers in Hillsboro."

Mr. Hicks spoke in a tone of bitterness. Annabel suspected there were lots of people in the world with whom the gruff old man did not get on. She pushed her empty plate aside. "Can I help with anything?"

"Give your hands a rest, kid. Take a walk around. There's a creek over yonder." Mr. Hicks took the pipe out of his mouth and used the stem to point. "And the horse and mule graze in a small meadow a mite down the hill. If you learn your bearings today, you can carry and fetch when your blisters heal."

He took a few more puffs in silence, then resumed talking. "I have a friend in Valverde, fifty miles north up the rail track. He puts provisions on the train and the conductor leaves the parcels in the mailbox by the water tower. If we run out, we hunt for food, or we go hungry."

For another ten minutes, they lingered at the table. Annabel learned the mine tunnel was narrow and the men took turns to work in the cramped space. When it was Clay's turn, Mr. Hicks took care of the chores around the camp. When Mr. Hicks went down the mine, Clay harnessed the

mule to the *arrastre* and crushed the ore. Mr. Hicks did not
like the task, for he did not get on with the mule.

"We had another saddle horse and two more pack mules
when we came out prospecting," Mr. Hicks explained. "But
we had to sell them to pay for supplies. As soon as we
have money to spare, we'll replace them, or at least the
saddle horse. It's no good for a man to be without transport of his own."

"What are the horse and mule called?" Annabel asked.

Mr. Hicks frowned. "The horse is called a horse, or
the buckskin. The mule is called the mule." His expression grew bleak. "Better not to treat them as pets. Makes
it easier to shoot them if you have to."

Clay's warnings about the old man's temper rang in Annabel's mind, but she steeled herself against an outburst
and asked the question that had been playing on her mind.
"Mr. Hicks, what do you have against women?"

He gave her a long look, then fastened his gaze on the
line of trees beyond the clearing. "They promise you paradise, but they give you hell. You're too young, kid, but
when you grow up you'll figure that a woman can be all
sweetness on the outside and poison on the inside. They
lure a man with honeyed talk but stick the knife of betrayal
between your shoulder blades when you turn your back.
Mark my words, kid. One day you'll find out."

Annabel hung her head, ashamed. What she was doing
now, interrogating him about his past while dressed as a
boy, was a betrayal, in a way. Uneasy, she got to her feet.
"I'll go and see if I can find my way to the creek." Casually, she added, "Do you ever bathe in the stream?" Her
scalp was starting to itch, from the way her hair was coiled
tight inside the bowler hat.

"Sure, kid. There's a good spot for bathing." Benign
again, Mr. Hicks gestured at her bandaged hands. "Take

your time, kid. If you peel off the dressings, the cold water will soothe your skin. I have some mending to do. There's a hole in my boots the size of Alaska. When you get back, you can help me prepare supper."

Clay lowered the pickaxe and blinked against the dust in his eyes. A lantern hanging from an iron peg hammered into the rock cast a dull sphere of light. Normally, Clay didn't mind the sense of being trapped inside the earth. There was peace in being underground, surrounded by silence, and the hard physical labor of a miner cleared a man's troubles from his mind.

But today his mind found no comfort in the steady clink of the pickaxe against the seam of ore. Clay told himself it was because the thin vein of gold was petering away, threatening the future of the mine, but he knew it was a lie.

The cause of his unease was the kid. The scrawny kid who filled his thoughts in the way no scrawny kid should be allowed to do. With a grunt of frustration, Clay lowered the pickaxe and bent to pick up the canteen by his feet. He uncapped the lid, tipped his head back to drink. Not a drop of water left inside. Clay sighed, reached to the rock ceiling to take down the lantern and used it to guide his way out. At the mouth of the tunnel, the bright sunshine made him squint.

As he waited for his eyes to adjust, Clay spotted the kid emerging from the cavern. There was something stealthy about the kid's movements, the way he glanced all around, as if to make sure no one was watching. Curious, Clay drew back against the sunbaked cliff, hiding behind the dried-up oak that shielded the mine entrance.

He watched as the kid set down the path, heading toward the creek. The kid was not carrying a bucket, so he was not fetching water. An empty flour sack hung draped over one skinny forearm, like a towel. In his other hand, the kid carried the bar of soap he'd been so proud about.

Clay hesitated. The kid seemed to relax, sauntering along. He was humming one of those sea shanties, not taking the time to study his surroundings. There could be anything out there in the forest. A bear. A mountain lion. Rattlers liked to coil up on rocks that reflected the heat of the sun.

Clay set off to follow the kid, but he kept his footsteps quiet and hung back, remaining out of sight. His gut seemed all tied up in knots. Guilt and shame and a terrible sense of confusion filled his mind, like a headache pounding at his temples.

The kid came to a halt by the creek. Bright rays of sunshine cut through the canopy of trees, like rich seams of gold. The water made a merry gurgle as it rippled over a boulder, gathering into the tiny pond they had dammed for bathing.

The kid hopped onto a flat rock and ducked to set the flour sack and the cake of soap by his feet. Then he removed the bandages from his hands and took a moment to study his palms. Next, he lifted his hands to the buttons on the front of his threadbare shirt. Peeking between the trees, Clay held his breath.

What was wrong with him?

Why did he want to watch the kid strip down?

Curious. He was curious. And concerned. There had been something odd in the way the kid had glanced about him before setting off to bathe. And those baggy clothes the kid wore, and the way he never took off his hat. Maybe he was covering up some injury—scars from an accident, or some defect he was born with.

Clay kept watching, the turmoil of emotions anchoring his feet to the ground. The kid pushed the cotton shirt down his narrow shoulders. Clay's brows drew into a frown. He'd guessed right. A wide bandage circled the kid's torso, covering him from armpit to waist.

With nimble hands, the kid undid the clasps that held the bandage secure and began unraveling it. Loop after loop, the fabric fell away, revealing an expanse of smooth, white skin. His shoulder blades protruded slightly on either side of the narrow groove of the spine. Angel's wings, Clay had once heard someone describe such a feature, but that had been on a woman.

He could see nothing wrong with the kid, no deformity, if you didn't count the lack of muscle and the oddly tiny waist. The final loop of the bandage fell away and the kid bent to set the bundle of fabric down on the stone. When he turned to pick up the soap, the curve of a small, rounded breast peeked into view.

Clay's mind seized up with the shock. He took a step back and sank on the ground, elbows propped on his knees, head cradled in his hands. The vegetation formed a barrier between them, but the sight remained burned in his memory.

The kid was a girl.

A huge wave of relief crashed over Clay. There was nothing wrong with him, no sudden change in his mental makeup. He didn't think of boys in such a way. It was simply that his body had figured out the truth before his mind knew.

Of course. Of course.

Fragments of recollection ricocheted around his brain. The voice. Mostly, the kid spoke in a low voice, but sometimes he forgot and the pitch climbed high. And that soft skin…those big eyes…the slender shape…and sometimes, when the kid prattled on, there was something downright feminine and coquettish about his manner.

Her manner.

A girl.

As the shock of the discovery faded, Clay's senses began to function again. He could hear the girl singing, could hear the splashing of water. He felt his body tighten. She was bathing.

Temptation tugged at him like a physical pull. He shouldn't look. It was not the gentlemanly thing to do. But he was powerless to resist the masculine inclination. Easing up onto his feet, he peered between the leaves of a scrub oak.

She was kneeling on the stone, bending forward, washing her hair. Long and black, it cascaded down in a sleek curtain. Now Clay understood why the kid never took her hat off in front of others. She couldn't have been pretending to be a boy for very long, for if she had, she would have been forced to cut her hair.

Turn around, Clay urged in his mind. *Turn around.*

But she did not. His eyes lingered on what he could see—the nape of a slender neck, the narrow span of those angel wing shoulders, an impossibly slender waist and the feminine curve of hips, hidden inside the mended wool pants.

Would she strip completely? Would she take off her pants? Would she turn around, giving him another glimpse of those small, rosy-tipped breasts? Clay felt his heart hammering away in his chest as he watched the girl. She was singing again, in breathless snatches while she soaped and rinsed her hair.

Cape Cod girls ain't got no combs,
They brush their hair with codfish bones...
Cape Cod kids ain't got no sleds,
They slide down the hills on codfish heads...

Cape Cod girls ain't got no frills,
They tie their hair with codfish gills...

As the afternoon sun burned in the sky, the girl straightened in her kneeling position. She canted her head to one side and wrung the water from her hair, taking care not to hurt her blistered hands. And then, turning a little, she reached for the flour sack on the stone, and Clay got the peek he'd been waiting for. The sight of those firm, tip-tilted breasts made his gut clench.

After patting her skin dry, the girl rose to her feet and picked up the long strip of linen and used it to disguise her feminine shape again. Hurrying now, she pulled her cotton shirt back on and leaned down to gather up her soap and the makeshift towel and the bowler hat propped beside her feet.

Without a sound, Clay retreated up the path to the small meadow where the horse and mule stood grazing. While he took a moment to allow the storm of agitation inside him to ease, he stroked the floppy ears of the mule and mulled over the situation.

How long could the girl protect her secret? Should he let her know he'd stumbled upon the truth? And what about Mr. Hicks? The gruff old man hated women. What would happen when he found out? And he *would* find out, for there was no way the girl could keep up the pretense for a month. No way on earth.

Chapter Six

As they sat down to supper, Clay stole curious glances at the girl in the fading twilight. The loose shirt and trousers swamped her slender frame, and the bowler hat was pulled low, but even then, how could he have failed to notice it before?

In his mind, he tried to recall their conversations. He'd never really talked to a woman before. Had he said things that might have offended her delicate sensibilities? He could not think of anything.

After they finished eating, Mr. Hicks lit his pipe, as was his custom. Using a mix of tobacco and herbs, he puffed out fragrant clouds of smoke that helped to disperse the insects swarming in the air.

Clay got to his feet. "I'll crush a bit of ore. The *arrastre* is too full."

Mr. Hicks spoke around the stem of his pipe. "Daylight's almost gone."

"I'll light another lantern."

Clay fetched a storm lantern from the cavern, topped up the coal oil, lit the flame and turned the wick high. Then he walked over to the stone slab, set the lantern on the ground and picked up the big hammer. Putting all his worry and troubled thoughts into the blows, he pulverized piece after piece of the gold-bearing ore.

Mr. Hicks tapped out his pipe, called out his good-night and took himself off to the cavern. Clay did not cease his pounding. From the periphery of his vision, he kept an eye on the girl. She'd finished clearing up and was standing on the edge of the kitchen, silhouetted in the glow of the lantern behind her as she watched him.

"Shall I leave the light on for you?" she called out.

"Take it with you," he called back. "I have mine."

The girl took the lantern down from the hook in the kitchen ceiling and used it to illuminate the short walk over to the cavern. It was a warm night, and they hadn't lit a bonfire under the overhang.

Clay saw her settle under a blanket, with the rounded bowler hat still covering her head. The lantern light went out. Up to now, he'd been puzzled why anyone might prefer to sleep with their hat on, the brim squashed against the ground, but now he understood she needed to hide her long, glossy hair from prying eyes.

For another hour, Clay labored, grappling with his thoughts, trying to decide on the right course of action, as well as attempting to drive his body into exhaustion, so he could overcome the needs that the sight of the half-naked girl had jolted into life.

Only when he felt certain she would be asleep did Clay cease his pounding. He stopped for a quick wash at the water barrel. Seeing his reflection in the mirror, he ran his palm over the stubble on his jaw.

Not pausing to consider the merits of the idea, he scooped fresh water into the enamel bowl and spread a thick layer of soap over the lower half of his face. He pulled out the knife tucked into his boot and scraped away the week-old beard.

By now, the moon had risen. He put out the flame in the lantern and waited for his eyes to adjust to the darkness. When he could make out the layout within the cavern, he eased over, keeping his footsteps silent.

He sat down, pulled out the gun tucked into his waistband, checked the load and laid the weapon down within an easy reach. Without a sound, he took off his hat and wrapped into a blanket. Then he rolled onto his side and let his gaze rest on the small shape next to him.

A man like him had little chance to meet decent girls. Up to now, those encounters had been limited to exchanging a few words with a girl working in a store or serving food in an eating house. And he'd never slept with a woman before. His only experience of closeness had been a few tumbles in a whore's bed. And now a girl lay beside him. A beautiful girl, with milky-white skin and hair as black as midnight and sleeker than an otter's pelt.

If he reached out, he could touch her. And he wanted to, so much it hurt. If nothing else, he wanted to simply rest his fingertips on her shoulder, to prove that she really existed, that there really was a lovely girl sleeping right beside him.

The willpower Clay had to exert to resist the longing told him what he had to do: he must take the girl back to the railroad. As soon as he could, he had to find some means to help her continue on her journey.

If he let her stay, not only would there be trouble when Mr. Hicks found out, but a month was long enough to start caring about another person. He didn't want to let her crack his emotions wide open and wriggle her way into his heart, only to rip it out and take it with her when she left.

It had been bad enough when Lee and Billy died. If he became attached to this girl, it would be a thousand times worse when he found himself alone again. There was only one solution. The scrawny kid who was a girl had to go.

Despite the bright morning sun, Annabel woke up shivering with cold. Beneath her hat her coiled hair covered her scalp like a damp cap. Next time, she would have to wash her hair in the morning, to allow it time to dry. At least the blisters on her palms no longer hurt and her muscles ached only when she made a sudden move.

She looked around the cavern. The men and animals were gone. She lifted her arms in a lazy stretch, then stilled as the world outside exploded into a cacophony of noises—crashing and grating and the clanking of iron chains.

Startled, even a little frightened, Annabel lowered her arms. Making haste, she pulled on her boots and went outside, driven by curiosity and alarm as much as by hunger and thirst and other physical needs.

On the far side of the clearing, she could see the mule, harnessed to the *arrastre*, plodding round and round in a slow circle. The pair of huge rocks hanging from the spokes of the *arrastre* smashed against the smaller rocks in the confines of the stone pit, grinding up the ore.

The noise boomed in her ears. A cloud of dust floated over the *arrastre* pit. On the other side of the *arrastre*, Clay was walking up the path, carrying a bucket of water. When he noticed her, his gaze lingered on her with an intensity that banished the last of the early-morning chills.

Halting in her approach, Annabel watched Clay as he set the bucket on the ground and then ran around the *arrastre* pit to catch up with the mule. Taking hold of the harness, he brought the animal to a stop beside the water bucket.

The grinding noises ceased, leaving a sudden silence. The mule buried its long nose in the bucket and drank, with eager blowing and splashing that filled the quiet. Clay stroked the animal's lathered flank and tugged at the harness, inspecting the hide to make sure the leather straps were not causing sores.

Annabel loitered over. She could tell Clay's touch on the mule was gentle, just as it had been when he bandaged her hands. A rebellion stirred in her mind. It seemed to her that kindness and warmth simmered behind Clay's cool facade, but he hoarded those emotions like a miser might hoard a bag of coins.

Something in her demanded that she force him to reveal those emotions, like her own emotions always flowed freely for others to see. She wanted to strike against the hard surface he presented to the world and make it crack, for no man could be made of stone the way he pretended to be.

She ambled closer. "You're very kind to that mule. You must love the creature."

Clay shot her a surly glance from beneath the brim of his hat. "No love to it. An injured animal is no good. It was the same with your blistered skin. You'll be no good as a laborer if you can't use your hands."

"Are you comparing me with the mule?"

"The mule is a darn sight more valuable than a scrawny kid."

His voice was deadpan, but Annabel could see a shadow of a smile tugging at his mouth. She edged closer and peeked into the circle of stones. "How can I convince you of my value?" she asked, glancing at him over her shoulder. "Will you teach me how to separate the gold from the gravel?"

She could feel Clay's attention on her, saw him shift uneasily on his feet. Again, Annabel could sense his sudden withdrawal. "No," he said curtly. "Not today. I need to crush the ore. There's another cartful waiting at the mine. You can work in the kitchen. See what you can put together for a noonday meal."

His rebuff ought to have offended her, but instead it triggered a frisson of excitement. She had little experience of young men, apart from the footmen and grooms at Merlin's Leap, and they had treated her with a formal respect. She had never had a chance to banter with a young man, and now the challenge filled her with a heady fascination.

Leaving Clay to tend to the mule, Annabel went into the kitchen. A pot of coffee, still warm, stood on the table, with a plate of biscuits. And next to them, a jar of honey! She sat down, poured coffee into a cup and spread honey on two biscuits and devoured them, not touching the rest, in case they were intended as a midmorning snack for the men.

Finished, she dusted the crumbs from her fingers and examined the skin on her palms. There was no sign of infection, just some ragged edges of burst blisters that were beginning to harden into calluses.

Satisfied with the signs of healing, Annabel got up to survey the kitchen contents, starting with the row of grain bins beneath the work counter. Flour. Evaporated vegetables. Rice. Beans. More beans. Jerked meat, perhaps venison.

Her inspection progressed to the shelves. Canned goods. Tins of evaporated milk. Another jar of honey. A crock of cooking oil. Kerosene for lamps. Matches in a waterproof tin. A bag of salt and small pouches of spices, not imported ones, such as saffron or pepper, but some kind of native herbs.

There was plenty of flour, and Liza had taught her how to bake bread. Dinner would be beans and rice, with bread and honey for dessert. Annabel rolled up her sleeves and set to work.

The mule had resumed its plodding circle. The grinding noise boomed over the clearing. Dust floated in the air. Annabel stirred dough in a bowl, gripping the wooden spoon with her fingertips to ease the pressure on her blisters.

She took to singing a sea shanty, altering the words to suit the occasion. After a few verses, she raised her voice to compete with the crashing and banging and the clatter of the mule's hooves.

They say, old Clay, your mule will bolt,
Oh, poor old Clay, your mule will bolt,
Oh, poor old Clay!
For thirty days you've ridden him,
And when he bolts I'll tan his skin,
Oh, poor old Clay!
And if he stays you'll ride him again,
You'll ride him with a tighter rein,
Oh, poor old Clay!

When she got to the end, she started again, increasing the volume until she was bellowing out the words. So engrossed was she in the competition to produce the most noise that when the mule stopped, she went on, her voice preventing her from hearing the sound of footsteps as they thudded over.

"There you go again, scaring every living creature in the forest."

Instead of pausing in the middle of a verse, Annabel put extra force in the final *"poor old Clay"* before she turned to face him.

The bowl nearly slipped from her fingers. He'd taken off his shirt! Standing on the edge of the kitchen, one arm lazily dangling from a timber post, Clay leaned forward and studied the evidence of her efforts.

"What are you making?" he asked.

Annabel tried to look away, but her eyes refused to obey. A strange new sensation clenched low in her belly. Her head spun, as if she'd been holding her breath for too long.

She gave up the attempt to avert her eyes and let her gaze roam over him. She could not recall ever seeing a man's naked chest before, not even Papa's, for a gentleman did not remove his shirt in the presence of his daughters.

Clay's body was lean, his arms roped with muscle, and beneath the sheen of perspiration Annabel could see a ridged pattern on his abdomen. Higher up, his torso broadened, and hidden in the sprinkling of dark hair on his chest, Annabel noticed two flat brown nipples, different from the pink tips of her own breasts and yet somehow the same.

"What are you staring at?" Clay stepped closer. "Your eyes are like dinner plates. Haven't you ever seen a man peeled to his belt before?" Reaching out, he pinched a dollop of dough from the bowl and popped it into his mouth.

Lips pursed, cheeks hollowed, he considered the flavor. Annabel studied the rugged features, now clean-shaven instead of covered with a thick coat of beard stubble.

Her attention settled on his mouth, and all of a sudden a wave of heat rolled over her. She knew she was blushing scarlet. Clay stiffened. The change she was learning to recognize in him came over again, as if a storm cloud had rolled in from the ocean, obliterating the sun.

"Better get back to work." His voice was gruff.

Annabel watched him go. And something tempted her to go after him. Curiosity. Devilment. Playfulness. The strange new tugging in the pit of her belly. Perhaps even the challenge she had set for herself earlier, to jolt him out of his carefully constructed coolness and indifference.

Quickly, she finished her kitchen chores. When the

bread was baking in the oven and a pot of beans simmering on the stovetop, she left the shelter of the kitchen canopy and strolled over to the *arrastre*. The mule was going round and round again, the stones crashing and grinding, dust rising in the air.

Clay was bent over a bucket to splash water over his face and arms. When he straightened, their eyes met. For a moment, they looked upon each other. Annabel held her breath. She could feel all those pent-up emotions seething within Clay, creating pressure, a force as powerful as the head of steam that drove the engine on the train.

Like a door closing, Clay's features hardened. Using the flat of his palm, he flicked away the droplets from his face, and then he turned to look the other way. Pointedly ignoring her, he went to coax the mule to a greater speed.

Bolder now, not even trying to hide her interest, Annabel watched him. She could feel his irritation rising, as if the storm clouds in his mind were about to burst into thunder and lightning.

When the mule needed a break, the noise ceased. At first, the world appeared silent in contrast, but an instant later Annabel could pick out the mocking call of a blue jay and the rustling in the trees as a squirrel leaped from branch to branch.

"Your skin is nicely bronzed," she called out to Clay. "You ought to always stay clean-shaven. Otherwise the top half of your face will tan but the lower half will remain pale. It will look funny. Girls won't like it."

"Girls?" Clay drawled. "What might you know about it?"

"Plenty. I have two older sisters."

"How old?" Clay stole a glance toward his shirt hanging on a juniper on the edge of the clearing, but he made no move to retrieve the garment.

"Twenty-four and twenty-two."

His shoulders shifted in a careless shrug. "Just right for me, then."

The jolt of jealousy at the imaginary prospect took Annabel by surprise. She brushed the feeling aside and went on with her probing. "How old are you?"

"Twenty-three."

"Twenty-three?" Her voice rose in surprise. "I thought you were older. Close to thirty."

"Everyone grows older at the same rate but some grow up faster."

"Mr. Hicks says you have been with him for five years. That means you were eighteen when he employed you. Are you an orphan as he says?"

"Yes."

"How old were you when your parents died?"

Clay took down his hat, raked one hand through his thick brown curls and replaced the hat on his head. For a moment, Annabel thought he might not reply. When he spoke, his tone indicated his patience was wearing thin.

"Six."

Six years old. So, he hadn't been abandoned at birth. He'd have memories. He'd have suffered the grief of loss, something they had in common. "Do you remember your parents?" she asked softly.

"I remember a woman's voice singing." He gave her a sly look from beneath the brim of his hat. "And a man's voice telling her to shut up."

For an instant, the cutting reply silenced Annabel. Then she launched into another attempt to get a peek into his mind. "What happened to you when they died?"

"Aren't you full of questions today?" Clay glanced up into the clear blue dome of the sky. "Could it be that the sun is frying up your brain?"

Annabel gave him an innocent smile. "Just passing the time."

Clay walked over to the mule, squatted on his heels to inspect the hooves and spoke without looking up. "Someone took me to the nuns. The nuns only looked after girl orphans, so they sent me to an orphanage that was little more than a workhouse. Boys as young as three were hired out to chimney sweeps and farmers and storekeepers—anyone who would pay."

Annabel could see the tension in Clay's naked back and shoulders, could hear the bitter note in his voice. Pity welled up inside her. They were both orphans, but the similarity ended there. Unlike her, Clay had no happy memories of loving parents to draw upon. He'd grown up with cruelty and neglect.

Had he ever felt love? Did he even understand such emotion? Did those hidden feelings of kindness and caring she had credited him with really exist, or had she merely imagined them, fooled by her own sentimental nature?

"How old were you when you left the orphanage?" she asked, aware that any moment now he might decide she was pushing too hard and react with anger.

Clay rose to his feet. Although his voice remained calm, there was no mistaking the warning in his manner. "I was fourteen, and I was not a scrawny kid like you. I was capable of doing a man's job, instead of loafing about in the sun and bothering other people who have better things to do."

Annabel eased back a step, then another. "I think the beans are boiling," she said and pivoted on her big leather boots. As she hurried away, her heart was pounding, her mind in turmoil. She'd been prodding at Clay, trying to stir his emotions, but it was her own emotions that had become stirred.

Poor, poor Clay, growing up without the comfort of a

loving home. Up to now, it might have been his good looks and his masculine strength and the air of self-sufficiency about him that had triggered such a strong response in her.

Now it was more.

Her tender nature reacted to suffering and pain, and she longed to heal some of the past hurt that had caused Clay to form such a hard shell around him. But could past hurts ever be healed? Could a barrier a man had put up around his emotions ever be knocked down? And what might it cost a woman if she tried and failed?

Chapter Seven

$\mathcal{C}\!\!\mathcal{D}\!\!\mathcal{D}$

For the rest of the morning, Annabel kept out of Clay's way and concentrated on preparing a meal. She wanted it to be a success, wanted to prove she was a valuable addition to the team. At Merlin's Leap, she'd sometimes felt overshadowed by her older sisters. Now she wouldn't be compared with them but would only be judged on her own efforts. She found the idea strangely liberating.

While she bustled about in the kitchen, Annabel kept an eye on the position of the sun. The day before, she'd noted that when the noonday meal was called the sun had lined up between the pair of tall pines to the left of the *arrastre*. The observation helped her to have the meal ready when she heard Mr. Hicks lumbering over from the mine.

His nose twitched. "I smell cooking."

"Beans and rice. And a loaf of bread with honey for after." Annabel gestured at the table she'd already laid out with plates and spoons. "Please, sir, sit down."

"Blimey—what is this, the Palace Hotel?"

Annabel smiled. "The Waldorf Astoria."

She heard Clay stroll over. He'd put on his shirt but had left the buttons undone, and the open edges of the shirt drew her attention even more to his naked chest, the way a frame might enhance a painting.

In silence, Annabel dished out the food. The men tucked in. She'd already noticed the way Clay ate, his focus totally on the meal, as if someone might snatch the plate away from him anytime. It made her suspect that at some point in his life Clay might have suffered from starvation. Another wave of compassion welled up in her at the thought.

"There's plenty more," she said quietly.

Clay glanced up at her, his eyes guarded. He made no reply.

Mr. Hicks nodded. "This is a fine stew. What did you put in it?"

"Just beans and rice. And salt, and a spoonful of honey to sweeten the beans while they were boiling."

"Go easy on the salt." Mr. Hicks adjusted his bulk on the log stump. "Too much salt makes a man thirsty in this heat."

"The heat also makes you sweat, which loses salt from your body," Annabel pointed out. "It is better to put salt in your food and drink plenty of water."

Mr. Hicks looked up from his stew. "How come you know such things?"

"My father was a seaman. Sailors are careful about nutrition, to avoid scurvy."

"Nutrition?" Clay lifted his brows. "Ain't you full of fancy words? Does it mean the food they eat?"

Annabel flushed. She fanned a hand in front of her face. "My, it's hot in here. I've had the stove going all morning."

Mr. Hicks unbuttoned his shirt and flapped the edges to create a current of air. "You can say that again." He winked at Annabel. "Kid, we might be at the Waldorf Astoria, but you can peel off your shirt."

Annabel stirred her stew, her eyes downcast. She had anticipated such a comment, was prepared for it. She kept her voice bland. "I'd like to, but I have pale skin that burns easily. I'll do better keeping my shirt on."

She scooped up another spoonful of beans and rice and slipped it into her mouth. She waited for a second, tension vibrating within her, and then she darted a quick glance at Clay. He was watching her with a strained expression on his face. A kick of panic jolted her on the log stump. Did he suspect? Had he noticed something?

The stew stuck in her throat at the idea. It had seemed harmless fun to tease Clay the way young women of her social class might do with their suitors. But now caution whispered in her mind. If he caught on to her secret, she'd have to face the consequences, and the anger of Mr. Hicks might not be the worst of them.

The mule was getting tired. Clay lined up beside the animal at the *arrastre* and added his weight to the task. Muscles straining, he pushed at the timber spoke with all his might, boots scrabbling for purchase on the gravel ground.

But even the hard labor could not dispel the unease that throbbed through him. When the mule halted and the noise ceased, Clay could hear the girl singing her sea shanties in the kitchen, softly now, instead of the mad bellowing of earlier.

He did not want to look. And yet, his eyes drew toward the timber canopy. The girl was working with a rag and bucket now, wiping down the shelves. As she bent down, the loose clothing molded to her body, revealing the feminine curves. The sight sharpened the restlessness inside Clay. He swiveled on his heels, curled his hands around the timber spoke. "Pull," he said to the mule.

Together they made the wheel turn, beast and man, working side by side, as the sun traveled across the sky. Clay's shoulders grew sore from bracing against the timber spoke. Dust itched on his skin. Thirst parched his throat. His body ached with the effort, but the fatigue failed to obliterate the tension that seethed within him.

Finally, the sun sank behind the hills and the evening cool crept over the landscape. Clay unharnessed the mule and rubbed down the dusty hide with a piece of wool cut from an old blanket, and then he led the animal down the slope to picket him in the small meadow where the saddle horse already stood grazing.

By now, the restlessness in Clay was turning into anger at the girl, at how she had taunted him earlier, with her prying into his past and the song about a misbehaving mule. There had been something downright coquettish about her teasing. She was using feminine allure to unsettle him, while at the same time hiding behind her boy's disguise.

Moreover, he hated lies, and she was forcing him to lie. In the West, if a man's honesty was in doubt, he found himself handicapped in business and without friends. There was a bond of trust between him and Mr. Hicks, and it added to Clay's sour mood that the girl was making him a participant in her deceit.

Boots thudding against the ground, Clay strode over to the kitchen. The girl was bustling about, stirring a pot on the stove, leaning in to taste, her lips pursing against the wooden spoon in a way that made his gut clench.

Alerted by his footsteps, she turned to look. Clay propped his shoulder against a canopy post and folded his arms across his chest. He'd put on his shirt but left it unbuttoned, and she was making those dinner-plate eyes at him again.

"So," he drawled, "those sisters of yours. Pretty, are they?"

A startled expression flickered across the girl's face. "Yes," she replied, flustered. "They are very pretty."

"What do they look like?"

"Miranda is tall with fair hair. Charlotte is a small and dark, like—" she caught herself just in time "—small and dark, with curly hair."

Clay sent her a bold smile. "Myself, I like a dark-haired woman. But I prefer straight hair—long and straight hair that flows down like a curtain of midnight." He made a smooth gesture in the air. "A man can lose his sanity running his hands through hair like that."

A pink flush was spreading over the girl's features. Her fingers gripped the wooden spoon tight. Her lips moved, but for once she appeared to find no words.

"What about you, kid?" Clay went on. He wanted her to feel some of the tension and confusion she had triggered inside him. "What kind of woman makes your blood run hot? You can tell me, man-to-man."

The blush on the girl's face deepened to scarlet. She turned away and made an attempt to sound casual. "Actually, I'm rather busy here, if you don't mind."

"Sure." Clay shuffled his feet and pushed away from the canopy post, getting ready to leave. "I'll let you get on with your work. We'll talk more some other time."

When he walked away, his frustration turned into guilt. He'd resented her for baiting him from the safety of her disguise, but had he not done the same himself just now? For what he'd done had been akin to flirting, and he'd best put a stop to it before he took it too far—before he betrayed her secret to Mr. Hicks or got his emotions even more tangled up.

It surprised Annabel how quickly life could fall into a routine. Again, she awoke to the morning sunshine slanting into the empty cavern. She no longer slept on the hard ground, for last night Clay had spread his bedroll out for her, with a comment that his back was aching and he preferred the firmness of the earth floor.

Today, it was Clay's turn to hack ore in the mine. The knowledge that she would see him only at mealtimes filled Annabel with a mix of relief and regret. Their strange conversation yesterday played on her mind. Was it a coincidence he'd talked about a woman with straight, dark hair? Or was there a chance he'd seen her without her hat and was teasing her?

It could not be. Surely, if he'd stumbled upon her secret, he would have confronted her, would have told Mr. Hicks. It had to be unintentional. A random match. But it added to Annabel's restlessness to know that she possessed the kind of feminine features Clay found appealing.

In the kitchen, she found a coffeepot cooling on the stove and biscuits and honey on the table. She took a cup from the shelf and poured. The coffee was thick sludge at the bottom of the pot, bitter, only lukewarm. She drank a few sips and ate some of the biscuits, watching a pair of cardinal birds hopping around in search of crumbs.

While she was tidying up in the kitchen, Mr. Hicks strode up the path. Shirtless, he carried a yoke over his shoulders, with a steel bucket hanging on an iron chain at each end. His boots and trousers were covered in mud.

Annabel hurried over to him. "Can I help with anything?"

The empty steel buckets hit the ground with a clatter as Mr. Hicks shrugged off the yoke. Annabel made a covert study of the man standing only three paces away from her.

Despite his age, Mr. Hicks was thickly muscled, as powerful as an ox. Surprised, she noted that the dark whorls of hair on his chest were going gray, just like the hair on his head and some of the strands in his bushy beard.

"Is there coffee?" he asked with a glance toward the kitchen.

"No," she told him. "But I can make another pot."

"Good." Saying no more, Mr. Hicks picked up a shovel leaning against the *arrastre* pit and set to work filling the steel buckets with the pulverized ore.

Curious, Annabel watched. "What are you doing?"

"I'm taking the dirt down to the creek to wash it."

"Wash it?" Her voice rose at the incongruity of the idea. "How is it possible to wash dirt?"

"If you come with me, I'll show you how."

Annabel stood aside while he bent to lift the yoke over his shoulders and straightened with a grunt. She followed him down the path. The horse and mule greeted them with a whinny as they marched past.

Mr. Hicks came to a halt by the creek a short distance beyond the small pond where they came to bathe and fetch water. He lowered the yoke and pointed at an elongated wooden box about four feet long. "This is a rocker box."

The box was tilted, one end higher than the other, with an extra tier attached to the higher end. Into this extra tier Mr. Hicks now tipped half a bucketful of dirt. A few paces upstream, where the creek formed a tiny waterfall, water cascaded through a funnel into a hose about five yards long.

When Mr. Hicks lifted the lower end of the hose, a current of water spilled out. With one hand, he directed the spray onto the pile of dirt in the box, and with the other hand he gripped a wooden handle and cranked it to and fro, making the box rock side to side, stirring the dirt inside.

"The water makes the dirt run down the slope inside the box," he explained, raising his voice to carry over the rumble of the gravel. "Gold is heavier than dirt and it falls to the bottom. The base of the box has slats across it. They are called riffles. Nuggets are caught in the riffles. A piece of coarse wool cloth at the end of the box catches the gold dust, leaving the worthless gravel to tumble out."

While Mr. Hicks lectured, Annabel craned her neck to watch. A fine mist rose from the waterfall, reminding her of the ocean at Merlin's Leap. The heat of the sun dispelled the chill of the night. She could smell trees and fresh mountain air.

A sense of contentment stole over her. She'd grown up in the safe confines of a loving household, and the enclosed world of their mining camp offered the same sense of security, the same sense of togetherness and unity.

Ever since her parents died, Annabel had felt a little lost, alone in the world despite the close relationship with her sisters. Now some of that emptiness inside her seemed to ease. In its place stirred a new desire to find her own place in the world, to forge her own future.

"Can I do anything to help?" she asked eagerly.

Mr. Hicks did not cease his rocking. "Let's see your hands."

Annabel held her palms out. The burly old man squinted to peer at her skin where calluses were forming at the base of each finger. "Leave it for another day or two," he suggested. "I'll see if I can find some smaller gloves for you."

"Holding the water hose would not hurt my hands."

Mr. Hicks gave an amused huff. "You sure are a hard worker, kid."

But he passed the hose to her. Annabel experimented. If she held the hose low, barely over the edge of the box, making the most of gravity, she could make the water gush out a little faster.

"That's good," Mr. Hicks said, surprise in his tone.

Annabel beamed. "If you show me how to make those

biscuits, I can get up earlier in the morning and have them ready for breakfast."

The benign expression faded. "I'll eat no biscuits apart from my own," Mr. Hicks bellowed. "Never met a body yet who can do them right."

The spray went wide as Annabel flinched. Clay had warned her that Mr. Hicks had a volatile temper, but so far she'd seen only a hint of it. Instinct warned that when fully unleashed his anger might be like a tempest that crushed everything in its way.

Carefully, she pointed the hose to the dirt in the rocker box. For the rest of the morning they worked together, fetching more gravel, emptying the riffles to take out the tiny nuggets of gold and rinsing the coarse wool cloth to remove the trapped dust. Occasionally, they paused to shovel aside the gravel expelled at the other end of the rocker box. By the time Mr. Hicks told Annabel to start preparing the midday meal, they had filled the bottom of an empty honey jar with gold.

"That's about two ounces," Mr. Hicks said, holding the thick glass jar to the sunlight. "A mite over thirty dollars."

Annabel admired the glittering product of their labors. "How long did it take you to mine the ore in the *arrastre* right now?" she asked.

Mr. Hicks considered. "I reckon that's about a ten days' work."

As Annabel hurried to the kitchen, she calculated in her mind. They had washed perhaps one-quarter of the pulverized ore in the *arrastre*. If she allowed fifty percent for expenses, at the current rate they were making around seventy dollars per person per month, but it might be less in the winter, and they would need to allow for a period without income if the mine played out, or if one of the men got injured or became sick.

But could they not increase the efficiency of their operation? The buckskin could carry the dirt down to the creek. And there might be a way to increase the flow of water to allow for a bigger rocker box. At the very least, when her hands healed, she could speed up the process by taking a turn on the rocker box while one of the men carried down the pulverized ore.

Her brain buzzing, Annabel explored ways to increase the profitability of their mining enterprise. She'd always been good at coming up with ideas, and now she could put that talent to use. Of course, she was merely passing through, and neither of the men had suggested she might become a permanent addition to the team. However, she refused to let the circumstance dampen her enthusiasm. She was developing a skill for dealing with obstacles, and she would deal with that one, too.

Chapter Eight

Clay spooned his stew, eager to get back into the mine. He tried to avoid looking at the girl, but his eyes kept straying to her across the table. She was chattering like a magpie, coming up with suggestions to improve their mining techniques.

Just the way the girl talked—cheeks flushed, voice high with excitement—ought to have been enough to betray she was a female. Clay glanced over at Mr. Hicks. Was the old man deaf and blind?

Putting down his spoon, Clay cleared his throat and set in motion the plan he'd made while he hacked at the seam of ore in the mine. "We're low on lamp oil. I reckon I ought to ride out to Hillsboro and buy some. I could take the kid with me, put him on the stage, and he could be off on his way."

Mr. Hicks mopped up his plate with a piece of bread. "There's another can of coal oil at the back of the cavern, behind the box of nails and iron chains."

Clay adjusted his balance on the log stump. "I reckon I ought to take the kid back to the railroad anyway. We don't have enough food for three to last a whole month."

Mr. Hicks looked up, frowning. "It's a two-day trip. I can't afford to let you go. We have work to do, and the kid can help. If we run out of grub, you can hunt for game." He shoved the piece of bread into his mouth and spoke around it. "The kid has brains. He did good today. I'll start him on the rocker box tomorrow."

The girl beamed at the praise. "Thank you, Mr. Hicks," she said with that solemn air of hers. "I appreciate your confidence in me, and *the invitation for me to stay*."

The last words were spoken with emphasis, and even though the girl was addressing her comment to Mr. Hicks, she was contemplating Clay across the table, her brows lifted in a meaningful arch. If Clay had ever seen a feminine display of triumph, he was looking at one now.

The old man raked his gray-streaked beard with his fingers. "Kid, a couple of days ago you asked to see the mine. Now's good a time as any. Clay will show you around."

Clay tensed. His fingers drummed against the edge of the tin plate as he sought for a way out. Women didn't go into mines. It was bad luck. And he didn't want the girl stumbling against him in the dark, tempting him to put his hands in places he shouldn't be putting them.

"The mine tunnel is no place for a—" he stopped just in time "—for a scrawny city kid. It's dark and dank. The walls are slimy. There are bats in the cave at the back." Clay racked his brain for more nasty prospects to scare a woman. "There could be snakes, and you don't see them until you step on them. The roof of the tunnel is unsound. It could cave in."

Frowning, Mr. Hicks stared at him. "What's gotten into you, Clay? If I didn't know better I'd believe you've developed a fear of the mine."

"I'm thinking of the kid. A tenderfoot."

The girl spoke up. "Are the snakes poisonous?"

Clay felt success within his grasp. "The deadly kind."

The girl tilted her head to one side and gave him a

rueful smile. "In that case, I'll make sure that you walk ahead of me."

Clay pushed up to his feet. He cast a longing look at the slices of bread and the jar of honey on the table, but the lure of the food was not enough to persuade him to stay around and continue the debate.

"Sorry," he said. "Today is not a good day to have a scrawny kid tagging after me. Mr. Hicks can take you tomorrow when it's his turn to work the mine."

A woman should understand when a man has said his final word. Clay marched off, heading back toward the mine tunnel. He half expected a protesting call to ring after him, but all he could hear was the incessant prattle of that too-feminine voice as the girl went on about reorganizing their business.

Annabel watched Clay retreat. Just before he disappeared out of sight behind the dead oak that hid the mine entrance, he lifted one hand and gave his hat a thump, ramming it deeper over his head.

She fisted her hands in her lap, fighting to suppress the forlorn feeling. Why did he suddenly want to be rid of her, send her away? It was not fair to have rescued her, lulling her into a sense of safety, and then withdraw his protection, as if she had become too much of a burden.

"Kid, have you done something to annoy Clay?"

Annabel snapped her head around and saw Mr. Hicks studying her with a curious look on his bearded face. "No," she hurried to reply. "Nothing…" She heaved out a guilty sigh. "I did ask him about his past…and perhaps I was a bit…*relentless*…in my questioning."

"Ain't you learned nothing, kid?" Mr. Hicks boomed. "In the West a man's past belongs to him and to him alone. Men have been shot for less. Count yourself lucky you're just a scrawny kid. Otherwise you might be sporting a bullet in your chest."

Why did they have to insist on calling her a *scrawny* kid, as if the adjective was chained to the noun? Annabel scowled but found nothing to say in her defense.

"Don't worry, kid," Mr. Hicks went on, his tone easing. "Clay will come 'round. He is just worried because the lode of quartz is petering out. But I'm the boss around here, and my word is the law. If I say Clay will show you the mine today, then he'll do just that."

Mr. Hicks got to his feet and took down the storm lantern hanging from the ceiling. He opened the stove, picked up a piece of kindling from the woodpile and held it to the fire until it caught. Using the burning stick, he lit the lantern.

"Never waste a match, kid," he said as he handed the lantern to her. "If you run out at the wrong time it might mean the difference between survival and freezing to death." He gestured down the path. "Push past the dead tree, and the entrance is right in front of you. There's only one tunnel. After a few paces it turns left and goes on for about ten yards. You can't get lost."

Annabel took the lantern. "Thank you, sir. And thank you for sticking up for me. I'll make sure you won't regret letting me stay."

Mr. Hicks nodded. He lowered his voice. "I'm counting on that, kid. When you look around the mine, pay close attention to the fissure on the right about halfway down. It connects to a cave beyond. But don't let on to Clay that I asked."

Why? Annabel wanted to know, but the old man's warning not to ask too many questions made her hold her tongue. She lifted the lantern high in front of her, as if to practice illuminating her way, and set off toward the mine entrance.

There had been an element of truth in Clay's warnings, Annabel discovered, for the air in the mine was dank, and after the sharp twist to the left very little daylight reached the tunnel. When she ran one hand along the rough rock wall, she could feel the slippery texture, a sign of high humidity. She picked her steps carefully, shining the light at her feet, to avoid tripping as well as a precaution, just in case Clay's threat of poisonous snakes was based on fact.

Even in the widest places the tunnel was no more than five feet wide, and sometimes so low she suspected the men might have to duck. After a few yards the last glimmer of daylight faded, and she had to rely on the lantern alone. She longed to turn up the wick, but was afraid to try, for she might turn the knob the wrong way and end up extinguishing the flame.

The steady clinking of a pickaxe warned her before she pushed through a narrow gap and saw the sphere of lamplight ahead. Judging by the position, the lantern was perched on a rock ledge at knee height.

Annabel found herself hurrying to reach the safety of another human being in the gloomy darkness. The swinging of the pickaxe ceased, and Clay turned to watch her approach. The faint light did not allow Annabel to see his expression, but the way he held his body rigid spoke of frustration, perhaps even anger.

"Did I not tell you not to come?" There was dismay in his tone.

Her heartbeat quickened. "Mr. Hicks sent me." She held her lantern high to shine the light on Clay's features, but he averted his face.

"Mr. Hicks suggested I look around," Annabel repeated her defense.

Clay swept one arm in the air. "Look around, then. The scenery ain't exactly varied."

Annabel wrinkled her nose. "What is that smell? Like burnt matches?"

"Bats. They must live in the cave behind the crack in the wall. They don't come out this way. There must be another exit somewhere."

She took a step closer to him. "Show me what there is to see."

Clay exhaled an audible sigh. He lifted his lantern high with one hand and took her elbow with the other, intending to guide her forward, but Annabel refused to budge. "You first," she told him. "Snakes, remember?"

The silence went on for a long moment. Annabel could guess Clay's dilemma. Either admit to exaggerating, or leave her to stumble after him. He chose to confess.

"There's no snakes that I know of. But there could be."

"And some of them might even be poisonous," Annabel replied.

She felt her anxieties melt away as Clay stood beside her, his hand curled around her elbow, strong and steady. Despite his resentment, she could feel protectiveness in his manner, and an odd sense of reverence, as if he worried about her safety more than he did of his own.

"Show me where the bats are," she told him.

"Over this way." Carefully, he guided her along.

As Clay gave her a tour of the mine, explaining how they had carved the tunnel following a natural fault in the rock, it dawned on Annabel that he held a deep interest in geology and mining. She'd never seen him animated like that before. From the terms he used, she surmised he must have read books on the topic. She longed to bombard him with more questions about his past, but she resisted the temptation, not wishing to spoil the moment of easy companionship.

The fissure was a jagged vertical crack halfway along the tunnel, just as Mr. Hicks had described. Twenty inches wide at the most, it spanned floor to ceiling. When Annabel eased her hand into the cleft, she could feel a cool draft against her fingers. Clay had to be right about another entrance on the opposite side. The current of air carried a strong smell of phosphorus and ammonia.

"Seen enough?" Clay said.

"Yes…but I'd like to ask you something."

Clay groaned out loud. Undeterred, Annabel continued. "I've already told you that I was on my way to the Arizona Territory when I got off the train."

"I've been meaning to ask you," Clay cut in. "Why was that gent in fancy duds chasing after you? Did you steal something from him?"

"No!" Annabel burst out. "He…he just thought I was someone else. It was foolish of me to run off like that, but I didn't want to borrow trouble. He seemed very insistent, and I didn't know what this other person might have meant to him."

She fell silent. Clay didn't comment. His green eyes glittered in the lamplight, sharp and unfathomable, as if he might have been able to figure out more from her words than she had actually said.

"I told you," Annabel went on, "I have two sisters. I was on my way to join them, in a place called Gold Crossing, Arizona Territory." She looked up at Clay, a plea in her eyes. "They'll worry about me. Is there any way you could take me to Hillsboro, so I could send a telegram to them, let them know that I'm safe? Or perhaps, if I write a letter, we could find someone to mail it, for example a miner on a nearby mining claim who has business in Hillsboro?"

"Those pretty sisters of yours," Clay said slowly, "what were their names again?"

Eager to talk about her beloved sisters, Annabel did not take the time to consider what might have prompted the inquiry and replied without hesitation. "The eldest is Charlotte. She is twenty-four. The middle sister is called Miranda. She is twenty-two."

As soon as she'd said *middle sister*, Annabel realized her mistake. She held her breath. It was a tiny, tiny slip. It would be a miracle if Clay homed in on the implication.

He spoke very softly. "And the youngest," he said. "What might her name be? Not Andrew, I'll wager. What is it? Ann? Anita? Annette?"

He knew. Annabel swallowed. At first, her nerves spiked, but then her quick mind shifted through the facts, and her unease changed to elation. Of course! He must have figured it out earlier. He wanted to send her away, not to be rid of her but to protect her, because a mining camp was not a safe place for a young woman.

"It's Annabel," she told him. "My name is Annabel." Then, in the spirit of honesty she added to her confession. "And I am eighteen."

She shifted her weight from foot to foot, waiting for Clay to react. When he said nothing, she peered anxiously up at him. "How did you find out?"

Those green eyes met hers. Annabel could feel Clay hesitate, could sense the sudden escalation of tension in him. When he spoke, his voice was low. "I saw you with your hair unbound."

"Saw me with my hair…?" Slowly, the revelation settled in her mind. There was only one occasion since she arrived at the mining camp when she had released her coiled hair—to wash it by the creek, when she'd also unbound her breasts.

"You watched me bathe?" It was as much an accusation as a question.

Clay replied with a silent nod. No excuses, no apology, even though he had spied upon her during the most private of moments. A fiery blush flared to Annabel's cheeks at the realization he'd seen her half-naked—had seen her the way no man except her husband should see a lady.

"How...how could you?" she stammered, aghast yet at the same time with a rush of heat that made her feel acutely aware of her body.

Clay shrugged, but it was an uneasy gesture. "I went down to the creek to check up on a scrawny kid, but I ended up seeing a girl." His eyes narrowed at her. "Nothing good ever comes from lies."

"I..." Annabel clamped her mouth shut. She'd been about to say she was sorry, but what would she be apologizing for? For being female? For teasing him from the safety of her disguise? She brushed aside her confused feelings and focused on the practical aspects of the situation. "Will you tell Mr. Hicks?"

"I don't know," Clay replied with a sigh. "He'll be mad as hell if he finds out. Women are bad luck in mines. Do you realize what you've done by insisting that you wish to see the mine? If he discovers you're a girl, everything that goes wrong with the mine will be your fault because you've jinxed the place."

He shone the lantern light on her face. "If the seam of gold peters out, as it looks it might do, he'll blame you. Are you prepared for that?"

"He seems a kind man."

"Kind?" Clay gave a bitter bark of laughter. "Maybe he can seem like a cuddly teddy bear when it suits his mood. But make no mistake, if you cross him, he'll be like a grizzly bear disturbed out of hibernation."

Annabel's mouth went dry, but she rallied. "So, it's best not to tell him?"

"Best not to tell him," Clay agreed in a somber tone. "But he'll be blind and deaf not to figure it out himself. When you belt out those sea shanties, you forget to lower the pitch of your voice. And your skin looks too soft, now that you don't have boot black smeared on your face. And you preen in front of the mirror in a way only a girl would do. And you prattle like a woman, asking too many questions."

"I'm sorry I probed about your past."

"And I'm sorry that I..." Clay made a rough sound. "Never mind," he added in a low mutter. He took her arm. "Let's get you out of here before you have a chance to jinx the mine and ruin what little might remain of our luck."

For the rest of the afternoon, Annabel helped Mr. Hicks with the rocker box. "So, kid, what did you think about our little hole in the mountainside?" he asked. "Do you think it is rich with gold?"

Subdued at the prospect of a superstition about women and mines, Annabel replied without her usual enthusiasm. "I have no way of knowing if it is a promising mine or not. It is the only one I have ever seen."

Later, after they had finished supper and Mr. Hicks was puffing out fragrant clouds of smoke with his pipe, he raised the topic again. "Kid, when you were in the mine, did you pay attention to the fissure in the rock?"

Annabel was squatting on her heels, washing the tin plates in a bucket of water. She glanced back at Clay over her shoulder. All through supper, she'd been aware of him watching her across the table.

She should be scandalized at the idea that he'd spied on her as she knelt down by the stream to wash her hair, her breasts unbound. But instead she found herself wondering if he'd liked what he saw and wished for another glimpse.

"I made a point of inspecting the crack in the mine wall," she replied to Mr. Hicks. "Cool air comes through. There must be another exit somewhere."

Mr. Hicks spoke with the stem of his pipe clamped between his teeth. "You reckon you might be able to crawl through the hole into the cave, kid?"

Annabel cast her mind back to what she had seen. A vertical gap, jagged and broken, a bit like a streak of lightning in the sky. Maybe twenty inches across at the widest point, tapering to only a few inches at the bottom.

"I could not do it on my own," Annabel said. "I might do it if you lifted me up and held me horizontal and fed me through the widest part of the opening, like pushing a piece of thread through the eye of a needle."

"No," Clay said bluntly. "It's a crazy notion."

Mr. Hicks took his pipe out of his mouth. His expression did not change, and yet an aura of controlled violence suddenly shimmered about him. A shiver ran over Annabel as she recalled Clay's warnings about the mine owner's fiery temper.

"It could save us," Mr. Hicks said. "The seam of gold is petering out. I have an inkling it might continue on the other side of the fissure, but I have no wish to spend a month hacking a passage through only to discover I was mistaken. If the kid can get into the cave, we'll know what's on the other side."

Clay held up a hand in protest. "It is too dangerous. The kid could get hurt. He could get stuck in the passage. He could have an accident while he is alone in the cave and we can't get through to help him."

He was speaking with caution, as if evaluating each word. Annabel suspected it was because he had to watch his tongue, to make sure he didn't slip up and say "her" instead of "him," accidentally revealing her secret.

"It's a risk worth taking," Mr. Hicks insisted.

"No." Clay's tone was implacable.

"I'd like to try it," Annabel cut in. "But I can't promise it will be possible."

Clay twisted in his seat to face her squarely. "Are you crazy?" His green eyes blazed at her in warning. "The cave might have no floor. There could be a sheer drop when you tumble through the gap. There could be a nest of rattlers. Spiders, scorpions. The air could be filled with noxious fumes."

Annabel suppressed a surge of fear. She straightened from the water pail and dried her hands with an old flour sack while addressing her words to Mr. Hicks. "What is our financial position? If there is no more gold, what does it mean?"

Mr. Hicks inhaled through his pipe, leaned back in his seat and glanced over at Clay, as if challenging him not to interfere. "If there is no more gold, we must abandon the claim and find a new one. It will be difficult, with the winter coming on. It's already September. We'll struggle to locate a new claim and build a shelter before the cold weather sets in."

Annabel directed her attention to Clay. "Do you agree?"

Clay shifted his shoulders. "It is a fair assessment. But if there's no gold beyond the fissure, we'll have to move on anyway. You'll have risked your life for nothing."

"But there could be gold?" Annabel pressed.

Clay gave a reluctant nod. "It is a possibility."

Annabel shuttled her gaze between the two men. When she spoke, it occurred to her that her future in the mining camp must have been weighing on her mind, for the words seemed to flow out without a conscious thought. "I will attempt to crawl through the fissure, but at a price," she told them. "I do not know what the arrangement is between the two of you, and I don't care."

Her mind crystal clear, determination reflected in the rigid set of her spine, Annabel put forward her demand. "If I get into the cave, and there is gold, I want a partnership. Any gold we extract will be divided into four equal parts."

She turned to the old man. "Mr. Hicks, I assume you have funded the horse and mule and the equipment, and for that you should get an extra share. The rest must be divided equally between the three of us, one share each."

Mr. Hicks stroked his beard. "You drive a hard bargain, kid."

"Partnership?" Clay frowned. "What's the point? In a month you'll be gone, on your way to join your sisters in Gold Crossing."

Annabel turned to the stove to shield herself from his glare. "I have decided to stay a bit longer," she said, striving for a casual tone. "When I get to Gold Crossing, I will need some occupation. I'd like to try gold mining. Working the claim with you will serve as an apprenticeship."

Chapter Nine

"Working the claim with you will serve as an apprenticeship."

Clay seethed in silence, unable to come up with a reasonable objection without revealing the truth. Of all the scrawny girl kids in the world, he had to end up with this one! Her mind was sharper than the knife he carried in his boot, and her stubbornness matched that of the mule.

All night, Clay lay awake, imagining the calamities that might befall the girl if she attempted to reach the cave. In the morning, as if by common consent, they all got up early and sat around the breakfast table. Defying the angry scowls of Mr. Hicks, Clay made another effort to dissuade the girl from the attempt.

"You could plunge into a bottomless pit on the other side."

"You can tie a rope around my waist to stop me from falling. And you can use the same rope to haul me back out again, should I become stuck in the fissure."

"What about snakes? The cave could be a pit of rattlers."

"We'll push an empty tin can tied to a rope through the gap first and bang it about inside the cave, to scare off any snakes."

"Scorpions?"

"Damp places don't attract scorpions." Anticipating his next argument, the girl went on demolishing his objections. "And the draft of fresh air from the cave proves the absence of toxic fumes."

Clay gritted his teeth. He'd been right. She possessed the stubbornness of a mule and a mind sharper than the blade of his knife. He drained his coffee and got to his feet. "What are we waiting for?" he said. "Let's get on with it."

The girl regarded him, a notch between her dainty brows. "No."

Relief flooded Clay. He sank back to his seat. It had all been talk. She wasn't really going to do it. It had just been boasting, childish make-believe.

Mr. Hicks spoke sharply. "You change your mind, kid?"

The girl lifted her chin, haughty as a queen. "Of course not. However, what is the purpose of my excursion into the cave?" When Mr. Hicks failed to offer a prompt reply, she supplied one herself. "To look for gold, of course. But how can I look for gold if I lack the expertise to identify a seam of gold-bearing quartz?"

She spread her hands, waited an instant, then went on, "Today, I shall study the mine. I shall learn what I am looking for, so that I'll not make a wasted trip into that bottomless pit full of snakes and scorpions and noxious fumes."

Annabel lay awake in the darkness, listening to Clay's even breathing. She could hear him, even though he'd moved farther away, putting a distance between them. It occurred to her that nothing troubled his back. It had simply been an excuse to hand over his bedroll, an act of chivalry after he discovered she was a girl.

And now she was defying his orders to stay out of the cave. A kernel of fear niggled in her belly. Had she taken on too much? Had she been foolish to volunteer for the task?

All her life, she'd been the youngest, a follower where her big sisters took the lead. Working as a shoeshine boy and living in the mining camp had offered an opportunity to be independent, to prove her worth.

And now she had a chance of a partnership with two experienced miners. However, without gold there would be no mine, no partnership. If she crawled into the cave, if she located the seam of gold, she would secure the future of the mine and take a big step toward establishing her place in the world.

It might be a dangerous thing to do, but success never came cheap. Moreover, Mr. Hicks and Clay would be there, supporting her with their expertise, and she would use her analytical brain to minimize the risks.

Already, she'd spent an hour in the dark, dank mine, studying the thin vein of gold-bearing ore. She'd learned that gold, mixed with quartz, had once upon a time burst from the molten depths of the earth and solidified into a stripe within the granite. The purer the gold, the brighter the color of the vein.

An owl hooted in the darkness. Something crashed in the woods. Annabel froze, strained her ears. The horse and mule, brought into the safety of the overhang for the night, did not stir. Slowly, she released the air trapped in her lungs.

Wriggling against the hard earth floor, careful not to make a sound that might awaken Clay, she inched closer to him. Surely, he couldn't deny her the comfort of his protection if he remained unaware he was providing it.

With a flare of guilt, Annabel accepted her foolish teasing might have caused a rift between them. She'd let Clay's handsome looks and his rugged masculinity go to her head like a potent wine. Too inexperienced to control the emotions he stirred up in her, she had plunged headlong into testing her feminine allure.

Now that he knew she was a girl, she had to put a stop to it. Anything else would be courting danger. They were alone, away from civilization, and it might be all too easy to give in to the attraction she felt between them. If that happened she might end up ruining her future.

Calmer now, Annabel burrowed into the blankets. Tomorrow, she'd do it. She'd apologize to Clay for taunting him, trying to flirt with him and pestering him with questions about his past. If she promised to stop behaving like a smitten schoolgirl they might find a way to be friends again.

Clay didn't know much about women, but when the girl ambled toward him, trying to look as innocent as a newborn, he knew she was about to make some bold request. He lowered the big hammer he'd been using to smash a piece of ore and turned to watch her approach.

Beneath the brim of her bowler hat, her skin was glowing with the beginnings of a suntan. Her body was slender, her posture erect, the big amber eyes fringed with long lashes. She was a pretty one, this. *Annabel.* He avoided thinking of her by her name, to reduce the risk it might accidentally slip out in front of Mr. Hicks.

"Could I take a moment of your time?" she asked.

"Take all you wish." Clay reached for the canteen by his feet, uncapped it and drank in greedy gulps. The heat of the day was building up. He'd been about to peel off his shirt, but he decided to wait and hear what the girl had to say.

"I owe you an apology." She peered up at him. "I've teased you, and I've pried into your affairs. I'm sorry if my behavior has given you a reason to resent me." She lowered her gaze, poked at the dirt with the toe of her clumsy boot.

A flare of sympathy rose in Clay. Just walking about with those heavy weights on her feet must tax her strength. And she must be used to a comfortable life, yet she made no complaints about the conditions in the mining camp.

"I know you want to send me away," the girl went on. "But I would very much like to stay. I'd like to try to crawl into that cave and find gold for Mr. Hicks. But I..." She took a deep breath, the way Clay had noticed was her habit. Beneath the sharp inhale, he heard something that sounded dangerously close to a sob.

"I don't think I can do it," the girl said, looking at him with a plea in those big amber eyes. "Not unless I have your support and friendship while I'm doing it."

"It's okay, kid," Clay said softly.

Not appearing to listen, the girl charged on. "Please give me another chance. I promise I won't try to flirt with you again, or engage in any feminine wiles, or ask questions about your past. It will be strictly a business partnership."

Clay wanted to laugh. Were women always so contrary? Before, she'd tried to break his shield of privacy with the same determination she'd used to swing the big hammer when she crushed the lumps of ore. Now she was proposing to put up a wall between them.

And yet, Clay knew keeping a distance was the right thing to do. He'd seen orphan boys, desperate for human closeness, become tangled up with a woman who took all they had and gave nothing in return, except perhaps a heap of trouble. He wouldn't let it happen to him. Although he could tell there was no guile in Annabel, it made sense to stand back, keep away from temptation rather than risk giving in to masculine needs that might lead him down a path of no return.

"Aren't you forgetting something from your list of sins?" he asked.

The big amber eyes stared up at him. "What else have I done?"

"If Mr. Hicks discovers you're a girl, he'll blame me. I brought you here."

"Of course." The girl snapped into attention like a well-trained soldier. "From now on, I'll make sure to behave with utter discretion. He'll never find out."

"I'm counting on that," Clay said and meant it, too. If the old man discovered Annabel was a girl, she'd have to go. He would have to send her off to face the dangers of the world alone, or he would have to go with her and say goodbye to Mr. Hicks. Although not exactly a father figure, the gruff old man was the closest to a parent Clay had known since the age of six, and he did not wish to face that choice.

"All right," he said to Annabel. "From now on, you'll stop pestering me and behave like a sensible young man should behave with his business partners."

The shine of gratitude on her face, the eager hope in her eyes, made something tug in Clay's chest. When she opened her mouth and burst into a flurry of thanks, he held up a hand to silence her. "That includes not prattling like a girl."

Clay finished tying the knot around the girl's waist and tugged at the rope. "How does that feel?"

She tested the rope, wriggled against it. "Make it tighter."

Clay adjusted the knot. The big leather coat the girl wore to protect her skin against abrasions from the rock bunched tight around her, making her look small and fragile.

Four lamps illuminated the mine tunnel, three coal oil

lanterns with a glass globe and an old whale oil lamp with an open flame. The whale oil smelled foul as it burned and gave out smoke, but they wanted as much light as possible.

It was midafternoon, but the darkness in the mine was timeless. The three of them had spent the early part of the morning in the tunnel, crowding close to each other as they studied the seam of gold, figuring out where it might continue.

At noontime, the girl had refused food, wanting her stomach empty. To finish her preparations, she had taken a slim piece of timber and burned marks on it with a hot nail, to measure inches. For greater lengths, she had tied knots at intervals into a long piece of rawhide string.

"Ready?" Clay asked, holding up a lantern.

"Almost." The girl stood still in front of him, her face pale as she looked up at him. Then she took a quick step toward him, flung her arms about him and pressed her face to his chest, the impact nearly knocking the bowler hat from her head.

Stunned, the lantern in one hand, Clay lifted his other hand to anchor the girl against him, but she was gone before he had a chance to complete the motion. For a second longer, he could feel the imprint of her warmth against him.

"I'll take the feet," Mr. Hicks said. "You take the head."

Clay put the lantern down. He wrapped his arms around the girl, but the contact was purposeful and efficient now, lacking the emotional charge of the fleeting embrace of a moment ago. Why had she done it? For courage? Or a farewell in case something went wrong and she didn't make it back from the cave?

Mr. Hicks bent his burly frame to grab the girl's feet, and together they lifted her high. One hand curled around her shoulder, steadying her, the other hand beneath her breastbone, supporting her weight, Clay balanced her in the air.

The passage through the fissure was perhaps six feet long. The girl extended her arms, like a diver, and they eased her through the widest part of the gap, carefully holding her high, so she wouldn't become wedged in the gap that narrowed beneath her.

"Back!" she cried out. "Pull me back."

Carefully, the men eased the girl backward and settled her on her feet. She drew swift breaths and spoke in nervous bursts. "Can't do it like that. The passage is too long. You can't reach far enough to hold me up. You'll have to let go of me, and I'll fall into the crack and get stuck."

She turned to face the fissure and gestured. "We'll have to fill the lower part of the gap with earth. Or we might be able to wedge a piece of timber into the gap, and I can slide along it."

They considered the problem, chose the timber beam as the best solution. Clay studied the shape of the gap to determine the size of tree they'd need, and then they trooped out into the open. The girl waited, basking in the sunshine, while the men scoured the forest.

They chose an aspen with a kink in the trunk where it grew past a boulder. After they'd stripped away the branches, Clay took a moment to whittle down the knots and peel away the roughest sections of the bark. To finish off, he ran his palm along the surface to ensure it had no splinters.

By the time they were done, the sun was sinking in the sky. The girl was sitting by the *arrastre* pit, arms wrapped around her knees, head bent, like she'd been when Clay went back for her at the water tower.

"Do you want to rest and try again tomorrow?" he asked.

She looked up, gave him a faint smile and shook her

head. "I'm not tired. I'm just concentrating. Something a friend taught me recently—if I imagine myself through a task ahead and see myself succeed in it, success will come."

After pausing to top up the coal oil lanterns and relight them, they went back into the dank darkness of the mine. Mr. Hicks helped Clay lift the length of timber in place, and they wiggled it about to ensure a snug fit, the kink in the aspen trunk curving around a bump in the rock wall.

"We'll lift you up and you can try it out," Clay said to the girl.

Mr. Hicks squatted to light the whale oil lamp on the ground. While he was busy with the task, Clay had Annabel make a final inspection of the toolkit she had gathered into an oilcloth pouch and strapped around her waist, in case they would be unable to pass anything to her through the gap.

One by one, she showed him the contents. Matches. Candles. Pencil and paper. Her measuring stick and the ball of rawhide string with knots in it. Clay watched her in the lamplight. She seemed so small, so fragile, yet determined as she checked off each item, muttering to herself and frowning in concentration.

She looked up. "I'm ready."

Clay tied the rope around her waist. For an instant, he stepped back, hoping for another one of those lightning hugs, but Annabel lifted her arms in her diver's pose. Clay took her shoulders. Mr. Hicks took her feet, and together they lifted her up and eased her into the gap.

"It's good." Annabel's voice grew muffled as they inched her forward. "The beam is not wide enough to crawl on, but it will stop me from falling into the crevice and provide support when I make my way back from the cave."

She wriggled along. Her hips vanished out of sight. Her

feet kicked in tiny jerks, the way a swimmer's feet might do. Clay fed through the rope tied around her waist, to keep it slack. Finally, her heavy boots disappeared into the fissure. The rope snapped taut and they heard a thud and an alarmed cry.

Then there was only silence.

Chapter Ten

A̲s Annabel pushed through the gap, she advanced into
almost complete darkness. There was nothing to guide
her but the acrid odors ahead and the faint coolness of the
draft on her face.

She'd not appreciated the difficulty of emerging out of
a narrow hole, like the neck of a bottle, with nothing to
hold on to, no means of knowing how far below the ground
was, how hard the landing. Once her head and shoulders
were clear of the passage, she reached down to explore the
cliff wall below with the flat of her hands. The surface was
vertical, smooth and damp and slippery.

Bracing her palms against the stone wall, wriggling
with her hips, kicking with her feet, Annabel inched forward along the narrow beam of timber, emerging into the
cave. When gravity took over, she popped out of the hole
and tumbled down in a wild somersault.

The impact of the landing knocked her breathless. The
drop had been no more than six feet, but the ground was
solid rock. Her bones jarred. However, the worst of it was
the sense of disorientation. It took her a moment to home in
on the streak of light through the gap and get her bearings.

She scrambled to her feet, lined her face with the opening, her only connection to the outside world. She'd been too stunned to realize that Clay's frantic voice was calling out to her. "Kid, are you all right? Kid? Kid?"

"I'm okay." She took a deep breath. "But I would have never agreed to this if I'd understood how terrifying the landing is." Not pausing to wait for a response, she added, "Pass me a lantern, and be quick about it."

The light in the gap intensified, and then a lantern hanging on a metal hook attached to the end of a wooden pole came through. Annabel rose on tiptoe to lift the lantern from the hook and turned around, holding the light high.

She wasn't sure what she'd been expecting to see, but if it had been sparkling stalagmites or a glittering emerald pond, she was in for a disappointment. The cave was roughly twelve feet wide and twice as long, made of gray rock that glistened damp in the glow of the lantern. At the opposite end, a black shadow indicated another fissure that connected deeper into the bowels of the mountain.

"Take the lamp!" Clay was calling out from the mine tunnel.

Annabel turned around, deposited the first lantern on the floor of the cave and reached up to take another one from the hook at the end of the pole.

"I'll pass you the third lantern," Clay called out. "We'll make do with the whale oil lamp."

"No," Annabel called back. "If I have an accident, you might need the lantern to rescue me. I'll manage with two."

Tugging at the rope tied around her waist, she began to explore the cave. Advancing a few steps at a time, she set down one lantern and returned for the other, always making sure there was enough light by her feet, even when she held one of the lanterns high to illuminate the walls.

Moving clockwise, she searched the rock face in a systematic pattern, left to right, ceiling to floor. Nothing but plain gray granite. The fissure at the far end was barely wide enough for her to poke her arm inside. She couldn't see through to the other side, but the draft of fresh air felt stronger here, indicating the presence of another exit.

Some kind of thick white substance that reeked of ammonia covered the rear wall. Bat droppings, Annabel guessed, but when she looked up into the ceiling she could see no bats, and the droppings seemed old, suggesting the bats had abandoned the cave a long time ago.

Clinging to a fading hope, Annabel took longer to inspect the final two walls. The surface was more broken in texture, and paler in color. Holding the light close to the rock, she examined every crevice, pausing to study every variation in color.

Nothing. No sign of gold. Her spirits sank. Just to make sure, she went back to the left wall, where she had started, and inspected it with the same thoroughness she had used to search the other walls.

Nothing.

Fighting the disappointment, she returned to the gap. "I'm sorry," she called out to the men. "No luck. No gold."

"In that case, you can damn well stay there," Mr. Hicks shouted back.

For an instant, terror gripped Annabel. Then sanity returned. She strained her ears and could hear the old man chuckling at his stupid joke.

"We'll get you out, kid," Clay shouted, his tone reassuring.

The rope jerked. The sudden tug around her waist caught Annabel by surprise. Clumsy in her big boots, she lost her balance. Her feet scrambled for purchase against the cave floor covered in a thick layer of bat droppings. One arm flailing, the other arm high in an effort to protect the lantern from smashing against the hard stone surface, she toppled backward, her rump hitting the ground with a bone-jarring thud.

"Ouch!" she cried out, and added a curse she'd picked up from Mr. Hicks. Carefully, she set down the lamp and rubbed her aching rear.

The rope snapped taut again, pulling her sideways. Unprepared, Annabel tipped over and flopped onto her belly. Bracing her weight on her elbows, she tensed her muscles to keep her face away from the stinking layer of bat guano.

Clay's voice came through. "What's wrong, kid?"

She turned her head toward the fissure and called back, "I slipped and fell. Give me a minute. I'll let you know when I'm ready to get out."

As she scrambled to her feet, a glint of color in the rock caught her eye. Right there, in front of her, something glittered in the floor. Holding her breath against the stench of guano, Annabel bent down for a better look.

A gleam of gold!

Her movements urgent, she dropped to her knees and studied the ground, the acrid smells forgotten. In the cave floor, where her boots had scrambled for foothold, cutting a groove through the layer of guano, a yellow stripe two inches wide sparkled in the lantern light.

Frantic now, Annabel scraped the bat droppings out of the way, grateful for the thick leather gloves that protected her hands. Fortunately, the damp air had prevented the guano from drying into a solid layer, allowing her to scoop the substance aside.

She scraped and scraped and scraped, the healing blisters on her palms getting sore despite the protection of the gloves. The smells of phosphorus and ammonia filled her breath, but she ignored the sour stench. Inch by inch she cleared the floor, following the golden stripe across the cave.

"Kid, are you all right?" Clay called out.

"I'm winded from the fall," she replied. "Give me a moment."

She'd already told the men there was no gold. She didn't want to raise their hopes, only to have to quash them again. She wouldn't say anything until she had made a thorough inspection and could be certain. Holding up a lantern, Annabel studied the texture and color of the seam in the floor. She found a small rock, used it to chip away a tiny fragment.

"Kid, talk to me," Clay yelled. "Are you hurt?"

"I'm fine," Annabel replied, impatience in her tone. Although well meant, Clay's concern kept interrupting her thoughts. She put the lantern down, lifted the hem of the big leather coat, untied the oilcloth pouch fastened around her waist and took out her tools.

Squatting on her heels, Annabel mapped out the vein, carefully measuring the width and length, taking the time to study the pattern. Gold was usually found mixed with quartz, but the bright yellow color indicated the vein was almost pure gold.

"Kid, are you hurt?" Clay shouted once more. "Don't lie to me."

"I'm not hurt," Annabel replied and put away the pencil and paper she had used to make notes. "I'm ready to come out."

She picked up the pair of lanterns from the guano-covered ground and made her way to the opening of the fissure. Sliding her feet carefully in order not to slip, she kept her eyes on the rope to stop any sudden tug from jerking her out of balance again.

"Take the lamps," she called out.

Tilting her head back, she lifted one of the lanterns high, ready for the pole with a metal hook to poke through. For a moment, Annabel stared at the fissure, a vague sense of alarm stirring in her brain.

Then it struck her—the opening had moved.

Not moved. But it was higher up.

No longer at shoulder height, she could barely reach the end of the aspen trunk with her fingertips, and only if she rose on her toes. When she'd received the lanterns through the opening, she'd failed to notice the height difference, for the lamps had been hanging by their handles and she'd gripped them by the base.

The floor of the cave must be lower than the floor of the mine tunnel, which put the fissure opening out of reach on this side. Fighting the surge of fear, Annabel put one lantern down, adjusted her grip on the other lantern to hold it by the base and slipped the handle over the hook in the pole as it came through.

The lantern vanished out of sight. The shadows in the cave deepened. A shiver of alarm rippled over her. There was something ominous about the darkness, as if some unseen force was waiting to swallow her up.

"Hurry up," she called out.

The wooden pole poked through again. Annabel hung the second lantern on the hook at the end and watched the light disappear into the gap. Solid darkness closed around her, gloomy and still and threatening.

"Don't pull the lamp all the way," Annabel yelled, a hint of panic in her tone. "Leave it halfway down the fissure until I'm crawling through."

The glow ceased fading, and the narrow band of vertical light from the fissure eased the darkness in the cave. Annabel felt her heart hammering in her chest. Despite the cool air, perspiration coated her skin.

Up to now, her focus had been on getting into the cave. She'd given little thought to getting out again. Was this what the lure of riches did to men? Did greed drive one blind to danger? Or was it only natural to assume that if you could complete the journey in one direction the return trip could be no more difficult?

But the fissure opening was two feet higher up.

And on the other side she'd had two men helping her.

"Hold the rope tight," she called out. "I need to climb. The floor is lower on this side. I can barely touch the aspen trunk with my fingertips."

Keeping on the thick leather gloves to protect her hands, Annabel rose on her toes and reached up to curl her fingers around the end of the aspen trunk. The rope pulled taut. She lifted up one foot, braced the toe of her boot against the rock face.

"Now!" she shouted.

The rope jerked tight, cutting into her body. She scrambled upward, slung one arm over the aspen trunk. Her boots scrabbled for purchase against the slippery rock wall. The muscles in her arms quivered as she tried to climb. She couldn't get a foothold, couldn't haul herself higher with her arms.

Her grip on the aspen trunk slipped, and she fell to dangle at the end of the rope. Her body swung sideways, her knees slamming against the solid rock. She tipped her head backward to protect her face. The rope bit into her rib cage with a crushing force.

"Let me down," she yelled. "Let me down."

The rope slackened. Her toes touched the ground. *Don't panic. Think. Stay calm.* Annabel tugged at the rope to ease the pressure against her ribs and took a step back to study the rock face. She fought the urge to ask for one lantern to be returned. They couldn't afford to leave any of their sources of light behind.

She reached into the pouch at her waist, took out a candle and a small waterproof tin of matches. The cave walls were damp, the soles of her boots muddy. Looking around, Annabel searched for a dry surface against which to strike the match. Finally, she bounced up on tiptoe and used a bit of bark on the aspen trunk.

In the flickering light of the candle, she examined the rock, searching for tiny dents and cracks, any unevenness she could use for a foothold, attempting to map a route upward along the wall. She took off one glove, felt the surface of the rock. It was damp and slippery.

"Kid, what's going on? Have you stopped to take a nap? We haven't got all day." It was Mr. Hicks calling, and to Annabel's surprise his coarse humor calmed her nerves.

"You gotta wait till I'm ready," she called back.

Perhaps, if she asked the men to make a torch for her—a rag soaked in kerosene—she could dry out the humid wall, making it easier to climb. *No, too dangerous*, Annabel decided. She sniffed at the air, thick with the odors of phosphorus and ammonia. The guano might be flammable. Using a kerosene-soaked torch could turn the interior of the cave into a fireball.

She concentrated on memorizing the footholds in the rock. On the left, a small depression at knee height. To the right, higher up, a tiny protrusion. From there on, the fissure widened to three inches. If she could get that high, she might be able to wedge the toe of her boot into the fissure and climb up.

"All right," she called out. "Haul me out of here."

The rope tightened. She bounced up, clung to the rock, scrambled madly. Left foot. The tiny depression. Right foot. The small protrusion. Clasping the aspen trunk with both hands, she lifted one foot high, fitted the toe of her boot into the fissure and tensed her muscles. "Pull," she yelled and surged upward.

The rope failed to tighten. She fell out of balance, flung backward and tumbled down. The rope snapped taut, leaving her swinging like a pendulum against the rock. The impact stole the air from her lungs. Rasping, Annabel fought to get her breath going again.

"Give me slack," she shouted in croaky voice.

"Can't." Clay's tone was stark. "The rope is stuck."

Despair seized Annabel. With all her preparation, she'd forgotten to take a knife. If she had a blade now, she could cut the rope. The men could pull the rope through and feed it out again. They could hammer metal eyelets into the aspen trunk to make sure the rope ran freely through the crevice.

But without a knife she was left dangling. The pressure of the rope crushed her ribs, making it hard to breathe. Was this how she was going to die? At the end of a rope in a dark, dank cave?

The dreams of gold and riches seemed meaningless now. Prospectors and miners who risked their lives in search of gold, did they not understand how little a fortune meant compared to human life?

Annabel fought the pain, fought the onslaught of panic. Tears burned in her eyes, but she refused to let them fall. This was the ultimate test. No one could help her but her alone. She had to make it up that rock face. Or she would die. Die alone in the darkness.

She thought of her sisters. If she didn't get up that rock, she'd never see them again. She thought of Clay, the sense of safety she'd felt when she clung to him on horseback, his gentle touch as he tended to her blistered hands, the thrill of excitement that ran through her every time she looked at him.

If she didn't get up that rock, she'd never see him again. She would never have a chance to build on those new emotions he stirred in her, would never have a chance to discover if the attraction between them could lead to something true and lasting.

She would never see another sunrise, would never feel the wind on her face again, would never see the ocean or the desert in spring bloom. She would die in this dark, dank, smelly cave with a fortune in gold right below her dangling feet.

"I'm climbing up," she called out. "Keep pulling the rope."

Flattening her body against the slippery stone like a lizard, Annabel eased upward. Her left foot found that tiny depression. Her right foot braced over the tiny protrusion. Gathering her strength, she lifted her left foot high, jammed the toe of her boot into the crevice and pulled with her arms, every muscle shaking with effort as she hauled herself up. She released her grip on the end of the aspen trunk and, for an instant poised in a precarious balance, extended her arms in the diver's pose and crammed her body into the fissure.

Her shoulders bashed against the rock. Her hips caught in the narrow passage, but she forced her way through, ignoring the abrasion against her skin, ignoring the bashes and knocks. Nothing could persuade her to pause until she was in daylight and fresh air.

"Move the lamp out of the way," she shouted. "I'm coming through."

Only when she could see the lit-up mine tunnel ahead, and caught her first glimpse of Clay peering into the fissure, did the panic that had taken hold of her recede. In those terrible moments in the cave, her greatest fear had been not seeing him again, and now a wave of relief propelled her into greater speed along the timber beam.

She longed to feel his arms around her, longed to nes-

tle against the solid strength of his body The light behind
Clay turned him into a silhouette, and she could not see
his expression. Did he feel the same? How stark had his
fear for her safety been while she remained out of sight,
how deep his relief on her safe return?

Reaching out with one arm, Annabel could touch him,
her fingertips grazing the locks of hair that tumbled across
his forehead. That physical contact acted like a lightning
rod that made her terror dissipate. Instead, a wild, gloat-
ing jubilation rose inside her. She'd done it! She had found
gold. As Clay pulled her out through the fissure, it occurred to Annabel she'd answered her own question.

*Prospectors and miners who risked their lives in search
of gold, did they not understand how little a fortune meant
when compared to human life?*

Of course they did. Every miner understood the dangers. But the triumph of success was a potent drug. The
moment one had a taste of it, the dangers became only a
distant memory, the fear akin to an illness one must overcome. And she had.

Chapter Eleven

Clay crammed his shoulders into the narrow fissure, eased the girl out and swung her up to her feet. He could feel her trembling. Without thinking, he pulled her into his embrace and held her close, one hand sweeping up and down her back in a soothing gesture.

She sagged against him and spoke in breathless relief. "I thought…for a moment I thought I would never get out…"

"Hush." He clutched her tight against him. She smelled of bat droppings and stale dampness, and Clay breathed in the smells, enjoying them because they meant she was out of danger and with him again.

The girl mumbled against his chest. "Get me into the sun."

Clay bent to scoop her into his arms and twisted around to look at Mr. Hicks, who was standing like a ghost a few paces away, disappointment stamped on his brooding features.

"You go first," Clay told him. "Hold up a lantern. When you get to the entrance, pull the dead tree out of the way."

"Why?" Mr. Hicks protested. "You can push through with the kid."

Clay addressed the old man with unaccustomed harshness. "Can't you see the kid is just about done in? Your joke about leaving him stranded in the cave was one step too far."

Mr. Hicks bristled but edged past, illuminating the way. Clay carried the girl out through the mine tunnel, ducking and turning sideways to avoid scraping any part of her against the rock walls. The last glimmer of sunlight formed a golden archway at the entrance. As soon as they stepped out into the open, the girl wriggled in his arms. "Put me down."

Reluctantly, Clay obeyed. The girl hurried along the cliff face to a smooth spot, leaned her back against the sun-warmed rock and tilted her face up toward the setting sun. Her lips were trembling, her skin pale, her lungs heaving.

So frightened yet so brave. Something twisted in Clay's chest as he watched her. He never wanted to see her put herself in danger like that again. He wanted to see her always in the sunshine, warm and safe, as she was now.

The girl stood there for long minutes, drawing deep breaths, until the sun disappeared behind the hills and the light began to fade. Mr. Hicks had gone into the kitchen, but now he strode back along the path, the heavy thud of his footsteps betraying his sense of defeat.

"Is the kid all right?" the old man asked in a low voice.

The girl opened her eyes. A smile spread on her face, banishing those lingering signs of terror. "I am all right." She pulled one hand out of the thick glove and jabbed a forefinger at the old man. "But I have a good mind not to tell you what I found."

Mr. Hicks frowned. "You found nothing. That's what you said."

"And that's what I thought at first. But then I slipped on the rotting layer of bat droppings on the cave floor." Her smile grew radiant. "There is gold—a thick seam of gold that runs like a creek along the bottom of the cave."

She pivoted on her big boots toward Clay. "Quickly. Find me a stick and I'll draw you a picture."

Clay turned to break a sturdy twig from the dead oak that had shielded the mine entrance. Not waiting for him to complete the task, the girl ran off ahead. Clay and Mr. Hicks hurried after her to the gravel clearing.

Brimming with excitement, the girl snatched the long stick from Clay and drew on the ground. "It starts about three paces after the opening, and twists to the right, like this…" She paused to take off the leather coat she'd borrowed from him and pulled a sheet of paper from the pouch tied around her waist.

Pausing every now and then to refer to her scribbled notes, she went on drawing. "There are two parallel veins, each about two inches wide. One of them peters out after six feet. The other one widens to three inches, like this…"

"You sure it's gold, kid?" Mr. Hicks cut in. "Not pyrite?"

Again, the girl reached into the pouch tied around her waist and rummaged inside. "I hacked away a tiny sample." After a few moments, she gave up the search with a careless shrug. "I must have dropped it in the darkness. No matter," she added and let go of the pouch. "It's gold, all right."

Eyes shining, talking in rapid bursts, she completed the drawing on the ground, to illustrate the seam of gold she had found. Finished, she tossed away the stick, spread her arms wide and rushed up to Mr. Hicks.

"We are rich," she yelled and gave the old man one of those fleeting hugs. Then she turned to Clay and did the same with him. Pulling away before Clay had a chance to react, she began leaping about.

"We are rich! We have gold!"

The old man spoke with a mix of hope and doubt. "Kid,

you're not taunting me, paying me back for saying I'd leave you stranded in the cave? There really is gold in there?"

The girl did not reply. Whirling on her big boots, she danced in the twilight and burst into one of those sea shanties, making the words fit the occasion.

Golden here, golden there,
Golden almost everywhere.
Golden up and golden down.
Golden all around the ground.

"I'll be damned." A huge grin split the old man's bearded face. Emitting a yell of triumph that echoed back from the cliffs, he launched into a jig, as clumsy as a dancing bear in a circus.

Clay stepped into the fray and seized the girl by the waist. Like quicksilver she was in his arms, and Clay told himself he'd best clasp her tight to his chest, for otherwise she might do herself harm with all that frantic leaping about.

She had done it! She had performed a perilous feat of courage and found a vein of gold! Annabel teetered on a log stump seat in the kitchen. Only a single lantern cut through the darkness, for they were low on lamp oil and wanted to save it for working in the mine. But what was darkness to her anyway? She'd ventured into a dank, dark cave that might have been a pit of rattlers, or an abyss leading all the way into the center of the earth.

"Go easy on the whiskey, kid," Mr. Hicks said.

Annabel giggled. *Kid.* She'd fooled the old man. A hiccup caught in her throat. She'd tasted only one small glass of the fiery liquid, but it had been enough to make her head spin and melt away the last residue of fear inside her.

Too elated to sleep, the three of them had eaten a cold supper of bread and venison jerky and were now sitting at the kitchen table, celebrating with a bottle of whiskey that Mr. Hicks had dug up from the stores under the overhang.

"It would take too long to hack a passage to reach the cave," Mr. Hicks said. "We'll have to blast our way through." He smiled at her, like a proud parent. "I'll teach the kid to use black powder and set a fuse."

"No," Clay said. "Absolutely not."

"Why not?" Annabel waved one arm at him, the pleasant glow of whiskey flowing through her veins. "I can do it. I can do *a-ny-thing*."

"With gunpowder you could even maim yourself or get killed." Clay's tone rang with irony.

"The kid is a quick learner."

Clay shook his head. "I said *no*."

Mr. Hicks spoke in a conciliatory tone. "Think about it, Clay. The winter will be here soon. We need to buy two more horses. The kid will need a saddle, and a warm coat and boots. If we spend weeks hacking through the rock, we won't have time to build a cabin, and we won't have enough money to pay for things."

Clay mulled it over. "It's too dangerous. A spark can ignite the powder, and *boom*! No more kid. I'll not allow it."

"*Not allow it*?" Annabel echoed. "You'll *not allow it*?" She lolled back in the seat and would have lost her balance if Clay hadn't reached out to grab her by the elbow.

"Excuse me, Mr. Collier," she said tartly, shaking off his supporting hand. "I do not require your permission to do anything." She was no longer Scrappy the deckhand, the youngest of the Fairfax sisters, the one who had to take orders. For the first time in her life, she had the chance to be the captain of the ship—even more so than she'd been as a shoeshine boy, for now she had a crew to command.

She turned her attention to Mr. Hicks. "Sir, I'll be happy to blast you a hole all the way to the center of the universe. You'll just have to show me how it's done."

Clay seethed in silence on the log stump seat. Had the girl switched off that razor-sharp mind of hers? Did she not understand the dangers? And Mr. Hicks, he just sat there, egging her on. Perhaps he should say it, Clay thought. Just blurt out that the kid was a girl.

He recalled how she'd felt pressed against him a moment ago, warm and vibrant and full of life. Icy fear enveloped him as he imagined the possibility of stones raining down on her, imagined the sight of blood and broken bones.

He could not let it happen.

He could not allow her to risk her life.

And if an order to stay away from explosives didn't work, maybe a bit of blackmail might achieve a better result. Clay pushed to his feet. "I'll move the dead tree back to hide the mine entrance. The kid can help." He picked up the lantern from the table and set off down the path.

Mr. Hicks, enthralled by the prospect of riches, made no protest that the task could wait until daylight. The girl, eager as always to prove her worth, bounced up and hurried along. In the darkness, Clay could feel her fingers gripping his elbow, in search of support and balance.

At the cave entrance, Clay halted, propelled the girl into the mouth of the tunnel and went in after her. He ducked to deposit the lantern on the floor and seized her by the upper arms, pressing her back against the rough rock wall.

"Haven't you forgotten something?" His voice was harsh.

"What?" the girl said. She tipped her head back, and the dull glow of the lantern by their feet made her features look mysterious and her eyes dark and deep, full of feminine allure.

Clay eased closer. "That your name is Annabel. Not Andrew."

"So?" Her dainty eyebrows arched. "I'm a girl. What difference does it make?"

Promise you'll stay out of the cave, or I'll tell Mr. Hicks and he'll toss you down the hill, Clay was about to say. But as he stared down at her face, the words scattered in his mind, like the autumn leaves scattered in the night breeze outside. Instead, he bent his head toward her. "This," he murmured, and settled his mouth on hers.

He could feel the girl's sharp intake of breath, could sense the shock that rippled along the length of her as he pressed his body against hers. Even through the sudden surge of passion that clouded his thinking, he could smell the scent of floral soap on her, could taste a hint of coffee on her lips, combined with the mellow burn of good whiskey.

Years ago, Clay had figured out that his emotions ran too deep to allow for casual intimacies. On the few occasions he'd paid for the company of a whore, he'd never allowed himself the make-believe that a tumble in the bed of a working girl was anything more than scratching an itch.

But now the recklessness from whiskey and the pent-up anger at the way the girl kept defying his orders combined into a volatile mix that made him forget every caution, ignore every warning, override every hesitation.

Again and again, he slanted his mouth across the girl's with a hungry demand. After that first startled reaction, she did not resist. Her lips parted, and she tipped her head back, offering him access. The softness of her lips, the eagerness of her yielding, the feel of her supple body in his arms made Clay forget the message of danger he had intended to convey with the kiss.

Soon he'd have to stop, but then he'd have to say something, explain his actions. Unable to justify what he'd done, even to himself, Clay finally found the strength to lift his head and draw apart from the girl. His heart was hammering, his muscles quivering, his breathing ragged.

"This," he said roughly. "This is what difference it makes you're a girl." Hiding his turmoil by turning around to face the darkness, Clay picked up the lantern from the ground. He took the girl's hand in his and led her out of the tunnel.

Not a single word passed between them as they walked back to the kitchen. The girl seemed in a trance, her lips trembling, her eyes wide and shining. Every step, Clay had to resist the temptation to whirl about and haul her back into the privacy of the mine tunnel and resume what he'd barely had the strength to stop.

Clay settled the girl at the table opposite to Mr. Hicks, who was now talking to himself, listing everything he would buy with the gold. With a quick glance at the old man, to make sure he was not listening, Clay bent toward the girl.

"That was the whiskey ruling our actions," he said quietly. "And the euphoria of surviving danger. Don't let it worry you," he added, his tone strained at the warning he knew applied to him just as much as it might apply to her. "In fact, best you forget it ever happened, and I'll do the same."

Annabel lay huddled up on the bedroll in the cavern. Despite the chill of the night, heat enveloped her, as if she had remained too long in the sun. Beside her, Clay slept with his back toward her.

Trying not to make a sound, Annabel shifted beneath the blanket and touched her fingertips to her lips. She traced the shape of her mouth, recalling the sensations. She'd never been kissed before. Not like that, on the lips, with hunger and passion. Her only points of comparison were the friendly pecks on the cheek she'd received from Mama or Papa and her sisters.

She'd expected a kiss to be cool and moist, like lips pressing against a glass of water. Instead, it had been warm and vibrant, with textures to it—the brush of Clay's dry, slightly chapped lips over hers, the scrape of his beard stubble against her skin, the slick slide of mouth on mouth when he'd tempted her into parting her lips.

It's best you forget it ever happened, Clay had told her. Annabel suppressed a groan at such masculine ignorance. How could she ever forget? Surely, for every girl, every woman, their first kiss remained branded in their memory, one of the rites of passage into womanhood.

She must have made a sound, for Clay rolled over on the hard earth floor. The moon was out, and she could see his features, could see the faint glint of his open eyes and knew he was looking at her. During the day, Annabel rarely saw him without a hat, but now a tumble of brown curls framed his face.

"Are you all right?" Clay whispered softly.

Annabel longed to reach over and rake her fingers into his hair. For a moment, she considered giving in to the temptation. She wanted him to kiss her again, wanted to feel those fiery sensations the kiss had awakened in her body. Frightened by her brazen thoughts, Annabel curled up beneath the blankets, like a hedgehog rolling into a protective ball. "I'm fine," she whispered back.

For a moment, Clay contemplated her, the moonlight

glinting in his green eyes, like a reflection on a pond. Then he nodded and turned away again.

So, he'd not been sleeping either, Annabel thought. Echoes of her fears from a few days ago pealed in her mind. It would be all too easy for a man and woman, isolated in the remote mining camp, to forget about the world outside. But for a woman, a virtue lost was lost forever. No such constraints applied to a man.

Clay was right, she decided with a sigh. It was best she forgot the kiss ever happened. But as Annabel closed her eyes and let fatigue overcome the tensions of the day, lulling her into sleep, she knew that she never would.

For two days, Clay wrestled with conflicting impulses. He didn't want the girl anywhere near explosives. But how could he stop her? He knew the answer. He had to tell the old man the kid was a girl, and Mr. Hicks would pack her off down the hill so fast the bowler hat would finally become unstuck from her head. And yet, he found himself unable to betray her secret and say goodbye to her.

Shirtless, water-soaked trousers clinging to his legs, Clay left the rocker box by the creek and walked up to the clearing. He found the girl and Mr. Hicks crouched over a big rock. The whirr of the hand drill against stone told Clay what they were doing even before he got close enough to watch.

"When you've finished drilling the hole, you pack it with gunpowder, like this." Mr. Hicks was using a handful of cornmeal to demonstrate. "And then you push in a metal needle, like this."

"Don't forget to tell the kid that if the needle makes a spark the gunpowder will explode and he'll blow himself to pieces," Clay cut in. That's how Lee had gone. Even now, almost six years later, nausea welled up inside Clay as he recalled the sound of the explosion and the smell of burning flesh.

The old man scowled. "We'll use a copper needle. There'll be no spark." He turned back to his demonstration. "Then you pull out the needle and insert a fuse into the hole where the needle was, like this." He fiddled about with a hickory ramming rod, using a piece of rawhide cord in place of a fuse.

"Then you cover the gunpowder with a dollop of mud to create a plug and let it dry. A strong plug is needed to confine the expanding gases that create the force of the blast."

The old man glanced up at Clay, his expression defiant. "When you have finished all the charges, you light the fuses and walk away and wait for the black powder to do its job."

The girl jumped up to her feet and sauntered over to Clay. Taking both his hands in hers, she looked up at him with those big amber eyes. "Please," she said. "I want to do it, and I know that I can. Instead of trying to stop me, can't you help? Teach me how to do it and remain safe."

Clay felt his breath catch as he looked down into her expectant face. With enough care and preparation, the risk would be minimal. And he could tell how much the girl wanted to do it, how much it meant to her to contribute to their success.

Ever since that impulsive, whiskey-driven kiss, the memory of her lips against his had refused to leave him in peace. Now his body quickened. His heart was beating too fast, his every sense heightened. He wanted to kiss her again, and almost gave in to the temptation, despite Mr. Hicks crouching no more than ten paces away, his sharp eyes watching them.

Shows the danger of casual intimacies, Clay thought with a flash of wry humor. *They can scramble a man's mind, make him think with the basement part of his anatomy when he should be thinking with the attic.*

"All right," he said with a resigned sigh. He brushed his thumbs over the back of the girl's fingers, enjoying the way her small hands fitted into his. "You can drill the holes and set the charges. But you can't light the fuses. I'll take care of that."

Annabel grew adept at crawling into the cave and spent hours working with the hand drill, in turn banging the end of the drill shaft with a hammer and rotating the handle to create a series of holes in the rock.

They were laying the charges in a horizontal line along the fissure. Clay was able to take care of the first two holes, reaching in from the mine tunnel, and she had to drill the final three, awkwardly balanced on the aspen trunk.

Sometimes, as they labored together, their bodies bumped. The physical contact made Annabel edgy and restless. At the same time she felt a new shyness in Clay's presence. She tried to ignore the sensations he created in her, tried to push aside the memory of how he'd kissed her. It was best forgotten, at least for now. When working with explosives, one needed a cool head and steady hands.

"We'll set the fuses now," Clay told her when they had completed the task of drilling the holes. "And then we'll cover the powder with mud and let it dry. When I'm ready to light the fuses, I want you to go down to the creek and stand next to the rocker box and not come up again until I fetch you."

"Clay, hold your horses a mite," Mr. Hicks cut in.

Perhaps the darkness of the mine tunnel made her ears more sensitive to nuances, Annabel thought, for she could hear an undertone of guilt in the old man's voice.

"What is it?" Clay asked tersely.

"We don't have much fuse wire left."

Annabel had learned the men used the Safety Fuze invented by William Bickford fifty years ago. Ordinary fuses could burn at an unpredictable rate, could break or be left smoldering, particularly if exposed to damp.

The Bickford Safety Fuze was waterproof, did not break or deteriorate, and burned at the steady rate of thirty seconds per foot, allowing the miners to know exactly how long they had to get out of the way before the charge went off.

"Let me see how much there is left," Clay said.

Annabel eased closer to him. Clay reached for what Mr. Hicks was holding out to him and inspected the coil of fuse wire in the dull light of the lantern.

"Did you know all along?" Clay's tone was grim.

Mr. Hicks did not reply. The silence spoke for itself.

Clay spun around, boot heels grating against the ground, and strode off. Annabel stared after him as he disappeared into the darkness, trailing one hand along the rock wall to guide his way since he carried no lantern. She longed to go after him but chose to remain, for out of the pair of them Mr. Hicks was the more likely to provide answers.

"What is it?" she asked.

"Well…" The old man's tone was evasive. "It's nothing, really. Only that we have less than ten feet of fuse wire left."

Ten feet. Five holes. Annabel figured it out in her mind. At a burn rate of thirty seconds per foot, whoever lit the fuses would have less than one minute to get away to safety before the gunpowder went off.

Annabel found Clay crushing ore at the stone slab. When he saw her approach, he lowered the sledgehammer. "No," he said, even before she'd opened her mouth.

"A minute is quite a long time," she pointed out.

"A minute is nothing when you're talking about the difference between living and dying."

He bent to place another piece of ore onto the stone. The autumn sun was still hot, but the air felt fresher now, and in the forest the aspens and oaks blazed in hues of red and gold.

"Keep out of the way," Clay warned her. "The stone chips fly about."

Annabel took a step back. Clay lifted the hammer and brought it down to smash the rock.

Watching him, Annabel began to count out loud, the way Papa had once taught her to measure time.

"One hippopotamus...two hippopotamus...three hippopotamus...four hippopotamus."

According to Papa, *hippopotamus* was a word comfortably spoken at a steady rate that helped to measure the passing of seconds.

"Twenty hippopotamus, twenty-one hippopotamus, twenty-two hippopotamus..."

Clay was speeding up his work, as if to prove her wrong. After Annabel reached thirty in her counting, Clay paused to take off his shirt. Throwing a quick, angry glance at her, he continued his pounding.

She watched the sheen of sweat on his bronzed skin, watched the play of muscles beneath. Not a heavily built man, like Mr. Hicks, Clay was lean but immensely powerful. Mostly, he smashed the rocks with a single blow.

"Fifty-nine, hippopotamus, sixty hippopotamus."

Clay wiped perspiration from his brow with his arm. Annabel waited until he glanced in her direction again. "See?" she said. "A minute is quite a long time."

"No amount of hippopotamuses is going to help you if a charge of gunpowder blows up in your face."

"Could we at least try it out? Do a trial run and time it, to see how long it takes?"

"With explosives you need a safety margin." Clay dropped the sledgehammer, walked up to her and placed his hands on her shoulders, his eyes intent on her upturned face. "How do you think I would feel if you died?" he asked. "How would *you* feel if you lost an arm or a leg? Lost your eyesight?"

He lifted one hand from her shoulder, curled the remaining hand tighter to hold her steady while he ran his fingertips over her forehead, over her nose, over her cheeks. "How would you feel if an explosion blew away that pretty face of yours?"

"I..." Annabel swallowed, not because of his words but because his touch was making her feel all quivery inside. He was leaning over her, the brim of his hat shadowing his face. His head bent lower, and for a moment Annabel thought he might kiss her again. But instead he muttered a curse, dropped his arms down his sides and moved away from her.

Annabel watched him pick up a stone. If there was no ore left in the mine, the men would leave the claim, and Clay would take her back to the railroad. The dream she'd had of forging her own path would die. She would have achieved no independence, made no mark as an individual, instead of the youngest of the Fairfax sisters. But if they found a way to get to the gold in the cave, they would mine the seam together, working in partnership.

"What about the gold?" she said. "Don't you want it?"

Clay paused, the rock in his hand. He studied the glitter of gold in the piece of ore in silence. Annabel hurried to press her case. "Think of what you could buy. You could buy land, stock a ranch. You could have the best of horses. A fine house. You could travel the world."

Clay turned to look at her. She could feel his gaze sweeping up and down her threadbare clothing and hand-me-down boots. "Is that what you want?" he asked. "A fine house and to travel the world?"

"Doesn't everybody?"

"I don't know," Clay countered. "Do they?"

"I…" Annabel swallowed. A blush flared up on her cheeks. Clay had a skill of using simple questions to ferret out excuses and half-truths. She had merely been trying to tempt him with what she thought all men wanted, instead of revealing her own hopes and dreams.

"I don't know either," she said quietly. "But I know what I want right now. I want a chance of a partnership. I want to achieve something, but I can't do it alone, and I don't think I'd even enjoy that. I'm used to doing things with others, and I'd like to share a successful mining enterprise with you and Mr. Hicks."

Clay set the rock on the flat stone and smashed it with the hammer.

"All right," he said. "We'll try it out."

Chapter Twelve

They practiced, and they practiced again. The holes drilled into the rock were empty, the charges waiting to be set. Stretched out on her belly over the aspen trunk, Annabel held a candle next to each hole in turn while Mr. Hicks counted out the passing of seconds.

"One fuse lit." She moved the candle along. "Two fuses lit."

Clay gripped her by the ankles and pulled her backward.

"Too far," she called out.

Clay scratched a mark in the rock face with a piece of charcoal, and they started again.

"One fuse lit," Annabel called out. "Two fuses lit."

Clay pulled her backward to the mark.

Annabel held the candle flame steady by a drill-hole in the rock. "Three fuses lit."

Clay yanked her out of the fissure and propped her on her feet. She passed the burning candle to him, bent to pick up one of the lanterns from the ground and raced out of the mine, silently counting hippopotamuses.

Carrying the lantern slowed her down, but they couldn't afford to lose their sources of light, so the only option was to transport them to safety. By the count of forty, she was lying flat on the gravel ground behind the *arrastre* pit and

Clay was hurtling down the slope toward her. By the count of fifty, he was lying beside her.

"See?" Annabel said. "A minute is a very long time."

"A minute is not a *very long time*."

Clay got to his feet, held down a hand to pull her up. "We don't know if we are counting too fast or too slow. The candle could blow out before all the fuses are lit. You could stumble and fall while running out of the mine."

Mr. Hicks walked up to them. "That went well." He combed his fingers through his gray-streaked beard, slanting an uncertain glance at Clay. "Are we going to do it or will we leave the gold to other men who possess greater courage?"

Annabel could see the flicker of anger in Clay's eyes. It was unfair of Mr. Hicks to hint at cowardice when they all knew Clay's concern was for her.

"We'll do it," Clay said in the end. "But we'll cut three long fuses and two shorter ones. We'll measure the longer ones to burn for one minute and fifteen seconds and the shorter ones to burn for forty-five seconds."

Annabel bit back a protest. On the face of it the suggestion made sense, since she lit her fuses first, which meant they would have more time to burn, but nowhere near the thirty seconds Clay had allowed. What he was proposing would jeopardize his safety in order to provide a greater safety margin for her.

Lantern light reflected from the damp walls of the mine tunnel. The charges were set, the fuses trimmed. Annabel stood beside Clay in front of the fissure, going over the final preparations.

"Candle." Clay held up a spermaceti wax candle. "I'll pass it to you once you are in position to light the fuses." The whale wax candles were expensive, but tapers made of tallow had a tendency to melt in the summer heat, and Mr. Hicks distrusted them.

Annabel patted the pocket she had sewn to the top of her shirtsleeve for the purpose. "Matches. Tested and dry." She didn't wear the heavy leather coat, for they had discovered clothing could become wedged between the aspen trunk and the rock wall, and her flimsy cotton shirt would be easier to rip free.

"Remember what we practiced," Clay said as he put aside the candle. "If the flame blows out, don't try to relight it. Drop the candle and use a match to light the remaining fuses. Call out to me so that I know what's happening."

He tapped a pocket on the front of his shirt, mirroring her action. "Matches. Tested and dry."

Annabel looked up into his face. For a long moment, their gazes held. She wanted to say something, to make some sort of declaration and hear him do the same, but Clay merely contemplated her in silence. Finally, he lifted one hand and cupped her chin and brushed his thumb over her trembling lips.

"It's going to be all right, Annabel," he said quietly. A crooked smile tugged at his mouth. "A pretty girl once told me a minute is a very long time."

"You'll only have forty-five seconds."

"I'll be fine." He withdrew his hand, efficient and focused now. "Let's get started."

Annabel took a deep breath, gave Clay one final glance, as if to memorize his features. Then she climbed up the wooden ladder Clay had built to provide easier access into the opening they had taken to calling *the funnel*.

Mr. Hicks had been banished to a safe distance by the creek. If disaster struck, they wanted him able to provide medical care or to ride out for help.

Annabel had written a letter to her sisters. She'd addressed it to Charlotte under her false identity as Mrs. Maude Greenwood, and had extracted a promise from Mr. Hicks to personally deliver the envelope to Gold Crossing if something went wrong.

It was late afternoon. The weather had broken, with a blustery wind sweeping along the hillside. Annabel could feel a new coolness in the current of air that flowed out of the cave.

Clay had suggested they might prefer to wait until morning, when they would be refreshed from sleep, but Annabel knew another night of worry would only serve to ratchet up her nerves.

"In position," she called, stretched out on the aspen trunk.

"Passing the candle," Clay replied.

The funnel was too narrow for her to reach back for the candle, and transporting it on her person might have damaged the wick, so they had rigged up a loop of rawhide cord beneath the aspen trunk, and now Annabel reeled the loop along to transport over the small leather pouch containing the candle.

She extracted the candle, examined the shape with her hands to check which way up to hold it. Her body blocked most of the light from the mine tunnel, and until she had the candle burning she had to work in near-complete darkness.

It took a bit of wriggling to extract a match from her sleeve pocket, but she'd practiced the movements. Annabel paused, candle gripped in one hand, a match in the other. Last chance to turn back. She filled her lungs with the damp air, held her breath for an instant and then released it in a whoosh, forcing her body to relax.

With her left hand, she scraped the match against a dry

spot in the rock, as high up as she could reach, well away from the fuses below. The flame flared with a hiss. She held the burning match to the candle. The wick caught. Annabel blew out the match and let it cool a moment before dropping it to the bottom of the fissure.

She waited until the candle burned with a steady flame, and then she held it up to illuminate the fuses. They had worried a wire dangling down might burn faster than one resting against a flat surface, so they had drilled the holes into a narrow rock ledge where the fuses could be laid out horizontally.

"Starting," Annabel called out.

She picked up the end of the first fuse and held it to the flame.

Clay began to count. *"One hippopotamus, two hippopotamus."*

The fuse wire sizzled into life. They had sacrificed a two-inch section for her to get a demonstration of how quickly the Bickford Safety Fuze caught and what it looked and sounded like as it burned.

"First fuse lit."

When Annabel moved the candle backward for the second fuse, a sudden draft from the cave made the flame flicker. She halted her motion, cupped her free hand around the flame until it steadied. The precaution lost her three precious seconds.

"Four hippopotamus, five hippopotamus," Clay counted.

Annabel picked up the end of the second fuse, held it to the flame.

"Second fuse lit," she called out. "Pull me back."

Instead of controlling her movement with her free hand, she used it to protect the flame, and her chest and stomach scraped painfully against the aspen trunk as Clay hauled her backward by the ankles.

"Nine hippopotamus. Ten hippopotamus," Clay counted.

The last fuse was slow to catch, but finally it glowed orange and Annabel heard the reassuring sizzling sound. "Third fuse lit," she called out.

In a smooth slide, Clay pulled her out of the funnel. As Annabel lifted the candle to cup her hand around the flame, her elbow bashed against the rock. With a cry of pain, she released her grip on the candle.

"Fourteen hippopotamus. Fifteen hippopotamus." Clay settled her on her feet, pointing her toward the exit.

"I dropped it," Annabel wailed and pivoted back to face him. "I dropped the candle."

"Start counting." Clay gripped her by the shoulders and gave her a sharp shake, scowling down at her. *"Eighteen hippopotamus,"* he prompted. "What comes next? Say it."

Annabel blinked. Panic clouded her mind. She clamped down on the fear and gathered herself. *"Nineteen hippopotamus."*

Clay spun her around once more, to face the route to safety, and gave her a small shove to urge her along. "I'll use a match," he told her. "Run!"

"Twenty-one hippopotamus. Twenty-two hippopotamus," Annabel called out.

She'd forgotten to pick up a lantern to carry out, and she ran stumbling in the darkness, her hands extended out in front of her. When she reached the sharp twist in the tunnel, sunlight guided her into the open.

"Twenty-nine hippopotamus. Thirty hippopotamus."

She was behind the times they'd achieved during their practice runs, for the damp air in the tunnel had made the fuses slower to ignite, and protecting the flame from the sudden draft had used up a few precious seconds.

Arms swinging, feet pumping, Annabel ran down the path. The ground thudded beneath her big boots. She passed the cavern…the water barrel…kitchen canopy. A blue jay screeched, flying up. The line of forest blurred in her vision, and then she was behind the *arrastre* circle and threw herself down on the ground.

"Forty-two hippopotamus. Forty-three hippopotamus."

By the count of fifty, Clay should have emerged, but there was nothing but the blue jay that had landed back on the ground, wings flapping, to resume its search for crumbs beneath the kitchen table.

"Fifty-four hippopotamus. Fifty-five hippopotamus."

Frantic now, Annabel rose to her feet. She wanted to cry out Clay's name or say a prayer and plead with God, but she had to keep counting.

"Fifty-seven hippopotamus. Fifty-eight hippopotamus."

The shorter fuses were timed to burn for forty-five seconds. What had been the count when she set off running and Clay began lighting his fuses? In their practice sessions they had achieved ten seconds, which meant fifty-five would have been the point of explosion for the shorter fuses. What would the point of explosion be now, with the extra delay? What number did she need to subtract from her count to know when it was too late for Clay to get out alive?

"Sixty hippopotamus."

Annabel's heart seemed to shrivel up in her chest. She took a step back up the slope toward the mine, then another, her feet moving of their own volition. Clay's image filled her mind, the tousled brown curls, the lean, stubble-covered cheeks, the carefree smile that was all too rare.

She couldn't let him die alone.

She was about to set off running when a blur of motion by the kitchen made her halt her steps. On the edge of the clearing, Clay burst into sight. His hat tumbled down to roll on the ground and he carried a lantern in each hand.

Hurtling along, curly brown hair flying in the wind, the flapping shirt molded to his chest, he raced toward her.

"*Sixty-two hippopotamus,*" Annabel shouted. "Drop the lamps! Run! Run!"

"Get down!" Clay yelled back at her. "Get down!"

Frozen, Annabel watched him advance, each step bringing him toward her. Barely slowing his pace, he ducked to deposit the lanterns inside the *arrastre* circle, and then he was beside her. He grabbed hold of her and knocked her off her feet and threw his body on top of hers, pressing her against the stone barrier that provided an extra shield.

"*Sixty-five hippopotamus.*"

A boom echoed deep within the cliffs, and the ground shook beneath them. Like thunder, the explosion reverberated through the air. A cloud of acrid smoke and dust billowed out of the mine entrance.

Annabel huddled on the ground, the warm weight of Clay on top of her, protecting her, his arms cradling her head. Her lips were still moving, but no longer to count the time. She was saying a prayer of thanks because her life with Clay was no longer measured in seconds.

As the sound of the explosion faded away, Clay could hear heavy footsteps pounding up the slope and the frantic hollering of Mr. Hicks. "Clay! Kid! Are you all right?"

Clay rolled his weight from the girl and shook her shoulder. "Kid?"

The girl lifted her head to look at him. He studied her face. Dust streaked the smooth skin, but he could see no visible sign of injury. In fact, she looked radiant, her eyes shining, her expression rapt, her lips parted and trembling.

Clay wanted to bundle her into his arms and hold her tight. He wanted to kiss those trembling lips, but Mr. Hicks had reached them, forcing him to restrain the impulse, for he could not predict the severity of the old man's reaction if—or when—he discovered he had a woman in his mine.

Clay got to his feet. Not waiting for him to reach down for her, the girl bounced up. She barreled into him, her arms clinging to him in one of those lightning hugs. Then she did the same to the old man and pulled away, a big smile on her face.

"We did it! It worked!"

"Hold your horses," Clay cautioned her. "The charges went off as planned. We don't know if we cleared a passage. We might have buried the gold under a mountain of rubble."

"But…" The light in her eyes went out, and Clay wished he could take back his words.

The old man spoke again. "You cut the timing a mite close."

Clay turned to him to hide his turbulent emotions. Even now, fear clawed in his gut. He should never have agreed to let the girl work with explosives, but it was the only way he could give her the mining partnership that seemed to matter so much to her. He forced a casual tone. "We didn't allow for the damp air in the mine and the draft that blows through the funnel. The fuses were slow to light. And I spent a moment pulling out the aspen trunk, in case it might constrain the force of the blast."

"But we did it," the girl said. "I'm sure it worked."

Mr. Hicks picked up one of the lanterns. "Let's go and see."

Clay held up a warning hand. "Don't be a fool. Wait an hour or two. Let the fumes clear and the dust settle."

"I've waited for thirty years. I'll not wait a second longer," the old man said and walked off.

Clay turned to the girl. "Go into the kitchen and stay there." When she opened her mouth in protest, he cut her off. "I don't want you in that mine until I can be sure it's safe, even if it means I'll have to truss you up and hog-tie you. Do you promise to keep out?"

Clay could see rebellion flash across the girl's dust-smeared features. Then she gave a reluctant nod. "I'll make coffee and start supper."

Clay picked up the other lantern and went after the old man. The mine tunnel smelled of smoke and gunpowder. Dust hung thick in the air, stinging his eyes and filling his lungs. Clay coughed, hurried to catch up with the old man. In the funnel, the edge of the fissure had broken off cleanly and loose rocks filled the gap.

Mr. Hicks spun around. "I'll get a pickaxe."

"Wait until morning," Clay cautioned him.

"No." Fevered impatience burned in the old man's eyes.

Clay shrugged. Sleep would elude them anyway, and it made no difference in the mine if it was day or night. "I'll get the mule," he said. "We can tie a chain around the bigger rocks and use the mule to haul them aside."

All through the night they worked, muscles straining, sweat pouring off their bodies, their skin scraped raw as they levered the rocks and rubble out of the way. Annabel kept her promise and stayed out, serving food and coffee in the kitchen.

Heavy clouds covered the sky, obliterating the moon. The wind had gathered force and howled along the cliffs. There seemed to be something ominous about the solid darkness of the night, but Clay told himself it was fatigue and tension stirring up his imagination.

When the first hint of dawn appeared in the sky, they had cleared away the loose rocks and rubble to open a passage into the cave. The opening was six feet high, straight on one side and curved in the other, in the shape of the capital letter D.

By an unspoken consent, the men had waited to inspect the seam of gold until they had finished the work. In the early-morning light Clay rubbed down the mule, led him out to pasture and strode back up the slope into the kitchen.

"Moment of truth," he said. "Is it gold or pyrite?"

The girl snapped her head up and stared at him, aghast. "Do you think…?"

He shifted one shoulder. "It's an easy mistake to make. You're no expert."

Her eyes pleaded at him. "Can I come with you?"

Clay considered a moment, relented. "All right. As long as you stay behind me."

They trooped into the mine, each carrying a lantern, and went through the hole, the old man first. Clay followed him and turned around to hold up his light for the girl. She entered the cave, took three paces forward, studied the layout and adjusted her position to the left.

"Here." She extended one arm ahead of her. "It runs this way."

Together, they lifted their lanterns high and lowered them toward the floor in a slow, ceremonial motion. When lamplight fell on a glittering snake by their feet, the old man gave a fraught cry and sank to his knees. He put his lantern down and scrabbled with both hands, cleaning away the layer of detritus that covered the bedrock.

"Is it gold?" the girl asked in a voice that trembled.

"It's gold all right." Dreamy, reverent, the old man traced his fingers along the sparkling seam, then lowered his head and touched the ground with his lips.

"Careful," Clay said wryly. "It's bat droppings you're kissing."

"It's gold," Mr. Hicks spoke in awe. "There must be a million dollars' worth beneath our feet. More, if the vein goes deep. And it will be easy to dig out. Almost as easy as shoveling sand into a bucket at the beach."

Clay held his lantern high above his head and inspected the ceiling. The air in the cave seemed unusually damp. He couldn't decide if it was just the change in the weather, or if an underground watercourse ran somewhere nearby.

He noticed a series of dark lines in the domed roof of the cave. Several thin cracks crossed over each other to form a straggly maze. He lifted one arm to indicate the pattern. "Kid, did you notice these cracks in the rock before?"

The girl tipped her head back to stare up at the ceiling. "I don't remember seeing them, but I'm not as tall as you, so the light from my lantern didn't reach as far. They could have been there but I failed to notice them."

Thoughtful, Clay studied the pattern of the fault lines. They could have been there for thousands of years. Or the gunpowder blast last night might have created them, destabilizing the structure of the cliffs.

He lowered the light and shined it on the faces of his partners. "I don't want the kid working in the cave. The roof may be unsound."

"But I—"

He cut her off. "If you don't agree to stay out of the cave, I'll ride out before sundown. You two can keep the gold. I hope you'll live to enjoy it."

Clay could feel his body shaking with anger as he strode out, the lantern light casting flickering shadows on the tunnel walls. Did Mr. Hicks not see the danger? Did he not value his life? The old man had no right to inject his craving for riches into the mind of the girl and lure her into taking crazy risks.

The girl had wanted to crawl into the cave and set the charges to achieve something, to prove equal in the partnership. Clay had sympathized with her need, had been willing to help, but he drew the line at letting her court death.

His mind filled with restless images. The charred remains of a burnt-out wagon. The sound of coughing and the memory of blood-spotted handkerchiefs. The rumble of an explosion and the smell of burning flesh.

He'd lost his parents. He'd lost the two closest friends he'd ever had. He might not be able to stop Mr. Hicks from sacrificing his life in search for gold, but he'd be damned if he stood by and watched the girl go the same way.

Chapter Thirteen

Thick clouds covered the dawn sky as they settled down to catch up on sleep under the overhang. An hour later, the sky burst into a deluge that drummed against the cliffs. Clay lay awake, listening to the sound of pebbles rattling down the slope and worrying about the fault lines in the roof of the cave.

At midday, when they got up, the downpour had passed but a cool mist hung over the hilltops and the paths were slippery with mud. Mr. Hicks barely paused for coffee before grabbing a pickaxe and heading off into the mine.

"You should pan the last of the gravel in the *arrastre*," he told Clay before he hurried away. "I don't want the new ore mixing with the old."

After extracting a promise from the girl to keep out of the mine, Clay left her in the kitchen, uncertain if he could trust her. She rewarded his faith by appearing at the creek. Without a word she took the water hose from him and directed the stream onto the pulverized ore.

As Clay cranked the handle of the rocker box, he couldn't prevent his eyes from sliding over the girl's slender shape. In the cave, while they practiced lighting the fuses, he had put his hands on her to pull her out, and during the blast he had shielded her body with his, but those times had been efficient, businesslike, and he had not allowed his thoughts to dwell on the kiss they had shared.

Now he gave his imagination free rein. He pictured the girl stripped half-naked, bending over the stone by the stream to wash her hair, the way he'd seen her once before. Then recalled the feel of her body beneath his, soft and warm, the way it had been when he lay on top of her by the *arrastre* pit. What would it be like, to combine those two memories? How would it feel, to press his body against hers without the barrier of clothing separating them?

"Penny for your thoughts," the girl said.

Clay contemplated her, unsmiling. "They are worth much more than that. They are worth all the gold in the cave."

"What…?" She flustered and let her voice trail away.

They both knew what she'd been about to ask. *What were you thinking?* As their gazes collided and held, Clay knew she could read the answer in his eyes, could see the hunger in them, and the hesitation, too.

A slow blush rose from the collar of the girl's threadbare shirt all the way up to her tattered bowler hat. She started to speak, appeared not to find the words, and chose to remain silent.

"You can take off your hat, you know," Clay said quietly. "You might like to wash your hair. Mr. Hicks will not come down here. You couldn't pry him out of that cave with a crowbar."

He could see the girl's throat ripple as she swallowed. Her neck was slender and very white. Once again, Clay wondered how he could ever have mistaken her for a boy.

"I don't have my soap," she pointed out.

"I'd like to see your hair."

Slowly, as if walking onto thin ice—which Clay recognized tempting a man might in a way be for a girl—she lifted one hand to her head and knocked down her bowler hat to reveal the shiny black tresses pinned into tight coils.

"Take your hair down." Clay could hear the roughness in his voice. *Take your hair down—or run away as fast as you can*, he wanted to add, for within him he felt the long-denied pressures snapping out of control.

As if sensing his dark, brooding mood and wanting to disperse it with a burst of sunlight, the girl laughed and shook her head. She made a move, as if to put the water hose down, so she could pluck the pins out of her hair, but at the last moment she altered the course of her action and lifted the hose, dousing him with the spray.

The stream was running high after the rain, the water pressure greater than normal, and the icy current hit him in the gut, cooling the surge of heat in his body, perhaps more effectively than the girl might have guessed.

Entering the spirit of fun, Clay let out a roar. He released his grip on the handle of the rocker box and dived for the girl. For an instant, they grappled for the hose. Clay restricted his strength to make the battle last a moment longer. Then he tossed the hose aside, scooped the girl into his arms and dunked her in the stream.

Shrieking yet laughing, eyes shining with merriment despite the scowl of indignation on her face, the girl clung to him, her arms wrapped around his neck. Clay's boots skidded in the mud, causing him to fall to his knees. His hat toppled from his head, and his hair, grown too long, flopped over his eyes.

Going still in his arms, the girl untangled one arm from around his neck and brushed back the curls from his forehead. Her touch was gentle, and when she looked up at him, Clay could see in her eyes everything a man could hope to see in the eyes of the girl he wanted—trust and tenderness and the spark of passion.

The sun broke between the clouds, making the ground steam on the banks of the creek. He was kneeling in the stream, the girl cradled in his arms, the current flowing cool and refreshing over them. Their wet clothing clung to their bodies, a barrier so insignificant they might as well be naked.

Clay lowered his head. Ever since he first kissed Annabel, he'd been burning with the fever to do it again. The strength of the urge baffled him, for he'd always told himself he derived no true satisfaction from casual intimacies. Emotionally, such encounters left him feeling even more isolated and alone, but now a storm of need raged inside him, a hunger like he'd never experienced before.

Slowly, he bent his head to the girl resting in his lap. At the same time, she leaned upward to meet him. He could feel the fine trembling in her body, could feel the warm puff of their breaths mingling when their lips were only a fraction apart.

For an instant, Clay halted, anticipating the pleasure, letting the desire build and build and build inside him, until it was so immense he would gladly have given up his share of the gold to feel her mouth beneath his.

Finally, he settled his lips against Annabel's. This time, her response was bolder. She made a small, eager sound in her throat, clung tighter to him and parted her lips, inviting him inside, inviting him to deepen the kiss. Again, the elation Clay remembered from their first kiss flowed through him—a strange mix of being at peace and a tension so overwhelming he felt he was about to lose his sanity.

For long moments, he kept the kiss going, while he fought to control his senses, but they refused to bend to his will. All he could think about was Annabel pressed against him, her body supple and slender, her lips soft and willing.

Finally, Clay lifted his head and studied her flushed

face. With his hand he touched her lips, as if to check if his kiss had left something there, like a brand of ownership. He saw the trusting look in her eyes, felt her mouth quiver beneath his fingertips, and a sudden feeling of contentment stole over him. Never had he understood there could be such pleasure in simply holding a woman in his arms.

Perhaps it was not casual intimacies that left him wanting, Clay decided, but intimacy without affection. Or maybe with Annabel there was nothing casual about it. The thought crossed his mind as he lowered his mouth to hers again.

And then, just as Clay was about to slide his hand along her chest to cup one of those rosy-tipped breasts he kept dreaming about, a low rumble echoed down the hillside and the ground beneath them shook with a slow, rolling tremor.

Clay raced up the path, past the *arrastre*, across the clearing, along the cliff face, his boots pounding against the rain-sodden earth. Like a yawning black mouth, the mine entrance gaped in front of him. Behind him, he could hear the girl's urgent footsteps.

"Stay back," he yelled, even though he knew she would refuse to obey.

He darted into the mine tunnel. The air was humid and heavy with dust. Somewhere ahead he could hear water trickling. After the sharp twist to the left, he lost the last glimmer of daylight. No lantern glow shone through the opening they had blasted into the cave.

"Get a lantern from the kitchen," Clay called out to the girl. Not only did he need a source of light, but the task would get her out of the mine for a moment, perhaps saving her life if another tremor rocked the earth.

Trailing his hands against the slippery walls now gritty

with dust, Clay found his way through the darkness to the funnel opening. He took out a match, scraped it against the rock. Once the match caught, he held it up. The flame did not flicker, indicating the lack of any draft.

He moved the match up and down, left and right, illuminating the barrier in front of him. He could see only a solid heap of rock and rubble, filling not only the cave entrance but also part of the mine tunnel.

"Mr. Hicks!" he yelled.

No reply came, but Clay knew the thick layer of earth would have dulled the sound. The flame burned away, scorching his fingers, and he dropped the spent match, letting it hiss out against the damp ground.

With a fevered urgency, Clay tackled the rockfall, rolling stones aside, scooping out loose gravel with his bare hands, working by touch in the complete darkness. From the corner of his eye he could see a sphere of light bobbing up and down along the mine tunnel as Annabel returned with a lantern.

When she got closer, Clay glanced at her. Hatless, her tightly coiled hair shining wet from the dunking in the stream, her eyes wide with fear, she looked feminine and fragile and frightened. Pausing in his labors for a second, Clay reached for the lantern and set it down on the ground past the rockfall.

"What is it?" the girl asked.

"Landslide...the roof was unsound...the rain brought it down." He spoke in bursts between heaving the stones aside.

Annabel stepped forward to join him in the effort. "No," he told her. "Get me a shovel and a pickaxe." He threw her another quick glance. "Can you find your way out without a light?"

She nodded. "I'll bring the whale oil lamp." They had

only one coal oil lantern they could use. The other two were in the cave with Mr. Hicks.

Not replying, Clay braced his shoulder against a boulder and strained his muscles to roll it aside. By the time the girl returned, he had made enough of a dent in the rubble to uncover a huge slab of rock that only gunpowder would shift.

Pickaxe in one hand, Clay banged the iron tip against the stone. The clang made a sharp sound in the dimly lit tunnel. They waited. The silence seemed impenetrable, as if the whole world had ceased to hold its breath.

Then from the other side came a muffled echo. *Tap-tap-tap.*

Clay lifted the pickaxe, banged the rock three times.

The answer came. *Tap-tap-tap.*

"He is alive." Relief pouring over him, Clay turned to the girl. "Set the whale oil lamp to burn halfway down the tunnel, so the light will guide you in and out. Then fetch a canteen of water and some food."

With a quick nod, the girl hurried off. A fleeting thought crossed Clay's mind that she was growing up, learning to overcome those weeping bouts of nerves he'd witnessed a couple of times before.

Dismissing all thoughts except those of getting through to his friend and mentor, Clay bent back to the wall of rubble and attacked it with the pickaxe. In a blaze of effort he worked, pausing only once in a while to tap at the rock and to hear the reply from the other side.

A terrible sense of guilt settled over him. He'd ordered Annabel to stay out of the cave, but he had given no such ultimatum to Mr. Hicks. Everything the old man had done for him, all the years of friendship between them, haunted him now. He should have spoken about the affection between them, used it to dissuade Mr. Hicks from risking his life in the cave.

Hour upon hour Clay labored. His muscles screamed with fatigue and his hands burned with blisters. The smoke from the whale oil lamp stung his eyes and the rancid smell made him retch, but he refused to slow down.

The girl was helping him now. He hacked at the rubble. She collected the loose earth into a bucket and tipped it out of the way a few yards deeper inside the mine tunnel. At times, she brought him a cup of coffee or a strip of venison jerky or a honeyed slice of bread, to keep his energy from flagging.

"He will live, won't he?" the girl said with a mix of hope and fear. "He has air. Even without water and food he can survive for days."

Clay didn't reply. He didn't have the heart to point out that the landslide might have cut off the current of air from the fissure at the opposite end of the cave, or that an underground stream might have broken through, posing an even greater danger.

Every now and then, while he'd been digging at the rubble, Clay had stilled for a few seconds, to catch his breath and to allow his body a rest. He'd listened, breath held, ears strained, and he'd heard it—water running down the cliff on the other side of the rockfall. If an underground stream had burst its way through the cave roof, had it found an outlet to drain away, or was water slowly filling the cave?

Chapter Fourteen

"Is it day or night?" Clay asked.

Annabel tipped the gravel out of the bucket onto the growing heap at the far end of the tunnel and straightened. "I don't know," she replied. "I'll go and see."

She trundled out to the mine entrance. While they had been working, darkness had fallen and a new day had dawned and now the sun was sinking again behind the hills. She trundled back to Clay. "It's evening."

Bending to the damp rubble, she hoisted the shovel. Pain arrowed in her back and shoulders, and her hands were scraped raw. Her feet weighed a ton, making her steps drag. She no longer thought in terms of death or survival. All she could think of was the next swing of the shovel, the next bucketful of earth, the next step, the next inhale of breath.

But if Clay could keep going, so could she.

The sound of the pickaxe against the rock altered, no longer a dull pounding but a hollow clang.

"I'm through!" Clay called out. He bent to the gap and shouted, "Mr. Hicks, can you hear me?"

A muffled voice came back. "How could I not hear such hollering?"

Annabel closed her eyes tight. Tears of exhaustion and relief spilled in a warm trail down her cheeks. *Thank you, God*, she said in a silent prayer.

"Can you come over here?" Clay asked.

Annabel opened her eyes and saw him gesturing at her. She eased around the rocks and rubble that still covered the ground and halted beside him. He lifted the lantern to illuminate the opening. "Do you think you could crawl through?"

The gap was at waist height, on the straight side of the D-shaped entrance. A boulder filled the bottom of the D, and on top of it a huge stone slab stood at an angle against the wall, leaving a triangular hole about eighteen inches wide.

Annabel eased her hands into the hole and felt the passage. The narrow part was no more than three feet long. "Maybe," she said. "I'll try."

Ducking, she pushed into the opening. Arms. Head. Shoulders. Caught in the narrow space, she emptied her lungs and wriggled along. She was inside, all the way to her waist. The rough surface of the rock crushed her rib cage, but the strip of cloth she used to bind her breasts protected her skin.

Behind her, Clay spoke. "I'll turn the bucket upside down and put it under your feet. It will give you an easier angle to push through."

She heard the hollow clang of metal, and then Clay curled one hand around her left ankle and lifted her foot onto the bucket. She moved her other foot, shifted her weight onto the bucket and inched forward.

Her hips were the widest part of her body and she got stuck, but by now her head and arms were clear of the passage. She braced her elbows against the side of the boulder, using the leverage to gain another few inches.

"Take my feet," she called out to Clay. "Push."

She felt him grip her legs and shove her along. Her trousers ripped, exposing her hip bones. Her skin scraped raw. With one final push and a grunt of determination, she emerged out of the hole and slid to the ground, bumping into some large obstacle.

A yelp of pain echoed around the cave, but although her skin burned from the abrasion and every bone in her body felt crushed, Annabel knew she had not cried out. Slowly, letting her muscles recover from the strain, she scrambled to her feet.

"Don't tread on me, kid," Mr. Hicks said. "I can't get up."

In the faint light through the gap, she could see him stretched out on the cave floor, but there was a dark shadow over him. Careful to avoid encroaching upon him, Annabel spun around on her toes and stuck one arm into the gap she'd just forced her way through. "Give me the light," she called out to Clay.

Clay passed her the lantern. She held it up and could not stifle the groan of despair. Only the top half of Mr. Hicks remained in sight. His legs were buried under a pile of fallen rocks.

"How is he?" Clay called out.

"He is…" Annabel bit back a sob "…alive."

"Look around," Clay said. "Can you see water flowing into the cave?"

"I'll tend to him first."

"Look around *now*." Clay's tone was sharp.

"Do as he says, kid," Mr. Hicks cut in. "Drowning holds no appeal."

Drowning? Only now did her ears pick out the steady trickling sound. With another cry of alarm, Annabel lifted the lantern high and eased her way past the piles of rubble and the huge stone slabs to inspect what remained of the cave.

In the far corner, a small waterfall gushed down the rock face to form a pond on the floor, but the water was seeping out again through a crack in the bottom of the cave and the pond did not seem to grow any larger.

"There is water coming in, but it flows out again," Annabel called out, loud enough for Clay to hear.

She tipped her head back and closed her eyes. She could no longer feel the current of fresh air against her face, and it appeared to her the air was getting stale. Fighting the onslaught of panic, Annabel set the lantern down by the injured man and went back to the gap.

"Give me the canteen." She held her arm out, and Clay passed the leather-covered metal canteen to her.

Annabel returned to the old man and knelt beside him. "Are you thirsty?"

"I could use a drink, but I'd prefer whiskey."

"Let's start with water." Annabel uncapped the canteen, slid one arm behind the old man's neck and lifted him up to drink. When Mr. Hicks had drunk enough, she tore a strip of cloth from the hem of her shirt, dampened it and bathed his dusty face, talking quietly. "We'll enlarge the hole, so that Clay can get in. He'll clear the rubble from your legs, and we can get you out. There'll be a doctor in Hillsboro."

"It's no use, kid." The burly mine owner's eyes glittered as he looked up at her. "My legs are crushed. Even if I made it out of here, I wouldn't live. And there is too much rock for Clay to clear in time. Do you not notice, the air is going stale?"

"Don't say that," Annabel pleaded. "We must try."

"I reckon not. No point in wasting the effort." He gave her a faint smile. "Don't fret over it, kid. Suits me fine.

I'll have a fine tomb, full of gold, like them ancient kings of Egypt."

Annabel stroked the old man's brow. His skin was clammy, deathly pale. She could feel the tension in his body and knew he was fighting not to show his pain. His eyes met hers. He watched her for a moment in silence and then spoke softly. "That's a woman's touch if I ever felt one."

Annabel nodded. The thought that had been weighing at the back of her mind broke free. "Mr. Hicks, I'm sorry for deceiving you. Do you think…do you believe a woman can jinx a mine?"

His face twisted into a rueful grimace. "In the old tin mines of Cornwall they believed so. If a miner's wife came to the pithead to ask what he wanted for his supper, the whole shift might walk out. Or, if a miner chanced upon a woman on his way to work, likely as not he'd turn back and go home, instead of risking his life."

"I'm terribly sorry. I didn't mean to…"

Mr. Hicks lifted his arm to brush aside her apology, flinching with pain at the motion. "Don't worry, girl. I think that kind of talk is nonsense. It is a relic of old times. I hold no truck with such superstitions. In America, women work their own mining claims, and some do a fine job of it. Seen it myself. Nevada. Californy."

Silence fell, punctuated only by the old man's labored breathing and the gushing of the small waterfall in the corner of the cave. Annabel tipped the canteen to dampen the cloth she'd torn from her shirt and mopped his brow again.

"Is there anything we can do for you?" she asked.

"Send Clay to fetch me the bottle of whiskey."

Annabel nodded. "Anything else? Blankets? Food?"

"I have no appetite. But bring me my gun. I reckon I'll

just lie here, enjoying the idea of all that gold beneath me, and wait for my time to come. But I'd like to have my gun, in case I get bored with the waiting."

Blinking back tears, Annabel got up and relayed the instructions to Clay.

"Bring candles, too," the old man shouted out, then lowered his voice and spoke to Annabel. "I want you to take the lantern with you when you go. The other two broke when the roof collapsed. I'll make do with candles."

A few minutes later Clay returned. One by one, he passed through the gap a bottle of whiskey, a glass, a blanket and a pillow of hay stuffed into an empty flour sack.

Annabel slipped the pillow under the old man's head and spread the blanket over him. She poured out a glass of whiskey and helped him to drink it. Then she sat down beside him, arms wrapped around her knees, and joined him in the waiting.

He turned his head to look at her. "When I go knocking on them pearly gates, you reckon they'll let me through?"

"Or course they will. You are a good man."

For a long while, they sat in silence. Mr. Hicks had two more glasses of whiskey. Then he spoke again, so low it took Annabel a moment to realize he was saying something.

"Her name was Sarah. Sarah Milford."

Annabel held her breath. It was clear Mr. Hicks was talking more to himself than to her, and she did not wish to interrupt.

"We grew up together. I was poor, but my mother came from a good family, and from her I received an education. My father was a no-good storekeeper who drank every cent of profit he ever made.

"Sarah and I...we promised ourselves to each other.

We were going to run away, but she got cold feet and worried how her folks would take it. She was an only child. So, being the fanciful young pup I was, I said I'd go off to Californy and get rich with gold. Then her parents would give us their blessing."

"Is that why you wanted gold so badly?"

He held up the empty glass, and Annabel filled it. She'd propped his head up so he could drink without assistance, and now he took another sip, swirling the drink around his mouth before swallowing.

"I found gold, all right. Not even a year had passed when I filled my pan with pay dirt so rich there were more nuggets in my pan than gravel. I worked the claim for two months and took out a small fortune in gold.

"I had a tailor make me a fine broadcloth suit and I bought a pair of good horses, one for me and one as a gift for Sarah. Then I rode home. And when I got there, I learned she had married some fancy dude and taken off to New Orleans."

Annabel hesitated. Mr. Hicks glanced up at her. It seemed he expected some kind of a prompt, so she gave it to him. "Sarah did not wait for you?"

"She did not. So, I took my gold, and I walked into the nearest saloon and got very drunk and sat down at the gambling table. By sunrise, I'd lost every cent of my gold and the pair of horses." He gave her a crooked smile. "Still had the suit, though."

Reaching out with a grunt of pain, he poured himself a shot of whiskey and downed it in one long swallow. "In a single day I'd lost the woman I loved and the fortune I'd found. It made me bitter. Set me against females."

"Did you ever see her again? Ask her to explain?"

"I wanted to, but without the money…" Mr. Hicks glanced up from the corner of his eye. "That's why I wanted to find the gold so badly. So I could hold my head high when I tracked her down and asked her why."

Silence settled again. There was something oddly serene about sitting in the dark cave, with the soft trickle of water and the muted glow of the lantern. Annabel found herself dozing off, the tension and the lack of sleep and the physical effort of the past two days taking their toll.

"Does Clay know?"

She jolted to wakefulness. "What?"

"Does Clay know you're a girl?"

"Yes," she replied quietly.

The old man nodded. "I've seen how he looks at you. I guess I knew, too, but I just didn't think of it, didn't pay enough attention. Promise me, girl…" Brows raised, he looked up at her with a question in his eyes.

"Annabel," she supplied. "My name is Annabel."

"Promise me, Annabel, that you'll do right by him. Don't let him down the way my Sarah let me down. Clay's never really known love, and he deserves some. He might be all grit and sandpaper on the surface, but he has a kind heart. Don't take from him all he has to give and leave him with nothing but bitter memories."

Annabel swallowed. There was something oddly prophetic in the old man's words. However, because Clay was so reticent with his emotions, she had no idea what he thought of her. The attraction might be merely physical, the affection no more than friendship, and his protectiveness simply gallantry toward a female instead of proof that he truly cared for her.

But she was happy to give such a promise and be bound by it. "I would never hurt Clay on purpose," she said quietly. "And I believe he would never hurt me."

Mr. Hicks nodded, pressed his head into the makeshift pillow with a sigh. "I reckon it's time for you to go now, girl. I have everything I need. My gold. My gun. A drop of whiskey and my memories. Don't weep for me. I'm not worth it."

Annabel knelt beside the old man and pressed a gentle kiss to his brow. She knew he could feel her tears falling, and she made no effort to hide them. "Goodbye," she said. "God be with you, and my love, and Clay's, too."

Exhausted, filled with grief and a sense of helplessness, Clay led Annabel out of the mine. Outside, the night had fallen. They did not talk much while they cooked a simple supper and settled down to sleep.

Autumn had turned the air cool and crisp. Clay could see Annabel shivering beneath her blanket. Without a word, he reached over and pulled her into the lee of his body. For the rest of the night, she slept curled up against him, her warmth like a shield that blunted the edge of his anguish. Clay merely dozed, unable to sleep despite his fatigue. Nerves taut, ears strained, he waited for a gunshot to echo deep within the mountainside.

Memories drifted through his mind. Five years ago he'd ridden up to Mr. Hicks's claim and the old man had taken him on as a partner. He could remember his initial reserve during those early months when the deaths of Billy and Lee had pushed him to take crazy risks in the hope of joining them.

Little by little, Mr. Hicks had won his trust. Clay recalled a thousand conversations by firelight—one-sided mostly, the old man rambling on about philosophy and history, giving Clay an education.

And now Mr. Hicks, too, would be gone, just like his parents and Billy and Lee had gone. Clay tightened his hold around the sleeping girl, seeking comfort in the feel of her in his arms. Would he dare let himself care? Would he be able to protect her, keep her safe, even while he let her flex her wings and join him as an equal partner in the mining camps?

Chapter Fifteen

When the first glow of sunrise painted the horizon with pink and gold, a gunshot boomed deep within the mountainside. Clay felt a sudden release of tension that left him numb. His lungs seemed to seize up, no longer drawing in air.

Annabel had been dozing. She came awake with a jolt. For an instant, she froze. Then she wriggled around in his arms and looked at him with grief-filled eyes.

"Was it…?"

"Yes." His voice was hoarse. "No more waiting. It's over."

Annabel pressed her face to his chest, fighting to suppress the tears.

"Hush," Clay said. The emptiness inside him eased a little, as if consoling Annabel was thawing some of that cold, numb feeling that had settled over him. "It's all right," he told her softly. "Mr. Hicks called his time, chose the moment of his death. That's more than most men can ask for."

"I know," she muttered against his shirt. "But it is so terribly sad."

Bracing up on one elbow, Clay laid Annabel down on her back on the bedroll and leaned over her. With his other hand, he stroked her hair. "Cry it out," he said. "Let your tears flow, for it is a good farewell for a man to have a woman weeping over him."

"He told me not to…but I can't help it."

"He would be pleased. Sometimes a man does not like to ask for something yet he is grateful to receive it."

Annabel gave in to the need to mourn. Her body shook with the force of her sobs. Lowering his head, Clay kissed away her tears, tasting the saltiness on her skin. He kissed her brow, the crest of her cheeks, her eyelids. Annabel clung to his shirt, her small fists clutching the fabric, and let her grief flow out.

Clay felt his chest tighten with tenderness. Perhaps this was how it worked between a man and a woman. Masculine pride did not allow a man to seek solace in tears, but if he had a woman to do the crying for him, it eased his grief, too.

His feelings in turmoil, Clay settled down beside the weeping girl and rocked her in his arms. She had to be exhausted, physically and mentally. She'd worked beyond endurance, helping him to clear a passage into the cave and crawling through, not knowing what she would find on the other side, and then caring for the dying man. Throughout the ordeal, her courage had staggered him. For the greatest courage was not the lack of fear, but the ability to keep going in the face of it.

Annabel knelt in the corner of the cavern overhang, sorting through the few items of clothing Mr. Hicks had left behind. Even though her melancholy refused to lift, the sharpness of her grief was easing. She'd always felt embarrassed by her emotional nature, but perhaps it was the best way.

Her grief was like the water in the creek, flowing free, letting the pain inside her heal. Clay's grief was like the dammed pond, building up inside him, creating a pressure that never had a chance to ebb.

She could see his suffering, as if it were branded on his skin. It was there, in the stark look in his eyes, in his stony expression, in the rigid set of his shoulders. In the way he threw himself into working at the *arrastre*, attempting to use the physical labor to blot out the grief he was unable to express.

Footsteps thudded across the clearing. Annabel turned to watch and saw Clay walking up along the sunlit path. As he entered the shadows of the cavern, the sunshine behind him turned him into silhouette, dark and brooding. The damp shirt clung to his wide shoulders, emphasizing his lean strength.

Empathy welled up in her. He'd given her so much. His friendship, his protection. The chance at a partnership. The comfort of his embrace as she wept in grief. How could she ease his suffering? How could she find a way to help him deal with his loss?

Clay sank to sit beside her, elbows propped on bent knees, head lowered. Annabel could feel his body shaking with fatigue and tension, the emotions he kept suppressed vibrating within him like a message along a telegraph wire.

"Why don't you let yourself mourn?" she said softly. "You cared about Mr. Hicks, and it is right to cry for him."

"I left tears behind in my childhood."

She reached out to touch his shoulder where the shirt had pulled tight over the hard muscle. "He spoke about you in his final moments."

Clay turned his head to glance at her but did not reply.

Annabel went on. "Mr. Hicks told me you've never known love."

For a long moment, there was silence. Outside the squirrel rustled in the fallen leaves, looking for acorns. The autumn wind whistled along the cliffs, like a train whistle warning them that soon they'd have to depart.

Finally, Clay spoke. His voice was low and halting. "I guess I must have loved my parents, with the love of a child who depends on an adult for food and warmth. And the two friends I had at the orphanage. Perhaps I loved them. And I did love Mr. Hicks, in a way." He turned to face her now, and the suffering in his eyes flooded out to Annabel like a wordless plea. "But every time I loved someone, they died."

"It doesn't have to mean you must never love again." She lifted one hand, traced his features with her fingertips.

Making a rough sound low in his throat, Clay gripped her wrist and pressed her palm against his mouth, as if to trap inside the sounds of sorrow. Tears welled up in his eyes, and he blinked to stop them from falling.

"No," Annabel said. "Let your grief flow."

A muscle tugged at the side of Clay's jaw as he clenched his teeth. She could hear his harsh breathing, could sense the battle of emotions inside him. Then a single tear spilled free to run down his cheek. Annabel rose up to her knees, leaned in and kissed the tear away.

She kissed his cheek, the side of his jaw, his forehead, his closed eyelids, in much the same way he had done to her while he comforted her. His shoulders were shaking now, with dry, heaving sobs that seemed to rise from the very core of him. Annabel wrapped her arms around him and held him close, cradling his lean, muscled body to her chest, his head resting on her shoulder.

For long moments, they clung together, the air cool and fresh outside, the setting sun gilding the autumn trees across the clearing. Then Clay stirred. He turned his head on her shoulder. Hungry and restless, his lips met the side of her neck, traced along the curve of her jaw and came to rest on her mouth.

There was no gentleness or sorrow in the kiss, only the hard edge of loss and despair and loneliness. The only way Annabel knew to respond was to let her own love flow with abandon, let her new and untested passions rise, hoping that the warmth of her emotions might thaw whatever was frozen inside Clay.

She could feel his hands fumbling at the front of her shirt now, his motions urgent and without restraint. Alarm bells pealed in her mind, but the sound seemed no more than a distant echo of a warning that came too late.

The threadbare fabric rent, and she could feel his calloused hand slide in to cup her breast, no longer bound with a linen cloth. His fingers curled around the shape as if created to fit. A shocking wave of pleasure rippled through Annabel. She emitted a small, startled sound at the new sensation, but Clay silenced her with another hungry kiss.

Frantic now, he was tearing at her clothing, his lips trailing hot kisses on her neck. Annabel felt adrift, helpless to resist. Being alive coursed through her veins with a reckless, pounding beat that obliterated all moral concerns.

Clay lifted his head to look at her. "Annabel." Her name on his lips was a rough, wild sound, and she took it for a plea to help him to deal with his loss.

She let her eyes roam over his features—green eyes that brimmed with grief, the sharp angle of high cheekbones, lean jaw darkened with stubble. Her heart seemed to swell and swell in her chest, making it hard to breath, making her body tremble with the need to comfort and console. "Yes," she said. "It's all right."

The death of Mr. Hicks had made her acutely aware of how precarious existence could be. Life was here and now, to be lived to the full. She wanted Clay to touch her, wanted to share with him the closest bond a woman could feel with a man, for there was no telling what tomorrow might bring.

Rising to his feet, Clay unbuckled his gun belt and let the heavy revolver slide to the ground. His eyes held hers as he quickly shrugged out of his shirt and pulled away his boots and tossed them aside before removing the rest of his clothing.

Annabel had never seen a naked man before, and it hadn't occurred to her that there could be such a blatant difference in their physical features. She stared at the sight, eyes wide, and then Clay was beside her, leaning over her on one elbow, and she could no longer see the part of him that had intrigued her so, only feel it, resting hot and hard and heavy against her thigh.

"Are you sure, Annabel?" Clay asked.

She swallowed, gave a tiny nod of assent. In truth, now that it was about to happen, she was no longer so sure at all. Then Clay lowered his head to hers, and his mouth settled over hers once more, hungry and insistent, and all hesitation scattered from her mind.

Time and time again, his lips closed over hers. She could feel the heat of him, could feel the rough stubble on his jaw scraping against her skin, could feel the strength of him, the power that throbbed in his body, but she felt no fear, only a wild excitement that tugged low and deep inside her.

And then she could feel Clay's knee sliding between her legs, easing them apart. His mouth left hers and his lips went to her throat, to her ear, to the side of her neck. Each new location ignited another spark of pleasure, throwing her deeper and deeper into the dark folds of passion.

Now his body was fully on top of hers, anchoring her to the ground. He was big and hard and heavy, his muscles like steel, his skin rougher and hotter than hers. The scents of leather and dust clung to him.

For an instant, Clay stilled above her. Bracing his weight on his arms, he studied her expression. "Are you sure, Annabel?" he asked for the second time, the gravelly timbre of his voice even more pronounced than usual.

"Yes," Annabel said.

Lowering his body, Clay leaned on his elbows. His hips moved in a quick twist, and something happened between her legs, a piercing flash of pain followed by a strange feeling of something pushing inside her.

It hurt! It hurt so badly tears sprang to her eyes. Startled, Annabel wriggled against the hard ground in an attempt to slide away from under Clay, but his hands, curled over her shoulders, locked her in place. Moving on top of her, he rocked his hips, sliding in and out of her.

The pain eased to discomfort, and the unfamiliar tension that had risen inside Annabel seemed to coil tighter and tighter. She longed for something more, but she had no idea what it could be. Her body seemed to scream for a release, and yet she found it impossible to attain.

She tried to join Clay in that rhythmic thrust and drag of his hips, but the intimacy was too new and frightening. She did not know what to do, what a woman's response ought to be to such a masculine invasion.

Soon Clay seemed to be reaching some kind of culmination, for his breath came in heavy gasps. His hips surged into her in one final thrust, and he stiffened above her, head tipped back, eyes tightly shut. The expression on his face could have been ecstasy or a grimace of great suffering.

After a moment, Clay eased their bodies apart. Rolling his weight away from her, he collapsed beside her. Hauling her into his arms, he scattered tiny kisses over her face. "It will be better next time, I promise," he said as he cradled her to his chest.

His warmth and strength wrapped Annabel into a safe cocoon, and the tenderness in his voice calmed her anxieties. With a sigh, she curled up against him and closed her eyes. If the minor discomfort of coupling was the price she would have to pay to enjoy this feeling of closeness, she'd be happy to pay it every night.

Chapter Sixteen

Clay cranked the handle of the rocker box and watched Annabel. She was crouching on the flat stone by the creek, washing her clothes in the pond, dressed in an old shirt that had belonged to Mr. Hicks. Billowing around her like a tent, the huge garment reached down to her knees. She had left her hair unbound, and it cascaded in a shiny curtain from beneath her bowler hat.

He'd hurt her.

He'd had no idea it could be so painful for a virgin. Bedding her had been wrong to start with, and he had compounded his transgression by not being gentle enough. He should have taken his time, coaxed her along, made sure she kept pace with him.

But he'd been unable to restrain himself. Once he had her beneath him, naked and willing, it had felt as though she had cracked his heart wide open. Even now, it daunted him to recall the surge of emotion. All his instincts had focused on being inside her, possessing her, reaching completion.

And when it came, the completion, the brief moment of total abandon that empties a man's mind of every thought, of every earthly worry, it had been so powerful, so shattering it had drained away every ounce of strength in him.

He'd always suspected it would be different with a woman one cared about, and now he knew it for a fact. No amount of money could buy that kind of pleasure in a whore's bed.

And such a gift should not be one-sided, Clay thought with regret. He longed to make it up to Annabel, longed to show her how good it could be. Make her feel those ripples of pleasure he had felt. He wanted to hold her in his arms while her body trembled through the aftermath of completion.

He wished he could talk to her about it, explain and apologize, but talking never came easy for him, and finding a way to introduce such a topic was beyond his capabilities.

Annabel jumped down from the stone, looking like a street urchin in her big boots, the tent-like shirt flapping damply about her legs. She said something to him, but Clay couldn't hear her. He stilled the rocker box, and the rattling noises ceased.

"What did you say?" he asked. "I couldn't hear you."

"Do we have to leave? Couldn't we stay here a bit longer?"

They had talked about the gold, agreed they would not mine it, for the cave had become a tomb and deserved sanctity as such. He'd been worried Annabel might feel differently, but her agreement had been instant and spontaneous.

Now he contemplated her, surprised. "You want to stay? With Mr. Hicks resting in his grave right beyond where you sleep?"

She gave a tiny shrug. "Why should it bother me? Surely, remaining near his grave is an act of kindness. We'd be keeping him company in death."

Clay weighed up the idea. It would take him a few more days to finish washing the ore. He did not wish to rush the task, to make sure he caught every grain of gold. *And,* his mind whispered, *if we stay, you might get a chance to redeem your actions, give Annabel pleasure instead of just taking.*

"The winter is on its way," he pointed out. "We don't have a cabin. We're low on food. The mine is closed. There is no reason to stay longer than we have to."

Annabel poked the toe of her boot at the heap of discarded mining tailings. She averted her eyes as she spoke. "What will happen when we leave here?"

Clay pushed his hat back on his head. They had talked about what to do with the gold, but they hadn't talked about what had happened between them. "We'll ride to Hillsboro," he said quietly. "Find a preacher."

The stiffness in Annabel's spine eased a little. A new maturity was developing in her, and Clay could no longer see all her emotions written on her face. But he could read relief in her expression now. So, she wished to marry. He owed it to her to offer, but what if the marriage didn't work out?

Faint memories of his parents flickered in his mind. They must have loved each other in the beginning, for he recalled laughter and kisses. And then the affection had died, turning into ugly fights that kept him awake in his cot at night.

Annabel had spoken very little about her past, but he could tell she was accustomed to physical comforts. How would she fare in hardship and poverty? Would the attraction between them be enough? Or would her feelings, instead of growing to a real, lasting love, crumble away into bitter recriminations?

Clay could think of no worse prospect than being married to a woman who ended up resenting him and wishing their paths had never crossed. But he was a man of honor, and it was too late for regrets.

"And then?" Annabel said, drawing him out of his troubled thoughts. "After we find a preacher in Hillsboro?"

"We'll see how much money we have left. I'd like to spend a few months prospecting. See if we can locate another claim."

"I'd like that," Annabel said quietly.

She settled down near him, sitting on the ground, arms wrapped around her knees, the way she liked to do. Clay washed the ore. When he went up the path to fetch another bucketful of gravel, he gave the glass jar with gold dust and nuggets for Annabel to hold, as a means of giving her a sense of purpose while he worked.

Annabel liked watching Clay work. When the sun reached its zenith, he took off his shirt. Watching the muscles play beneath his bronzed skin gave her that tugging low in her belly she was learning to recognize and enjoy.

It didn't matter it had hurt. It was supposed to, the first time. Mama had educated her daughters on such matters, and although Annabel had been too young to be included in those talks, her sisters had passed on the information—including an understanding of the basics of human procreation.

She refused to regret what had taken place, and yet, she felt ill at ease. Only now did she fully appreciate the extent of her recklessness. She could have brought ruin upon herself, shame upon her sisters, shame upon the memory of her parents.

Why had she done it? Had it been loneliness and longing? Need to ease Clay's grief? The euphoria of first love and awakening passions? Or, could it be something less noble? Could it be that subconsciously she had wanted to make sure Clay would have to marry her, keep her under his protection, making it impossible for him to end their partnership? And if that was the case, she should be ashamed.

On impulse, acting quickly before she could change her mind, Annabel gestured for Clay to cease the cranking of the rocker box. He stilled, straightened, pushed a stray curl from his forehead and settled his attention on her.

"What is it?" he prompted when the silence dragged on.

"What you said about finding a preacher...only if you really want to."

The merry gurgle of the creek, the birds hopping near the water, the wind rustling in the trees suddenly seemed very loud as the seconds ticked by.

"I want to," Clay finally replied.

Her anxieties easing, Annabel rested her chin on her upraised knees while Clay resumed his task, the muscles on his arms and shoulders bunching and leaping. In the back of her mind she knew she would need to think about the future, talk to Clay about her sisters, make plans, but for a bit longer she wished to live only in the present, not letting the outside world intrude.

When Clay paused to collect nuggets caught in the riffles, the noise of the rocker box died away, allowing conversation. Annabel longed to reach out to him, to understand him better. Perhaps, after what had taken place between them, she was no longer bound by her promise not to pry into his past.

"What is Clay short for?" she asked. "Clayton?"

"No." Previously, his features had drawn into a scowl whenever she questioned him, but now one corner of his mouth kicked up into a crooked smile. "It's short for a clay cup with a dragon painted inside it."

"Clay cup? What do you mean? You were named after a clay cup?"

"Exactly," he said and handed her a few nuggets to add into the glass jar. "A clay cup, and a necklace with green stones. Collier. That's the French word for a necklace, I've been told."

Curious now, Annabel contemplated him. "Tell me more."

Instead of replying, Clay knelt by the creek, splashed water over his arms and chest to rinse away the dust from the ore. Then he ducked down to drink. When he'd had enough, he rose, wiped his mouth with the back of his hand and walked over to her. Leaving a couple of paces between them, he stretched out on his side, facing her, his weight braced on one elbow.

"I told you, I'm an orphan."

Annabel nodded. "You were six years old."

Something flickered in Clay's eyes—surprise, but perhaps also pleasure that she'd paid enough attention to remember. He picked up a pebble from the ground and toyed with it while he spoke, keeping his tone light.

"Someone took me to the nuns, and they asked for my name. I told them I didn't know. But I had been holding a clay cup, and hidden in my clothing they found a necklace of green stones. Clay cup—*Clay*. Necklace—*Collier*. One of the nuns was French, and she came up with the word. And so Clay Collier was born."

"At six years old you did not know your own name?"

He gave her a wry smile. "As it happens, I did. A whole dozen of them, and I had no idea if any of them was real."

Intrigued, Annabel leaned forward. "What do you mean?"

"My parents were actors in a traveling theater show. Every few months, they left one troupe and joined another.

And every time they gave me a different name. They had drilled into me not to tell my name if anyone asked, so it hardly seemed to matter, but I learned and memorized each new name anyway. Charlie, Benedict, Claude, Jeremy, Joseph. I've been them all."

"But why?"

"I assume they were on the run. They changed their own names, too. Perhaps they had committed some crime. Perhaps one of them already had a wife or husband and was running away from responsibilities."

Her mind painted a different picture. "Or maybe your mother was the daughter of a nobleman who had eloped with a penniless cowboy and they were fleeing from her enraged papa."

Clay shook his head gently. "Don't build up foolish dreams, Annabel. They were low-class people, drunk as often as sober, and they burned to death in their wagon when one of them knocked over a lamp and they were too full of cheap whiskey to get out in time. I know that's how it happened, for I was down by the riverbank, trying to catch a fish for my supper because half the time they forgot to feed me."

Annabel held her breath. Clay's tone remained even, but she sensed a store of hidden grief beneath his quiet words. To suffer a childhood of such neglect…and then to lose one's parents in such a terrible way…

She and her sisters had never mentioned it, but she knew they all had imagined how it might have been for their parents when they drowned. Did they know life was about to end? Did they share their final moments, or had the storm tossed them apart? Were they frightened? Did it hurt when the sea took your life?

"Did you…?" Her voice faltered. "Did you see them burn?"

Clay shook his head. "By the time I came up from the river, there was nothing left but the charred remains of the timber wagon and their burned bodies. They were buried in a pauper's grave, and I was taken to the nuns."

"And then you went to the orphanage?"

"I went to the orphanage and stayed there until I was fourteen." Clay seemed to hesitate, as if reluctant to go on, but the words trickled out anyway. "At the orphanage I made friends with two younger boys, and I tried to look out for them. When it was time for me to leave, they were afraid to stay behind, so I took them with me."

Annabel heard the bitter note in his voice. Her pulse quickened. When they first met, she'd longed to put a crack into his stony facade. She had an inkling that she might be about to get her wish.

Very softly, she asked, "What happened to those boys?"

"They died." Clay's reply was bland. He picked up another pebble and tossed it along the ground, to scare away a squirrel venturing too close. "I should not have taken them with me. I was not equipped to look after them. If I had left them behind, they might still be alive."

Along with pity over Clay's troubled past, Annabel felt a sting of disappointment. She'd been so close to getting a glimpse into his feelings, and then he had hidden behind that stony facade of his again.

"What was it like, growing up in an orphanage?" she asked, hoping to push through the barrier that shielded his emotions. "Were you unhappy? Did you suffer? Did you have enough to eat? Did you get any schooling?"

"I was not happy. I did not suffer. Much of the time I was hired out as a day laborer to a stone quarry. When I was small, I sorted out stones. When I got bigger, I pounded the rocks." He shifted one shoulder, as if to cast aside the past. "The food was tasteless and scarce. I learned to read and write, but the education I have is from Mr. Hicks. He was a learned man, and he enjoyed sharing his knowledge."

Clay fell silent. Annabel waited. A cloud drifted in front of the sun, and a cool breeze rustled the autumn leaves. Even the rippling of the creek sounded darker, as if nature was announcing an overture for the winter.

Then Clay spoke again. "Growing up in an orphanage seemed to affect boys in two different ways. With some, all softness goes out of them. That's often boys who've been abused. They don't know how to love. They turn hard and cruel.

"The rest…most orphan boys…are the opposite. When they grow up, they are so desperate for the comfort of love, for the bond of human warmth, they give their heart to the first woman who asks, even when they should not."

His eyes met hers now, with a storm of emotion in them. Annabel's pulse was racing wildly. She knew they were on the brink of some turning point, as if they had been teetering on a slippery surface ever since they met, and now they would either recover their balance or tumble into something unknown.

"Which kind are you?" Her question came on a whisper.

"I thought you would have figured it out by now."

And then Clay rolled onto his feet and walked over to her. He scooped her into his arms and carried her up the path. Past the *arrastre* they went, across the clearing, beyond the kitchen and the water barrel, his eyes holding hers as he clasped her to his chest and took her into the cool shadows of the cavern.

Clay laid Annabel down on the earth floor while he went to fetch his bedroll and spread it out. She was silent, but he could feel her watching him with concern in her eyes. Gently, he lifted her up, positioned her on the bed-roll and knelt beside her.

"I'm sorry," he said. To his surprise, the words came easily after all. "I hurt you last night. Let me make it up to you. Let me show you how good it can be."

"I didn't know..." She took a sharp breath, then spoke on an exhale. "I didn't know what to do...you have to teach me..."

"There is nothing to teach," Clay said. "Just follow the natural instincts of your body." He adjusted his position, reached out with one hand and slipped a button free on her borrowed shirt...and another...and another, all the way down the front until he could ease the edges of the faded fabric apart.

She no longer wore the strip of cloth tied around her chest, and her naked breasts shone white in the muted sunlight that spilled into the cavern. Her amber eyes held his, trust and longing burning like a flame in them.

Clay felt something shatter within him, as if the layers of defense he had carried inside him most of his life were crumbling away. How could he doubt what was between them? He should have more faith in Annabel. Again and again, she had proved her courage, her loyalty, her compassion.

"You are shivering," he said. "Are you cold?"

"A little," she replied. "My hair is damp, and my shirt got wet."

"Let's get it off you." With a new gentleness, Clay lifted Annabel's shoulders and eased her arms free of the worn garment. He got to his feet, found a clean blanket and used it to rub her skin warm.

A snatch of saloon talk drifted into his mind. Once, he'd seen a man haul a passing girl onto his knee and tell her he could make her purr like a kitten. The girl laughed and led the man upstairs, not even taking the time to negotiate the payment.

Once, a long time ago, before his parents died, he'd had a kitten. He had enjoyed making the tiny tabby purr so hard its body vibrated with the motion. Now he was determined to do the same with Annabel.

When she was lying down, dry and warm, Clay eased his hand beneath the blanket, letting it slide over her breast. Annabel sucked in a startled breath and quivered beneath his touch. Clay repeated the caress, then caught the pebbled nipple between his thumb and forefinger. Annabel made a tiny sound that conveyed as much protest as delight.

"Did that hurt?" he asked.

"No." Her voice was dreamy, her posture languid on the bedroll.

"Good," Clay replied. "And neither should what we do together." He slid the blanket out of the way to reveal Annabel's nakedness. Lifting her hair aside, he pressed a kiss to the nape of her neck. "Do you remember what I told you once?" He spoke softly. "That a man can lose his sanity when running his hands through hair like yours. That's what you do to me, Annabel. You make me lose my sanity. I'm sorry I was rough with you last night."

"It's all right."

Clay ran his hands over her naked skin, seeking out new places to kiss…the curve of her shoulder…the dip of her waist…the narrow groove of her spine between those angel's wings shoulder blades. He paid homage to her beauty, like a sculptor might admire a statue he had just completed.

Only when Clay could see a languidness of arousal take hold of Annabel did he shed his own clothing and lie down beside her. "Just relax, let me touch you. Don't think of anything. Just concentrate on feeling the pleasure."

She gave him a wordless nod and closed her eyes. Clay

resumed that slow, gentle stroking with his fingertips, paying attention to her reactions. If she made a small, whimpering sound, it meant she liked what he was doing. And the low, throaty moan meant she liked it even better. And when she pressed her head back against the bedroll and let out a frantic cry, she liked it most of all.

For long minutes, he touched and stroked her body, finding the places that rewarded him with those sounds of pleasure. Her breasts, the line of her collarbone, the shell of her ear, the inside of her elbow, the dip of her waist, the bend of her knee. He kissed all those places and many, many more.

He turned her over onto her stomach, and kissed his way down her spine, then nipped at one rounded buttock with his teeth. She cried out and arched up on the bedroll.

"You like that, don't you?"

Only when she was writhing with impatience, only when her breathing was swift and that throaty moan almost a constant sound, did Clay roll her over onto her back again and settle over her. He nudged her legs apart, cradled her face between his hands and looked deep into her eyes.

"Tell me you want this, Annabel."

She gave him a hesitant nod.

"Tell me with words."

"I want you to make love to me."

Carefully, taking his time, Clay eased inside her. He stilled and looked into her face. "All right?"

"Yes."

He gave an easy thrust, then another.

Annabel wriggled beneath him. "Wait."

Clay stilled again. "What is it?"

"You didn't mean...when you said an orphan boy can give his heart to the first woman who asks for it, even when he should not…you didn't mean…you didn't imply that it would be unwise for you to give your heart to me?"

"No," Clay said. "I didn't mean that." He flexed his hips and began thrusting deep, as if those simple words had sealed the bond between them. He studied Annabel's reaction, ready to slow down if she showed any signs of distress. After a few moments of hesitation, her hips began rocking to meet his.

This time, she was with him. Encouraged, Clay increased the speed and power of his strokes and felt her respond. Lowering his head, he kissed her, deep, consuming kisses that added to the heat between them.

Slowly, he felt a tension build up in Annabel, felt the rising urgency in her movements. Clay held back his own climax, waited, waited. Finally, Annabel flung her head back, arched beneath him and cried out. Clay gave in to the release, let it roll over him and sank down on top of her, taking care not to crush her with his weight.

Just as he had dreamed, Clay held Annabel in his arms while the tremors of completion buffeted her. Watching her in the throes of pleasure—pleasure he had given her— peeled away another layer of his defenses. In that moment, he decided there would be no other woman in the world who could offer him the same sense of belonging, the same sense of unity, the same hope for the future as Annabel did.

Chapter Seventeen

Annabel sat cross-legged on the ground by the creek, mending her torn trousers. Her body still tingled from the pleasures of the afternoon. Papa had taught her that if a person failed at a task, it was important to try again. She doubted making love was quite what Papa had in mind, but the lesson had served her well.

Clay was operating the rocker box, shirtless but with a hat on his head and a gun belt around his hips. Occasionally, Annabel glanced up at him while she kept the needle rising and falling.

She knew she was in love with him, but she possessed no yardstick against which to measure the emotion. Could it be merely a schoolgirl infatuation, a rite of passage that would soon pass? Or was it something deeper, something that could bridge the gulf between their backgrounds and survive the pressures of the real world?

Not having told him about everything she had left behind had become a source of discomfiture, like a fishbone stuck in her throat. Cousin Gareth was her legal guardian, after all, and they were planning to marry without his consent. She should reveal the truth, soon, but for a little longer she wanted to hold on to her anonymity—be just herself, instead of the youngest Fairfax girl, the sheltered daughter of an affluent family.

After Clay had finished washing the ore, they took out the pair of gold scales from their protective wooden case and weighed the dust and nuggets, adding gold into one cup until it balanced with the weight in the other cup. They kept repeating the action until they had weighed the full quantity.

"Just under fourteen ounces." Annabel held the glass jar up to the sunlight, making the contents sparkle. "Together with what we already have, it makes almost twenty-one ounces in total. At sixteen dollars on ounce that's worth three hundred and thirty dollars."

Clay glanced at her. "How can you count so quickly?"

She shrugged. "I just can."

Impressed by her skill, Clay put away the jar with gold. He didn't mind having a woman who outshone him in cleverness. She would never match his physical strength, so a more agile mind balanced the power between them.

"Do you know how to shoot?" he asked as he moved along to inspect the boxes of rifle shells stacked in a metal box on the shelf.

"Only an old-fashioned musket."

"I'll teach you to use a handgun before we leave, and we'll buy you a revolver in Hillsboro. It pays to go around armed in the mining camps."

When going through the small stack of papers Mr. Hicks had left behind, they found the location notice for the mine. If they didn't submit evidence of labor at the claim every year, the notice would lapse and another miner could stake a claim—a possibility they could do nothing to prevent.

In the papers they also found a Bible, with Mr. Hicks's given name written on the flyleaf, and beneath it the name of a woman.

Aaron Hicks.
Sarah Milford.

"Sarah Milford?" Clay said with a frown. "Never heard Mr. Hicks mention her."

He could see hesitation flicker across Annabel's face. She spoke softly. "She was a woman he loved. She betrayed him by marrying another man, even though she had promised to wait for him. That was the cause of his bitterness toward women. He told me about it as he lay dying in the cave."

"A woman who can't stay true is not worth a man's love," Clay said, scorn in his tone.

Annabel gave him one of her wide-eyed looks and started to argue, one woman defending another, but gave up when she found nothing to say. Clay moved on and studied the pile of goods they had stacked on the floor, ready for packing.

Kitchen utensils, pots and pans, blankets, mining equipment—shovels, pickaxes, blasting tools, buckets, a small tin of black powder, iron chains and bottles of mercury, magnets, gold pans, everything needed to work either a lode or a placer claim.

"We need to cut the quantity in half." Clay dropped down to his haunches and began shifting through the items. "The mule can't carry this much."

"He could, if I ride the buckskin with you," Annabel suggested. "The equipment is worth money. Anything we can do without, we can sell in Hillsboro. And I don't want to ride into town bouncing on the back of a mule."

Clay considered. "It's only ten miles, and you're light. We'll do that and take everything for now." He smiled at her, the happiness he could read in her expression easing his worries over their future. "It is not every day a man gets to ride into town with a beautiful bride in the saddle behind him."

For three more days they stayed at the camp, roaming the forest, bathing in the creek. Clay taught Annabel how to load the big Walker Colt and fire it with enough accuracy to stop an attacker at a close range. Annabel cut his hair and mended his clothing and taught him to sing some of her favorite sea shanties.

Clay called it a vacation. Annabel saw it as a farewell to their mountain sanctuary—a place where she had found happiness and a sense of purpose, despite the tragic death of the old man she had come to like and respect.

At night, they slept in each other's arms. "We won't do it again, until we are wed," Clay whispered in the darkness as Annabel snuggled up against him.

"We couldn't anyway," Annabel whispered back. "I have my monthly flow."

Women's reproductive cycles were a mystery to Clay, but he understood it meant she couldn't be with child. Relief flooded over him. It had been wrong to succumb to the temptation, but at least they had avoided consequences that would have added to his sense of guilt.

And yet the thought of a baby stuck in his mind. While Billy and Lee lived, he'd gained a sense of pride from looking after them. What would it be like, to be responsible for a child? He tried to imagine a little boy with green eyes and unruly curls, but it kept turning into little girl with amber eyes and straight, midnight black hair.

Before they got ready to leave their claim, Clay climbed up on a ladder and hacked an inscription above the entrance to the mine.

Aaron Hicks 1834–1889

He added a large cross, turning the cliff into a headstone.

After he came down, they tore down the kitchen canopy and burned the timber, including the ladder and the handcart and the *arrastre* spokes. They scattered the gravel from the mine dumps and rolled the stones that had formed the *arrastre* into disarray, in the hope of disguising any signs of the mine.

Anything they couldn't feed to the flames or take with them—the stove, a few empty grain bins, loops of rusty iron chain—they hid inside the mine tunnel. To cover up the opening, they dragged back into place the dead oak that had served as a screen and transplanted saplings around it, spruce and oak and aspen.

If the trees took, they would form a thicket that hid the entrance, even if someone ventured close by. And if another prospector found the mine by chance, the inscription would warn him it was a tomb, and he might choose to move on.

Annabel sat behind Clay on the buckskin as they rode into Hillsboro at sundown. It was the first boomtown she had ever seen. The noise was deafening. Up on the hill, a huge stamp mill smashed the ore. In town, music and raucous voices blared out from the saloons that seemed too many to count.

In the street, horses stood tethered at hitching rails and people milled about. Among them Annabel could see women, dressed in gowns with a narrow waist and wide skirts. With dismay, she considered her own ragged clothing. No longer pretending to be a boy, she wore her hair in a single braid that hung down her back. Tomorrow she would buy a pair of boots that fit her feet. And before she took her wedding vows, she would purchase a gown.

Dodging a speeding cart and a pair of snarling dogs, Clay rode up to the livery stable at the end of the street. He swung Annabel down and dismounted. The hostler, a tall man with a huge drooping moustache, came to take their horse and mule.

"Two dollars a night," he said. "Half for the mule."

Clay's brow puckered. "That's twice the going rate."

"It's the going rate here. If it doesn't suit, go elsewhere."

"Is there a good hotel in town?" Annabel cut in.

"Mrs. Orchard runs a clean establishment." The man pointed down the street. "Her husband runs the stage line, in case you're looking to travel out."

They made their way along the crowded street to the hotel. "We only have a suite, with its own bath," the portly, balding clerk informed them. "Five dollars a night. Payment in advance."

"Can I pay with gold?" Clay asked.

"Cash only," the man replied. "The bank will change your gold. They open at nine in the morning."

Clay turned to leave, but Annabel tugged him back. "I have money." She pulled out the leather poke hanging around her neck, lifted the rawhide cord over her head and offered the poke to Clay. "There is twelve dollars in there, enough to tide us over until we get to the bank."

Clay balanced the poke in his hand. Annabel could read his thoughts. Accepting her savings hurt his pride, but he turned to the clerk, counted out five silver dollars and took the key the clerk handed out.

When they got upstairs, Annabel rushed around the airy room with a small bathing alcove and a pair of tall windows overlooking the street. "A bath," she exclaimed. "And clean linens. It seems forever since I slept in a bed."

She caught Clay watching her with a thoughtful expression on his face. Annabel bit her lip, wishing to take back the words. She'd have to watch out, to avoid giving him the impression she missed the everyday luxuries of her former life.

In the morning, they had breakfast in the hotel dining room, then went to the telegraph office. Clay wanted to send a message to the man in Valverde who sent the supplies and settle any debt Mr. Hicks might owe. Annabel wished to let her sisters know that she was safe and well.

The small office attached to the drugstore was empty, but they could hear the telegraph key clacking behind the low partition at the back. Pencils and blank telegraph forms lay scattered on the wooden counter.

"I've got it down to four words." Annabel picked up a pencil and wrote: *"Hicks dead. What owing?"*

While Clay filled in the address for the merchant in Valverde, Annabel composed a telegram for Charlotte. At ten cents a word she did not wish to waste them. After several attempts, she was satisfied with the balance between brevity and clarity.

Missed train. Stranded in Hillsboro. Will ride west. Have trustworthy escort. Please send funds. Annabel.

"Please" was not strictly necessary, but she was willing to sacrifice ten cents in the name of polite manners. She considered adding she was fit and well, but decided to save the money. Her sisters would figure it out. After a moment of hesitation, she glanced over at Clay. Satisfied his attention was on the mining notices tacked to the wall, Annabel inserted an extra line.

Spotted Gareth Southern Pacific train month ago. Watch out.

If Cousin Gareth had been on his way to Gold Crossing, most likely he had already arrived, but if he had not, she wanted to alert Charlotte and Miranda to his presence in the area.

Unease filled her at concealing her affluent background from Clay. Why was it that when you didn't tell something because it didn't seem to matter, keeping the information a secret seemed to blow its importance out of all proportion?

The clacking of the telegraph key ceased, and a small, sharp-featured man with a visor over his eyes and garters on his shirtsleeves came out from behind the partition. Appearing harassed, he accepted their forms without as much as a greeting and added up the words. "That will be four dollars and thirty cents."

"When can we expect a reply?" Clay asked.

"Just as soon as the person at the other end sends it" came the surly answer.

The operator took their five dollars, made change and hurried back behind the partition, where the telegraph key had burst to life with an incoming message.

When they stepped out into the sunshine, Annabel nearly collided with a tall man coming out of the drugstore. He swerved to avoid her, his walking stick tapping against the boardwalk. Annabel caught the flash of silver on the handle—a handle shaped like a wolf's head!

Her eyes darted upward. Her throat closed up. *Cousin*

Gareth. And his eyes were sweeping up and down her ragged clothing with a glint of recognition in them.

She could run. But Cousin Gareth had seen her come out of the telegraph office. He might go inside, bribe the operator—Cousin Gareth was good at bribing people—and get his hands on her message addressed to Mrs. Maude Greenwood in Gold Crossing, the false identity Charlotte was hiding behind.

She had to distract him, to avoid exposing Charlotte. Boldly, Annabel stepped forward. "Sir, I don't know if you remember me. I ran from you on the train." She lifted her bowler hat and flicked her long braid over her shoulder.

"I am sorry I ran off like that, but you said I reminded you of a girl you knew, and I thought you might have caught on to my secret—that I was a girl masquerading as a boy. I fled from you to avoid exposure."

Cousin Gareth contemplated her, a baffled frown on his face. "Oh, yes, I remember," he said after a moment. "I did indeed think you reminded me of someone, but the recollection has faded now. You see, I've lost my memory." He touched the scar on his brow. "I go by the name Gareth Wolfson. See here." He lifted the walking stick. "The handle is shaped like the head of a wolf. That gave me the name Wolfson. My first name I got from a woman who thought I resembled a relative of hers called Gareth."

He gave a small, self-deprecating shrug. "I seem to be an educated man, and I am rather good with cards. I earn my living as a gambler, and I don't cheat."

He exhaled a long, slow sigh. "I hoped you could shed some light on my identity. I've only had one lead up to now. A saloon singer, by the name Miss Randi. She is the one who gave me my first name. When she saw me, she blurted out *Gareth*, but when she took a closer look at me she decided she had been mistaken."

"Gareth?" Annabel breathed.

"That's right."

"What....what did this Miss Randi look like?"

"She was quite tall for a woman. Blonde, with blue eyes. A very beautiful woman. Married to a Cheyenne Indian. The strange thing is, when I looked at her, my mind conjured up the roar of the ocean and the smell of salt spray, and yet we were in Wyoming."

"In Wyoming?" Annabel echoed.

"Yes. Miss Randi—Miranda something, her real name was—was on her way to the Arizona Territory. I tried to follow her, in case she held a key to my past, but I lost her trail. I decided to head south anyway, and then I crossed paths with you."

His eyes narrowed, and the easy manner vanished. "And now I shall have to look for the key to my past in your pockets. Figuratively speaking, of course. Are you certain we're not acquainted?"

"No," Annabel blurted out. She pushed past him and fled, her boots stamping a frantic beat against the boardwalk. Her mind was reeling. Miranda, in Wyoming, as a saloon singer, married to an Indian? Could it be true? Blindly, Annabel rushed ahead, almost toppling over when the boardwalk ended and she stumbled on the steep step down to the rutted street.

Clay caught up with her. "What was that all about?"

"I..." Annabel shifted her shoulders and fell silent. Anxiety clouded her thinking. Unable to make a rational assessment of how to best navigate between honesty and caution, she clammed up, putting loyalty to her sisters first.

"Do you know that man?" Clay studied her with a suspicious look in his green eyes. "He claims he has lost his memory, and yet he thinks he knows you. Are you running from something?"

"No." Annabel's tone was fraught. It had been bad enough not to tell him that she grew up in a mansion and her sister Charlotte was the heiress to a great fortune. Now she was adding an outright lie. "He is known to me…but the secret is not mine to reveal…it concerns my eldest sister… I will tell you once I'm able to secure her permission to speak about it."

Chapter Eighteen

Clay perched on a rickety chair in the corner of Miss Jolie's Fashion Emporium and watched a Frenchwoman with red hair rifle through the rack of dresses, occasionally pulling out one and draping it in front of Annabel.

They'd been to the bank to exchange their gold for cash, and the teller had charged them twenty dollars in commission, putting another dent to their funds.

The redhead held up a dress. "Thees ees very becoming for Madame."

"No," Clay said. "She will need a dress she can ride astride in."

"Ride astride in?" The woman looked aghast. "But a true lady like Madame does not ride astride."

"This one does." Clay crossed his arms over his chest. "And no corsets. No feathers. No plumes. No sequins. And something warm enough for the cool evenings when the winter sets in."

"*Poof.*" The woman, around thirty-five, short and plump, threw her arms up in the air. "I sell no such gowns." She pursed her mouth and tapped her forefinger to her lips. "Perhaps there ees something..."

She delved into a box of clothing beneath the rack,

wiggled her rear end and pulled out a bundle of green and brown.

"Thees is a split skirt for riding. Very petite. Made for a lady who…" her brows made a delicate leap "…has lost the *amour* of the gentleman who was going to pay."

Clay watched the woman unravel the parcel of leather and velvet and push it at Annabel. "Madame try eet on. *Vite. Vite.*" She flapped a hand to usher Annabel along. "*Monsieur* is getting bored."

Annabel vanished behind a curtain. Boots thudded against the plank floor. Fabric rustled. The curtain flung aside, and Annabel stepped into view. Clay held his breath. He'd seen her naked, he'd seen her in rags, but he had never seen her in clothes designed to enhance female beauty.

She wore a split riding skirt in brown cowhide and a green military-style velvet jacket, trimmed with brown and decorated with brass buttons at the front. She looked like a miniature general in charge of the troops.

"How much?" Clay asked.

"Feefty dollars."

It was more than they could afford, but Clay could see the shine in Annabel's eyes, could feel her pleasure as she twirled upon her feet, making the skirt flare. "Can you throw in a wide-brimmed hat in the same brown cowhide?" he asked. "A waterproof one?"

"*Oui. Oui.* Madame will need a hat. That bowler hat is *'orrible.*" The woman reached for a shelf, lifted boxes, pulled out a hat that was slightly battered but exactly the right color and style to complement the outfit.

Clay rolled up to his feet and dropped five gold pieces on the counter. Turning to Annabel, he smiled at her open delight and spoke in a tone of affection. "Let's get out of here before we go bankrupt."

They made another stop at a boot maker, where they

were able to exchange Annabel's huge boots for a second-hand pair of boys' riding boots. Annabel seemed reluctant to make the switch, peering inside her old boots as if something lay hidden there. Eventually she succumbed to the lure of the better fit, even though at the door she still turned back, craning over her shoulder, as if sad to leave the old boots behind.

The next day at breakfast Clay surveyed the elegant dining room, just as he had done the day before, and at supper last night. Women wore fashionable gowns, the gentlemen fine broadcloth suits. The coffee cups were rose-patterned china, so fine he was afraid they'd shatter in his calloused hand.

In his worn clothing, he felt like a crow among parrots. But Annabel fitted right in. What did he know about her? *A true lady*, the Frenchwoman in the dress shop had called her. And that dude in fancy clothing—he knew Annabel, yet she refused to admit the fact. What secrets was she keeping? What shadows might there be in her past that could reach all the way out to the Western Frontier?

He poured coffee from the polished steel pot on the table, filled Annabel's cup. "I want to go to the livery stable, to pay the man for another night and check on the horse and mule. While I'm gone, you can have a rest in the room."

"I'd rather go to the telegraph office, to see if there are any replies."

He frowned at her. "Are you sure you'll be safe walking around the town on your own?"

Startled, she looked up from her coffee cup. "The telegraph office is only a few doors down."

"Don't underestimate the dangers in a boomtown. They contain an explosive mixture of men in possession of sudden riches and others who wish to relieve them of their fortunes."

"I'll be fine." Annabel gave him a rueful smile. "After all, I have nothing to offer to a thief."

Pointedly, Clay took in her appearance in her new clothing. Leaning across the table, he lowered his voice. "You have everything to offer to a violent man who has no respect for the law, no decency toward a woman and no mercy for the weaker. Remember that, and be on your guard."

She made those dinner-plate eyes at him. "But you'll let me go?"

Clay leaned back in the padded chair. "I intend to be your husband, not your jailer. You have a good head on your shoulders. I trust you to use it."

Annabel sat straighter, appearing to grow taller. Clay felt a surge of affection. He'd noticed how much importance Annabel put on being treated like an equal, on being independent. He had little material gifts he could offer her, but he had done his best to give her a sense of pride and confidence in herself.

Annabel hurried down the street, her steps light, her heart brimming with pride. Clay had a knack of making her see the truth, and he'd done it again. She'd worried her feelings for him might be a naive girl's infatuation with the first handsome man who came along, but she'd been wrong. She loved him with a true devotion that would last, for he had given her the encouragement and support she needed to forge her own identity as a capable young woman.

She'd summed it up herself when he pressed her about her demand for a partnership. *I want to achieve something, but I can't do it alone, and I don't think I'd even enjoy that.*

She didn't have the temperament for solitude. With Clay, she could have independence as well as togetherness, be an equal partner yet enjoy the safety of his protection.

At the telegraph office, the surly operator came out from behind the partition when he heard her enter. "I wonder if there are any replies to our telegrams," Annabel said. "Clay Collier and…" She glanced around, to make sure Cousin Gareth was not lurking about. She lowered her voice. "…and Annabel Fairfax."

"I hardly recognized you in those clothes." The man lost his surliness and rifled through the bundle of telegrams waiting to be collected. He pulled out two. "Here you are."

Propping one hip on the counter, he appeared eager to engage her in conversation, but the bell above the door jingled and another customer walked in. The operator hopped to his feet, and Annabel took the opportunity to retreat.

Outside, she halted in the shade of the building. The message from the man in Valverde was short and to the point.

Owing $18.
Settle Hagstrom's Mercantile.

The other telegram filled an entire page. It appeared Charlotte had no need to economize with words. Annabel unfolded the sheet with such haste the paper tore.

Married now. Have my inheritance. Very happy. Miranda married, too. Rich husband. Very happy. Can send private railroad car. Cousin Gareth suffering amnesia. Aware possibly traveling to Arizona Territory. Be careful. Have arranged credit line with Percha Bank in Hillsboro. See manager Jim Drum-

mond. Send message if need more money or want
railroad car to collect Las Cruces. Love, Charlotte.

Her sisters were safe! And now that Charlotte was married and had claimed her inheritance, there was no need
to worry about leading Cousin Gareth to her. And lack of
money had ceased to be a problem. With jaunty steps, Annabel set off toward the bank, the telegram clutched in her
hand. Tonight she would talk to Clay, explain everything.

Outside the bank, three men loitered beside their horses.
Perhaps the bank was not open yet. Annabel climbed up
the front steps and tried the door. It yielded. She stepped
through and found two customers already waiting inside.

The building she'd already visited with Clay the day
before was small, just one room, but the interior reflected
the wealth pouring out of the mines. A full-height carved
oak panel separated the customers from the employees.

When the two businessmen dressed in neat suits had
been served and Annabel's turn came, she walked up to
the window in the partition and introduced herself to the
teller, a young man with fair hair and rosy skin.

His expression brightened. "Miss Fairfax? Of course.
The manager, Mr. Drummond, isn't in today, but I am
happy to be of service."

"How much is the credit line for?"

"Two thousand dollars. But I would advise you not to
draw it all out at once. If you wish to take more than six
hundred, you will need to wait for the manager to return,
for I don't have the combination for the safe."

Two thousand dollars! Annabel's head spun. Five hun-
dred would be ample until she and Clay reached Gold
Crossing. She arranged to draw the amount in gold eagles.
Only when the teller had counted out fifty gold pieces on

the counter did she realize how heavy the money would be to carry.

The teller reached beneath the counter and produced a drawstring pouch in sturdy cowhide. "A complimentary service for our premium customers," he explained with a smile as he scooped the coins into the pouch. He tightened the cord on top and slid the pouch across the counter to Annabel.

She thanked him and turned to leave. She'd barely taken a step when the door flung open and two men with bandannas tied over the lower half of their faces burst into the room. Each brandished a gun.

"Sorry, ma'am." One of the bandits, a tall man with a black hat, seized her by the arm and shoved her into a corner. "Just keep out of the way and you won't get hurt."

The other bandit, a short man with spurs that rattled when he walked, was kicking down the paneled partition. When he'd crashed through, he grabbed the teller by the front of his shirt and pointed his gun at the young man's head. "Open the safe," he ordered, speaking with a thick Mexican accent.

"I can't." The teller's voice came in a frightened croak. "I don't have the combination."

"Not waste my time." The bandit released his grip on the teller's shirt and pulled a knife from his belt. The blade sliced across the teller's cheek. Blood seeped from the wound. "Ees your eye next." The bandit gestured with the tip of his knife. "What go first? Right eye? Left?"

The teller was shaking but made a valiant effort to remain calm. "I told you, I don't know the combination for the safe. Only the manager knows, and he isn't here. I only have enough for the daily business needs."

The bandit rammed his gun against the teller's temple, stuck the knife back in his belt and reached with his free hand to the cash tray beneath the counter. Coins rattled as he rummaged around. "Ees only a hundred dollar here."

"There have been withdrawals."

"You lie." The bandit stuffed the coins in his pocket and turned toward the teller. "Only three customer come in since the bank open ten minute ago." The blade glinted in the sunlight through the window as he pulled the knife out again. "Right eye?" he asked. "Left eye?"

Annabel huddled in the corner. The taller bandit had turned his back on her to aim his gun at the teller. She eased toward the door. One step. Two steps. If she could slip through, she could summon help.

"Ma'am." The taller bandit's tone was polite. "I told you, you won't get hurt if you keep out of the way. Do you want me to hurt you?"

Annabel shrank back against the wall. The man had to have the hearing of a cat, for only the rustle of her cowhide skirt must have given her away.

The shorter bandit behind the counter lifted his knife again. Annabel cringed. *I have it*, she wanted to yell, but nausea clogged her throat. Her heart was pounding, her hands damp, panic clouding her thoughts.

The clerk arched backward, trying to escape the tip of the knife. The bandit was toying with him, pricking at his eyebrow, his forehead, his cheek. Tiny streams of blood trickled down the teller's rosy skin.

"Right eye? Left eye?" The knife shuttled in front of the teller's face.

Finally, Annabel found her voice. "I have it," she shouted. "I withdrew five hundred dollars!" She hoisted up the leather pouch with the bank's name printed on it.

The bandit with the knife halted his cat-and-mouse game. He jerked his chin toward his partner. "Jeb, check the lady, see if she tell the truth."

The taller bandit whirled toward her. "Let's have it, ma'am."

Annabel had tied the string of the pouch around her wrist. Now she lifted her arm and swung the heavy coins with all her might, aiming at the bandit's head. The blow struck, sending the man staggering backward. Annabel lurched toward the door, but the bandit recovered his balance and jumped after her. A big fist shot out, delivering a blow against her skull that knocked her off her feet.

Annabel crumpled to the floor. Black waves of unconsciousness rolled over her. Something tugged at her wrist, and then she could hear a muffled cry of pain from behind the counter, followed by the rattle of spurs and a pair of rough voices talking above her as she lay slumped.

"Jeb, the lady hit you. You want I kill her, too?"

"No. We'll take her with us. If she can withdraw five hundred dollars in one day, she must be worth a lot more. We'll ransom her."

A nasty gust of laughter. "Now, why I not think of that?"

Chapter Nineteen

The livery stable smelled of hay and manure. Clay stood in the shadowed interior and stroked the neck of the buckskin. He'd already paid the hostler, but he was lingering to give attention to the horse. Missing human company, the buckskin had greeted him with an eager whinny and a reproachful look in his eyes.

A commotion burst out in the street. Horses thundered by. The sharp retort of gunshots punctuated the steady pounding of the stamp mill. Clay gave the buckskin one final pat and headed out to investigate. In boomtowns, trouble was a daily occurrence.

A crowd had gathered in the street, staring at something on the ground. Clay shouldered his way through the throng. A man lay in the dust, clutching his belly with both hands. Blood spurted through his fingers. On his face, a web of small, superficial cuts marred the smooth-shaven skin.

"That's Kjell Sandelin, the bank teller," someone said.

A storekeeper in a long white apron was kneeling by the injured man. "Bart's gone for the doc, Kjell." His tone was calm. "You just hold on a mite."

"They came…to rob the bank…two men…" The teller,

a fair-haired man not much over twenty, spoke in labored bursts.

"Did they get the money, Kjell?" a coarse voice shouted out.

"No…only five hundred dollars…the girl had it…"

"The girl?" The man in the white apron bent lower. "What girl, Kjell?"

The teller closed his eyes. His head flopped to one side. His chest ceased rising and falling, and his hands fell away from the wound in his gut, where the surge of blood had already slowed to a trickle.

The storekeeper straightened on his feet and addressed the crowd. "Did anyone see what happened?"

Like branches rustling in the wind, the crowd sent out a flurry of replies. The girl was with the robbers. She'd gone in ahead of the others and waited inside the bank. No, no, the girl was not part of the gang. She'd been taken hostage, hauled out with her hands tied behind her back. No, no, that was wrong. The girl was one of them.

The cold, frozen feeling inside Clay told him he already knew the answer, but he had to ask anyway. "What did the girl look like?"

"Young and pretty. Dark hair in an upsweep. Wore one of them split riding skirts and a green coat with brass buttons."

Clay surveyed the crowd. Madame Jolie was staring at him with a shocked expression on her face. The fancy dude who'd spoken to Annabel was using his walking stick to clear his way through the circle of onlookers.

Careful not to draw attention, Clay eased back from the crowd and hurried to the livery stable. The good citizens of Hillsboro might debate the question of the girl for hours. Eventually, they would figure out the truth and form a posse to go after the bandits, but by then it might be too late.

Chapter Twenty

Clay tracked the bandits southwest, the hooves of the buckskin thudding on the desert trail as they cantered along. An echo seemed to follow. Not slowing down, he craned to look behind him. A long-legged black thoroughbred was catching up.

Clay reined to a halt, both to allow the buckskin a rest and to find out what trouble might be chasing him. It was the fancy dude in a peacock blue coat. "Why are you following me?" Clay shouted as the man drew near.

"Thought you might like help to rescue the damsel in distress."

"There'll be bullets flying."

"That's fine." The man lifted the hem of his coat to reveal the holster hidden beneath. "I have a new Smith & Wesson revolver I'm keen to try out."

For an instant, Clay let curiosity distract him. "Why would you risk your life for a stranger?"

"Because that is the gentlemanly thing to do." A frown flickered across the man's features. "And there is something else… I feel I know her…like it is my duty to keep her safe…" His lips curled into a rueful smirk. "Or maybe I'm acting out of self-interest because I think she possesses information that might be valuable to me."

Clay nodded and kicked the buckskin into motion. Once again, he wondered what connection there could be between Annabel and such a fine gentleman—a connection so strong that he was willing to face death for her but so unwelcome she sought to run away from it.

Brushing the question aside, Clay concentrated on following the trail. Now was not the time. He must ignore every distraction, shut away every fear, think only of the task ahead. If he let his thoughts dwell on the mystery about Annabel's past, or if he allowed images of her in the clutches of the robbers to occupy his mind, he'd be less effective in rescuing her.

They located the bandits late in the afternoon. The last mile was along a dry riverbed, heavy going for the horses but an easy trail to follow—unless it rained, and already a few drops were splashing down from the heavy clouds.

Ahead, a line of cliffs rose like a solid wall from the scrub-covered desert floor. Clay halted as soon as he saw a thin plume of smoke drifting up toward the sky. Confident of their escape, the robbers were not bothering to hide the signs of their campfire.

Clay dismounted, waited for his companion to get down. "What's your name?"

The man flashed him a wry smile. "Wish I knew. I go by Wolfson."

Clay pulled his rifle from the saddle scabbard, checked the action and did the same with the heavy Walker Colt at his hip. "You handy with that pistol, Wolfson?" he asked, with a quick glance up from his task.

"Haven't had much chance to find out. I am a skilled marksman, but I don't know if my nerve will hold under fire."

Clay took the measure of the man. His clothing immaculate, his expression bland, Wolfson appeared as calm as on a Sunday stroll. "It'll hold," Clay said. "Can you picket the horses? Keep away from the streambed, in case the skies open and there's a flash flood. I'll go and take a look."

The rifle in his left hand, Clay set off on foot, crouched low, skirting around an outcropping of rusty red rocks. When the bank of the dry wash no longer kept him hidden, he dropped to his belly and crawled along, taking cover behind the sagebrush.

From twenty yards away he could see why the bandits were so confident. They were holed up in a small box canyon, perhaps thirty yards wide. A stone column and a heap of rubble protected the opening, preventing easy access. As long as the men's ammunition held, the place was as impenetrable as a fortress.

Clay surveyed the vicinity. If he could find a path to the top of the cliffs, an attack from above might be feasible. He discarded the idea. The distance meant he'd have to use the rifle, and the first gunshot would alert the men. They might kill the girl, and even if they chose not to harm her, ricochets posed too great a risk in the confines of the narrow canyon.

His only chance was to wait until darkness fell and then pick the men off one by one, a silent death that struck too quickly to allow a shouted warning. For an hour, he watched, studying the slightest movement in the camp.

He could see three men. Their horses were picketed near the entrance, where water trickled from the cliffs into a rock basin. One man remained with the horses, watching the access path, rifle poised for shooting. It was the same man all the time, a young Mexican with flared trousers decorated with metal studs along the side seams.

The other two men moved around the camp, cooking supper. At first, Clay could not see Annabel, but then the bundle of blankets at the base of a stunted cottonwood rippled with motion. She had to be huddled beneath, drugged or asleep or too terrified to do anything but keep out of the way.

Clay eased back. He found Wolfson by the horses, rubbing down the shiny coat of the black thoroughbred with what looked like a silk neckerchief.

"I'll have to go in alone," Clay said.

Wolfson protested, but Clay cut him short. He explained the situation. "I don't know if you can move without a sound, and there's no time to teach you. When it gets dark, I want you to take up position ten yards from the mouth of the canyon. The moment you hear a gunshot, storm in. Don't shoot unless you are sure not to miss. In such a tight space, ricochets can kill."

He left Wolfson to tend to the horses and crawled back to his vantage point. He could do nothing until darkness fell. Hiding behind a clump of prickly pear, Clay settled down to wait, facing the longest hours of his life.

"Girl." Annabel felt the toe of a boot poking at her through the cocoon of blankets. "It's supper, girl, if you are hungry."

Slowly, she pushed the blankets aside, hope penetrating the icy layers of fear. If they planned to kill her, they would not bother feeding her. She'd regained consciousness on a horse, slumped in front of the tall one called Jeb, her hands tied in front of her. One of Jeb's arms had circled her waist to keep her from falling, but his touch had not been intrusive or lewd.

As they rode through the desert, stopping only to let the horses drink or to answer the call of nature, Annabel kept silent, pretending to remain dazed from the blow on her head. Whenever she could, she left some mark on the ground—a disturbed rock, a broken twig, anything to mark a trail for Clay to follow.

In town, people had seen the bandits haul her off. Clay would ask questions, would know it was her. He would raise a posse and rescue her, before the rain came and washed away the trail. A lot of *ifs*, but Annabel refused to lose faith.

Once they struck camp, Jeb had tossed her a blanket and told her to keep out of the way, just as he had done while they were robbing the bank. All afternoon, Annabel had huddled in silence, listening and watching.

Jeb was the leader. Calm, intelligent, he seemed to possess a shred of decency. The short, square man who'd cut the teller's face was called Credo. He was cruel, swaggering, a bully who needed to prove his manliness at every turn.

The third man was young, with a short beard and moustache. He hardly spoke at all. It took Annabel a while to realize he knew no English, only Spanish. His name was Nunez, and he stayed by the horses, just as he had done during the robbery. The few times he'd been by the campfire, he'd given her bold glances that made her skin crawl.

It was Jeb who'd come to talk to her now. He cut the cord around her wrists, walked away and came back carrying two tin plates heaped with beans. He handed one to her, pulled a spoon from his pocket and offered it to her. Then he squatted beside her and ate, using the blade of the knife he pulled from his belt.

Ravenous despite the terror, Annabel tucked into her portion. The meal was surprisingly good, spiced with chili peppers and herbs.

Jeb gave her reassuring look. "Girl, we don't mean to harm you. You must have a rich daddy or a rich husband. If you let us know the address, we'll send them a note.

They'll pay the ransom, and we'll let you go. You have my word on it."

Annabel's brain kicked into motion.

"Ransom?" she said in a startled tone. "The five hundred dollars was from my sister. All her savings, to buy us a share in the bakery. She won't pay you a ransom. She'll kill me with her own bare hands when she learns I've lost the money."

Jeb stared at her. "You're not rich?"

"Rich?" Annabel gave a snort and put the tin plate down. She pushed up the sleeves of her green velvet jacket and stuck out her hands, turning them this way and that. "Look at these hands. Full of scrapes and calluses. Are they a rich woman's hands?"

Jeb looked at her hands but did not reply. Annabel stuck out her feet. "Look at these boots. Boys' riding boots bought secondhand. Are they a rich woman's boots? Is my battered hat a rich woman's hat?"

Frowning now, Jeb got up and walked over to Credo. The short, squat man was making coffee by the bonfire, the rowels on his spurs rattling every time he moved. The two men held a muttered conference. Jeb kept his voice too low to carry, but Annabel could hear some of Credo's words. "Sell her…south of the border…pay well for virgins…"

Her appetite vanished, yet it was important to keep up her strength, so Annabel kept spooning the spicy beans into her mouth and chewing. Beneath the brim of her hat, she watched Jeb amble over. With the sinking sun, deep shadows filled the east-facing canyon, but she could see the troubled frown on his face.

"Girl," he said as he sank to his haunches and picked up his plate of beans. "Have you ever had a man?"

"Man?" She pretended to be dimwitted. "I had a father before he died."

Credo swaggered up to them, raked a glance over her. "You a virgin?"

Annabel put her nose in the air and spoke in a haughty tone. "I am eighteen years old and unmarried. What else could I be?"

She could see a flash of disappointment on Credo's swarthy face. He gave a reluctant nod and moved away again. Annabel released her trapped breath. It had worked. Being a virgin added to her value as merchandise, and for the time being Credo was prepared to let her stay that way.

Darkness descended soon after they'd finished their meal. The air turned cool. A quick burst of rain fell, for only a minute or two, but enough to soak Annabel's velvet jacket and make her shiver with the chill. The terror inside her flexed its claws. The heavy drops would have wiped out the trail, making it impossible for Clay to find her. No longer could she expect him to come and rescue her. Perhaps it had been a mistake to fool the bandits about the prospect of a ransom.

Jeb got up again, went to the bonfire and argued with Credo. Annabel sensed trouble brewing between the pair. She calculated the odds in her mind. If Jeb killed Credo, she'd go free. If Credo killed Jeb, she might be left unharmed until she'd been sold into slavery in Mexico—it depended on how much influence Nunez had on Credo. If the silent young man with silver studs on his trousers got his way, she'd be raped before Jeb had finished twitching in the throes of death.

The darkness was solid now, not even a single star in sight. The clouds held the threat of rain, like a thrifty man unwilling to part with his wealth. A few distant flashes of lightning and a rumble of thunder broke the night quiet, but the storm was far away.

Clay eased to his feet. Slowly, letting the horses get used to his smell so they wouldn't raise an alarm, transferring his weight carefully from foot to foot to avoid making a sound, he edged toward the canyon entrance.

The young Mexican guarding the horses was a heavy smoker. Every now and then, the flare of a match cut the darkness. At other times, Clay could use the orange tip of the burning cigarette to guide him.

He reached the stone pillar, melted like a ghost against the rock and waited. The young Mexican threw the spent cigarette down to the dirt and ground it out with the toe of his boot. Clay waited, his eyes riveted on the darkness. Usually, it took the man a couple of minutes to light up again.

A match flared. Clay watched as the man cupped the flame with his hand and dipped his head to hold the cigarette to the flame. His cheeks hollowed as he puffed. The light fell on his short beard and neatly trimmed moustache.

While the man had his attention on his smoke, Clay darted closer. He'd left his rifle behind and carried the knife in his right hand. Halting like a shadow behind the Mexican, Clay waited until the man straightened and took a deep drag from the burning cigarette, then removed it from his mouth to exhale.

Like an uncoiling snake, Clay pounced. He pressed his left hand against the man's mouth and used his right hand to slice across the man's throat. The Mexican emitted a faint gurgle, but Clay covered the sound by scraping his boots against the ground.

Warm blood poured over Clay's arm. The cloying, metallic scent made nausea rise in his throat, but he conquered the feeling. In utter stillness, he waited until the man went limp, and then he quietly lowered the body to the ground.

The horses were shifting restlessly, alerted by the smells of death and danger.

"Nunez?" Jeb called out.

Clay lowered his voice and called back. *"De nada. Solo un culebra." Nothing. Only a snake.*

The Mexican had a habit of talking with a cigarette in his mouth, which made his voice slurred, not too difficult to imitate.

Silent on his feet, Clay retreated ten yards, then faced the entrance, raised his voice and called out, "Hello, there in the camp. May I come to the fire?" He dropped his voice to the sullen growl. "Boss, *puede pasar*?"

"Tell Nunez to check him for weapons," Jeb ordered Credo.

Credo repeated the order in Spanish.

"I have a Walker Colt snapped into a holster," Clay shouted back. "No rifle."

"Come in with your hands held high," Jeb replied.

Clay walked into the camp, hands raised in the air. It was down to Annabel now. If she didn't hold her nerve, they would both die. He stepped up to the bonfire, lowered his hands and held them to the flames to warm them. "My horse went lame almost two miles back. Have been walking ever since."

"We hear no gunshot." Credo was covering him with a pistol and watching him through narrowed eyes.

"Didn't shoot him," Clay replied. "Bandaged the lame foot. Reckon I'll walk back in the morning and see if it's any better." He kept his hands to the fire but took care not to stare at the flames, for the bright light would blind him for a minute or two in the darkness. He spoke to Jeb over his shoulder. "You wouldn't have a spare horse to sell?"

"Sorry, stranger. No spare horses."

"Shame," Clay said. "But if you have coffee, it was worth the walk anyway."

Jeb hesitated, jerked his chin at Credo. The shorter man knocked a tin cup empty against a stone and poured from the pot. Instead of handing the cup to Clay, he set it on a stone by the fire and stepped back. Both men had their guns out, at least one of them covering Clay at any time.

Clay sat on the ground, took a sip of coffee, nodded his approval. He racked his brain for how to get them talking about the girl. The horses were getting restless about the presence of death. He couldn't waste time, in case one of the men decided to go and check on Nunez.

In the end he decided he had to take a chance and open the conversation himself. "I had to walk slowly in the dark, not to trip, and I heard your voices. You know how sound carries in the desert. You were talking about a girl for sale. If you tell me where she is, I might ride over and take a look, provided my horse is up to it."

"You want a girl?" Credo asked.

"Not for me. But I know people who pay well."

Credo swaggered, sending the rowels on his spurs jangling. Ignoring Jeb's warning frown, he went on, his Mexican accent thickening. "Thees one is especial. A virgin."

"How much?" Clay asked.

"Credo, shut up," Jeb warned.

Credo spun around. "We sell now. It ees too slow riding with the girl. And Nunez…he ruin the goods if we not stop him." He turned back to Clay. "One thousand dollars."

Clay whistled. "That's a steep price for a girl."

He glanced over to where Annabel huddled beneath a blanket, beyond the glow of the fire. After the men had fed her, they had tied her hands again and had left her alone.

"All right if I take a look?" Clay asked.

"*Si*," Credo said. "You look. One thousand dollar."

Clay finished his coffee, got up and stretched his feet, appearing to be in no hurry. He walked over to Annabel. She was watching him with wide, frightened eyes. Her face was pale, her hair disheveled, her hat dangling down her back by its string, but he could see no cuts or bruises.

As he lifted away the blanket, he paused for a fraction of a second to curl his hand over her shoulder, his touch delivering comfort and reassurance. Then he grabbed her by the rawhide cord that tied her wrists together, hauled her to her feet and pulled her to the light of the bonfire.

"She ain't a blonde," he complained. "No dark-haired woman is worth a thousand dollars. She's no different from the Mex women."

"She's a virgin," Jeb said, no longer reluctant to do business.

"So what?" Clay threw back. "How do I know it's true? By the time I've checked for myself she won't be one no longer. Five hundred is the most I'll pay for a dark-haired girl, even one that looks as unspoiled as this one."

He could see a notch of worry appear between Annabel's brows and understood she was trying to figure out if he had the money or if he was bluffing.

"Eight hundred," Jeb countered.

Clay pretended to consider the offer, circling Annabel, lifting up her hair, rubbing a strand with his fingers to feel the texture. He lowered his arm down by his side and kicked a pebble with his feet, making a noise to cover the sound as he unsnapped the flap on his holster to free up his gun.

He came to a halt between Annabel and the fire, his back to the flames, his body casting her in shadows. He turned his head to address his words to Jeb. "Do you mind if I untie her wrists? The way her arms are now, I can't see what she's got beneath that jacket. Looks a bit on the scrawny side to me."

Jeb nodded. "Go ahead."

Slowly, keeping his motion casual, Clay reached down to his boot and pulled out his knife. After he'd killed Nunez he had wiped the blade clean, and the shiny steel glinted in the orange light of the bonfire.

He jerked Annabel's bound hands upward, stepped close to her and spoke in a voice that was no louder than a rustle of the night breeze. "When I cut you free, grab my gun and spin me around, using me as a shield. Point at Credo. Don't shoot until I tell you."

Annabel's chin dipped in the tiniest of nods. With the tip of the knife, Clay snapped the cord around her wrists. He made a show of nudging her arms aside to get a better look at her breasts, a motion that served to position Annabel's left hand near the gun in the holster at his hip.

He could feel the gun slide out. With her other hand, Annabel grabbed his arm, spun him a quarter turn and darted around him to hide behind his back. "Don't move," she yelled, pointing the gun over the top of his shoulder. "Stay back."

Clay lifted his hands, still holding the knife. "Don't shoot," he called out to the men. "I'll deal with the hellcat."

Jeb and Credo crouched, guns at the ready. Clay tensed his muscles against the impact of a bullet. He inched forward. The bonfire was to his left, Jeb directly behind the fire and Credo in front of it.

"Now," Clay roared. He took a leap forward and aimed a kick at the fire, scattering the firewood. At the same time, he let his arms swing, hurling the knife at Jeb. By his right, Annabel fired the big Walker Colt, too close to his ear. The noise boomed in Clay's head. He could hear nothing but the thundering echo of it. A fraction of a second later he felt the scrape of a bullet at the top of his shoulder.

On the ground, the burning timber hissed against the earth, still damp from the burst of rain. The flames flickered, sending shadows leaping. The last image before the light faded remained imprinted on Clay's consciousness.

Jeb, falling to the ground, knife in his heart. And Credo, up on his feet, the barrel of his gun spitting flame. Then there was nothing but darkness, eased only by the glow of orange coals on the ground, like the eyes of the devil peering up from hell.

"Annabel," he roared. "Give me the gun."

He could not hear his own voice, only the ringing in his ears. A small hand fumbled at his shoulder, slid down his arm. He felt the heavy Walker Colt pressed into his palm. He adjusted his grip on the handle and moved in the darkness to push Annabel behind him.

"I can't hear you," he yelled. "How many times did you shoot?"

She tapped his shoulder once.

"Get down." He could not tell if he was shouting or speaking too quietly.

Annabel gave his shoulder a quick series of taps, like a head shaking. He felt the current of air as she hurried away. The burning coals moved on the ground. For a moment, Clay thought he was becoming disoriented, but then he realized Annabel was kicking the coals back into a heap.

The campfire flickered into flame. From the corner of his eye Clay could see Annabel crouching to add more wood into the fire. He surveyed the darkness around them, saw no movement. Annabel came to stand in front of him. Her lips were moving.

He shook his head, pointed at his ear. "Can't hear."

She nodded, held up one finger, jabbed it against her

heart. She held up two fingers, jabbed her forefinger against her head.

"Dead?" Clay said. "You shot Credo?"

Annabel shook her head and spread her hands wide, palms up, looking baffled. Then she held up three fingers, her brows lifted in question. *What happened to the third man?* Clay held up three fingers, slashed his hand across his throat. Annabel's eyes widened, but she said nothing, merely stepped into him. Clay wrapped his arms around her and hauled her to his chest and held her tight.

He could have lost her. The thought filled him with an aching emptiness that felt worse than the neglect of his childhood, worse than all those lonely years in the orphanage, worse than the combined deaths of everyone he'd ever loved.

There were things to do, but he didn't want to let go of Annabel just yet, didn't want to break the contact that reassured him she was safe. Lowering his head, he kissed her, hard and deep. Emotions buffeted him, frightening in their intensity—relief and something else, something so bold and powerful he found it impossible to deal with now, with death all around them.

Clay lifted his head and cupped Annabel's face between his hands and studied her features in the flickering light of the fire. Looking at her filled him with a strange new awe that had something timeless and solemn about it, but figuring out what it meant had to wait. With regret he eased their bodies apart.

"Sit by the fire," he told her. "I'll look around."

He could still hear nothing but ringing in his ears. The lack of sound surrounded him with an eerie sense of isolation. He picked up a stick of wood, held it to the fire until the tip blazed and he could hold it up like a torch.

He checked Jeb first, retrieved his knife and wiped the

blade clean on the dead man's shirt. Next, he inspected Credo. A neat hole punctured the man's forehead, just as Annabel had indicated. The bullet she'd fired from his Colt had grazed the man's shoulder, a minor injury but enough to spoil Credo's aim as he fired at them.

The bullet that killed Credo must have come from Wolfson's gun. Where was the man? Clay straightened on his feet, lifted the torch high to illuminate the darkness. "Wolfson!" he yelled, his voice muffled inside his head. "It's okay to come out now."

Annabel tugged at his sleeve. Clay turned around. Her lips were moving, her brows lifted in concern, and he could guess her question. The thoughts he'd suppressed earlier crowded into his mind. What was Wolfson to her? What power did the man have that made her so afraid to admit the connection between them? And was that power something that could come between them, destroy their partnership?

"Yeah," he replied. "The fancy gent rode along. He must have shot Credo and taken a hit. We need to find him, see if there's anything we can do for him." He held up the torch to shine the light on Annabel. "Will you be all right on your own while I search for him?"

Her eyes were full of fear, her face deathly pale. Instead of replying, she reached up and grabbed the torch from him. Rushing around in the darkness, she searched the ground for an injured man.

As Clay stood by and watched, something hard and unyielding settled in the pit of his belly. Time after time, Annabel had told him she didn't know Wolfson, but her panic was not for a stranger.

He hadn't had a chance to tell her that the preacher in Hillsboro had gone off for a tour of the mining camps, to raise funds for building a church. They would have to wait for his return before they could be married. Just as well, Clay thought as he heard Annabel calling out in the darkness. He couldn't make out the name, but he could tell it was something other than Wolfson.

Chapter Twenty-One

$\mathcal{O}\!\!\!\!\!\sim\!\!\!\!\!\!\sim\!\!\!\!\!\!\sim\!\!\!\!\!\!\sim$

Annabel found Cousin Gareth slumped on the ground, a dark shape hidden by the night shadows. She fell to her knees beside him, illuminating him with the flickering flame. "Gareth! Cousin Gareth!" She shook his shoulder, flinched when her hand came away soaked with blood.

She jumped to her feet. "Clay!" she yelled. "Help me!" Somewhere at the back of her mind she was aware he couldn't hear her, but the sound of her voice rippling through the night eased her sense of helplessness. She waved the torch in the air until Clay stepped into the sphere of light.

"I've found him," Annabel said.

Clay crouched to examine the fallen man. "He's been shot twice," Clay said. "One bullet made a groove along his skull. I don't know how serious it is. The other bullet is at the top of his arm. It will not kill him, provided we can stop the bleeding." He turned to look up at her. "Find some string."

Annabel hurried back to the campfire, took a moment to make a fresh torch in the fire. Then she found her leather hat and took it to Clay. With his knife, he cut away the rawhide cord and used it to fashion a tourniquet.

"Is it not too tight?" Annabel asked and gestured to explain her meaning.

"Ever heard of *life or limb*?" Clay replied. "With the tight cord he might lose the arm, but without the pressure he'll bleed to death."

"We need to get him to a doctor," Annabel said. The depth of her anguish came as a surprise. Memories flooded her mind, how Cousin Gareth had once been, a dashing young man with a deep sense of honor and family loyalty. Had he risked his life for her because he was a gentleman? Or because in the mists of his mind he had recognized her as kin? Either way, she owed him.

Clay glanced at her over his shoulder, a thoughtful look on his face. She could read the questions in his eyes. *Who is this man? What is he to you? Why are you fretting over him?* She longed to pour out explanations, but his lack of hearing made it impossible. Perhaps it was for the best, Annabel thought, for her turbulent mind would have struggled to put together words that made sense.

"Is it important to you that he lives?" Clay asked.

Annabel gave an eager nod. She held up the torch and mimed a procession, using her other hand to portray a cantering horse and point into the distance.

"Ride through the pitch-black desert by torchlight?" Clay said.

Annabel nodded, this time hesitant. She might be asking for the impossible, but Clay gave her another long look and pushed up to his feet, making room for her beside Cousin Gareth. "Watch over him," he said, and took the torch from her. "I'll get the horses."

With silent steps, he vanished into the darkness. Annabel could hear him crooning to a horse, and then the clip of hooves. It seemed an eternity before Clay returned, the sound of the hooves multiplied as he led over the buckskin and a black horse that gleamed in the torchlight.

"We need to take the bodies with us," Clay said. "There's no time to bury them, and we can't just leave them to the buzzards." He went off, moving carefully in the darkness. A wind had picked up, and the clouds were breaking. Occasionally, a shaft of moonlight came through, bathing the desert in silvery light.

Annabel watched Cousin Gareth, her lips moving in silent prayer. She wanted him to live. For what he had once been to her, for being family, for risking his life to save her, and if those were not enough reason, to finally provide an explanation for what had sent him down the path of ruin.

Cousin Gareth looked elegant even when unconscious, Annabel thought as she sat by his bedside at the doctor's house in Hillsboro. They had reached the town when the first hint of dawn painted a streak of gray in the sky. Riding double on the buckskin by the pale glow of the moon, they had brought in four men strapped to their horses, three of them dead and one clinging to life.

The doctor, a brusque man in his forties, with the smell of whiskey on his breath, had opened the door when they pounded upon it. He had removed the bullet in Cousin Gareth's arm and cleaned the cut in his head.

"Will he live?" Annabel had asked.

"That's for God to decide. I expect that if he comes to, he'll recover."

She heard the door open behind her, but no footsteps. Only Clay knew how to move as silently as a cat. "How did you get on?" she asked, not turning to look. His hearing was back to normal, and he'd gone to take in the bodies of the three robbers and make a report to the sheriff.

"They need you to sign a statement. The bank clerk had

entered your withdrawal in the ledger, which confirms you were an innocent bystander."

Clay didn't ask anything, didn't press for explanations. *Why don't you talk about it?* Annabel screamed in her mind. *Ask me how I could draw such a sum! Ask me about Cousin Gareth!* Explanations would be easier if she could answer questions instead of having to navigate her own way to the truth.

"I went to the telegraph office," she said quietly. "There was a reply from the merchant in Valverde. Mr. Hicks owes eighteen dollars. You can settle at Hagstrom's Mercantile."

"Fine," Clay said. "Thank you."

The cool formality of his words stung. She wanted to jump to her feet and whirl around and hurl herself into his arms, tell him that she could explain everything if he just gave her a moment to gather her thoughts, but the rustling of the bedclothes stopped her short.

With a moan, Cousin Gareth stirred beneath the pristine white sheets. His eyelids fluttered and lifted. Squinting into the morning light, he swept a glance around the room and let his attention settle on her. "Annabel?" he said. "What are you doing here?" He took another quick survey of his surroundings and homed in on her again, a baffled expression on his face. "What am I doing here? Where are we? How did we get here? Where is Miranda? Where is Charlotte?"

Cousin Gareth was back. Despite the wave of relief, the accumulated resentments of four years put tartness into Annabel's tone. "Isn't Charlotte dead and buried in the Fairfax family cemetery at Merlin's Leap?"

Cousin Gareth had the decency to look ashamed. "She chose to run away and deserved to be written out of existence."

"It's your fault she ran away. You were beastly to her."

A flush rose on Gareth's skin. "I'd been drinking," he muttered. "I didn't mean to... I wouldn't have... I was merely angry at her." He cast another look around the room. "Where are we? Who is dealing with the business?" He fumbled at the sheets, attempting to get up. "The *Northern Star* is due for repairs at the dock, and the *Morning Light* has no outbound cargo to Shanghai...*ouch!*"

He slumped against the mattress, a grimace of pain on his patrician features. "Why is there a hot poker in my head and my arm feels like it's been on a butcher's block?"

Clay stepped forward. "You've been in a gunfight."

"Gunfight?" Cousin Gareth stared at Clay. His mouth curled into a rueful smile. "You look like the Western type. I guess I'm not in Boston. Who are you and what are you doing with my cousin?"

He is my husband, Annabel wanted to say, but they hadn't been to see the preacher yet. All those social constraints she'd been so eager to discard crashed upon her now, making her hesitate about the right way to describe their relationship.

Before she had a chance to organize her thoughts, Clay spoke up. "The name's Collier. The lady got stranded on a train stop, and I've been escorting her to her sisters."

Cousin Gareth nodded and addressed his words to Annabel. "The last thing I remember is following Miranda to Chicago. You might be kind enough to fill me in with anything you know about my fate since then."

How typical of Cousin Gareth, Annabel thought with a touch of bitterness. Barely back from death's door and already taking charge. At least she no longer needed to worry that he might stumble upon his old boots she'd exchanged with the boot maker and notice his name inked into the lining.

Behind her, Clay shifted on his feet. "I'll leave you

to catch up with your cousin, Miss Fairfax," he said in a formal tone of politeness. "We can meet later at the hotel and…settle up."

Annabel flinched. Settle up? What did he mean? Was it just a phrase to stop Cousin Gareth from guessing too much, or was he implying their partnership had come to an end? As she watched Clay walk away, she wanted to jump to her feet, run after him, but her rational mind whispered it made more sense to postpone the confrontation until they were in the privacy of their hotel suite.

Clay stormed out of the doctor's house, every muscle taut. Emotions collided in his head, like rocks smashing against each other in the *arrastre* pit. Had he gone and done exactly what he'd sworn never to do? Had he given his heart, his love, to the first woman who came along and asked for it?

Annabel had lied to him.

She was not a helpless orphan, alone in the world, in need of his protection. She was a rich man's daughter, with a family that could take care of her. Fairfax was a gentleman, and he lived by a gentleman's code of honor. How would he deal with a poor drifter who had interfered with his cousin? Icy sweat rose on Clay's skin as he considered the possibilities. If Fairfax felt so inclined, he might persuade the townsfolk to string him up. No one would believe that a girl like Annabel had given herself freely to a man like him, and ugly jeers of rape would follow him all the way to hell as a rope tightened around his throat.

Annabel, Annabel. Clay pictured her in his mind, her amber eyes shining with pride at every new achievement, the soft mouth curving into a smile of delight and triumph. How much of their partnership had been real? Did she really want to make a life away from her affluent background, or was she a society girl on an adventure holiday, ready to head home when the lure of a primitive life wore thin?

Clay had no destination in mind as he strode along the crowded boardwalk, the morning sun bouncing back at him from the dusty street. When he found himself outside the hotel, his thoughts sharpened and he went inside.

The portly clerk behind the counter looked up when he walked over. Without a word, Clay reached for the open ledger, swung it around and located the entry.

Mr. and Mrs. Clay Collier

"Give me the pen," he said and put out his hand. Frowning, but prompted into obedience by Clay's curt tone, the clerk took out a pen and dipped it in the inkwell before passing it over.

Clay pressed the nib against the page. A blot formed to cover up the beginning of the line. He made another, smaller blot, to cover up the *s* in Mrs. He examined the result. Mr. Clay Collier, and a blot to the left of the name, as if the pen had been loaded with too much ink.

On a new line, he wrote "Miss Annabel Fairfax," and then turned the ledger around for the clerk to see. While the man inspected the entry, Clay dug in his pocket and dropped a gold eagle on the counter with a clatter that drew the clerk's attention.

"Do you think you could be persuaded to forget you've ever seen me walk up those stairs?" Clay asked.

Comprehension flashed in the clerk's eyes. "Sir, I can do better than that. I can swear that Miss..." He glanced down at the ledger. "...Miss Annabel Fairfax has been the sole occupant of that suite."

"Good." Clay took a step back from the counter. "Close

your eyes one more time while I go upstairs and collect my things."

His boots thudded with a heavy beat as he slowly climbed up the stairs, as if he wanted to postpone the first stage of removing his presence from Annabel's life. It was fortunate the clerk had been so amenable, Clay thought. Hating lies himself, he did not believe he had the right to force another man to tell untruths on his behalf.

Upstairs, Clay picked up the sailor's duffel Annabel had made for him and stuffed his belongings inside. There was not much. The sum of his worth as a man, Clay thought grimly. Two books on mining. The Bible that had belonged to Mr. Hicks. A few items of clothing. A tattered postcard and a small bird carved from hickory, keepsakes from his friends at the orphanage. He looked around, spotted a green hair ribbon and slipped it in his pocket. A keepsake of Annabel. The idea cut like a knife, making the prospect of their parting real and imminent.

Refusing to linger in the room, Clay went to the livery stable. For the rest of the day, he helped the hostler, earning free board for the buckskin and the mule. Night fell, but he waited. He waited until the small hours, when the saloons grew quiet and the town slept. Only then did he make his way along the empty street and drift like a ghost up the stairs into the suite that now belonged to that affluent stranger, Miss Annabel Fairfax.

Annabel waited in the hotel suite, a lamp burning on the nightstand. Guests moved in the corridor, entering their rooms. Voices echoed through the thin walls. Then it grew quiet, with everyone settling down to sleep.

Midnight came. The lamp guttered out, and she didn't take the trouble to get up and replenish the oil. She huddled beneath the quilt, dressed in the simple cotton nightgown she'd bought from the mercantile when they arrived two days ago. It seemed forever now. Would Clay come? Or would he simply vanish from her life?

She heard a faint scratching by the entrance and felt a cool draft as the door opened and closed. The floorboards creaked. Annabel eased up to a sitting position against the headboard and strained her eyes into the darkness.

The scent of dust and leather and horses alerted her before she felt the weight of someone sitting down on the edge of the bed. A match rasped, and in the flame she could see Clay's features. His expression appeared closed and stark.

"You lied to me," he said.

The match flickered out. Talking in the darkness, Annabel hurried to offer the explanations that had rattled inside her head for hours while she waited. "I didn't lie, not really. I just didn't talk about my background."

"Twice I asked you if you knew that man."

"I..." She took a deep breath, launched into her tale of how she and her sisters had been orphaned, how Charlotte had inherited Papa's money and Cousin Gareth had tried to force her into marriage. "See?" she finished. "I had to keep my identity secret. I couldn't risk leading Cousin Gareth to my sisters."

"How could telling me have jeopardized their safety?" Clay's tone was curt. "There was no reason not to reveal your secret, unless you suspected I would betray you to your cousin."

"I wanted to tell you. I was waiting for the right moment, but it never seemed to come." She tried to find the right words to justify her actions. "I was only fourteen when my parents died. Since then, my life has been limited to the confines of Merlin's Leap. I didn't have the chance to grow up. When I left home, I was desperate to forge my own identity. To be something other than the child of my parents, the youngest of the Fairfax sisters. I wanted to be myself, without the baggage of my background. My purpose was not to deceive but to be judged by my own merits."

She reached out in the darkness, laid a hand on Clay's arm. "I told Cousin Gareth about us. That we plan to marry."

Clay stiffened beneath her touch. "Did you tell him that we've anticipated our wedding vows?"

Annabel hesitated, flushed in the darkness. There should be no shame in what they had done, but Cousin Gareth would think otherwise. "No," she admitted with reluctance.

"That was wise," Clay replied. "If you tell him, he'll most likely kill me. He has every right to. He might even get the citizens of the town to string me up with a rope. A penniless miner does not interfere with a decent girl and get away with it."

Annabel could not deny the truth in his words. "We'll find the preacher tomorrow." She stared into the darkness, trying to discern Clay's features. His voice sounded too bland, too cool, and it made her shiver, as though the autumn chill had invaded the room. "We'll get married," she told him. "It will be all right."

"The preacher has gone off to tour the mining camps." Clay's voice was strained. "But it makes no difference. You're only eighteen, and I assume your cousin is your legal guardian. Now that his identity is known, the preacher won't wed us without his consent."

Annabel held her breath. Fear knotted in the pit of her belly, like a heavy weight. For weeks now, she'd fooled herself into believing it didn't matter if she was economical with the truth, but all the time she had known it would.

"What should we do?" she asked.

The bedding rustled as Clay adjusted his weight. She heard him sigh, and then quiet words that sounded reluctant to her ears. "I'll have to speak to your cousin and hope that he does not put a bullet in me. Then I'll decide what is best for both of us."

Rebellion sparked in her. "Don't speak to me like that. Like we are not equal and I'll have to meekly follow orders, accept what you decide."

"You lied to me, Annabel. I've never lied to you. Not even when I wanted to, about having spied on you when you bathed by the creek. I hate lies. I remember sleeping in my cot and hearing my parents scream at each other, accusing each other of lying. I will not have my life turn out like theirs."

"I didn't really lie…not much."

"You told me you used to live in an old house by the sea and your father was a seaman."

Annabel tugged at the covers, gaining time to formulate a reply. "Merlin's Leap *is* a house by the sea," she finally said. "Quite a big house, actually. And Papa *was* a seaman. Even though he commanded his own fleet of ships. The only lie I told you was that I didn't know who Cousin Gareth was."

"And that you were a boy. And your name was Andrew Fairfield—"

"Stop," she burst out. "Don't focus on my record of dishonesty. Just tell me if you forgive me or not."

She heard Clay make a small, resigned sound. "I guess I could forgive you almost anything," he said roughly. "Except betraying me with another man. That I could never forgive or forget."

The mattress dipped again, but this time Clay's arms closed around her, hauling her tight against his chest. Annabel could feel the tautness in his body and understood how much his cool indifference was a front. Behind it, he must be just as frightened as she was about the pressures of the external world that had finally caught up with them. For those pressures might turn out to have greater power than they had assumed—enough to break their partnership apart.

Clay thanked the doctor for showing him in and nodded at Gareth Fairfax, who sat propped up against pillows in the bed. On the small table beside him, a stack of telegrams jostled for space with pen and ink and sheets of paper crammed with neat handwriting.

Last night, Clay had left Annabel alone in the hotel suite and slept in the hayloft above the livery stable. The only redeeming aspects of their situation were that Annabel's cousin remained unaware of their liaison and she was not pregnant. Clay wanted to keep it that way.

In the morning, he'd woken to the prickle of straw on his skin and the tickle of dust in his throat. Likely as not, bits of hay still clung to his clothing, making him look like a saddle tramp. Which was not far from the truth.

Clay turned his hat in his hands and balanced on his feet, trying to figure out how to best open the conversation. Fairfax spared him the trouble. "I understand you wish to marry my cousin."

Early thirties, with blue eyes, well-cut fair hair and patrician features, Fairfax cut an elegant figure, even with one arm in a sling, a bandage around his head and two-day beard stubble on his chin. The difference in their backgrounds was evident at a glance.

"We've talked about getting hitched," Clay replied gruffly.

"Do you love her?"

Something within Clay seemed to lock up. He had not given those words to Annabel yet, not in such plain terms, and she should be the first to hear them. But he refused to lie. Even if Fairfax asked if he'd bedded her, he'd be honest, and take the consequences.

"Yeah. I love her." His tone was grudging.

Fairfax smiled. It was an odd smile, wistful and harsh at the same time. For a moment, a faraway look came into his eyes. Then his gaze sharpened and settled on Clay. "I guess you expect I'll withhold my consent."

"Crossed my mind."

"And yet you are here, asking."

"I promised Annabel I would."

Fairfax nodded, slow and measured. A shadow crossed his face. *He knows*, Clay thought. He couldn't fight an injured man. He'd just have to take it, whatever came, bullet or angry words. But instead of challenging him for ruining his cousin, Fairfax spoke calmly. "How do you propose to support her?"

"I'm a gold miner."

"Do you have a claim?"

"Not right now. We had one, a good one—" Clay flicked his hat in his hands to brush aside the comment. "Never mind," he said. "I don't have a claim."

"I see." Fairfax pursed his lips. "Well. Mr. Collier, I happen to believe that lack of funds should not stand between a man and the woman he loves. You have my consent."

"But—" Clay caught himself, gritted his teeth.

Fairfax smiled again, a grim smile tinged with amusement. "You thought I'd make it all easy and neat for you, didn't you? That I'd rant and rave and throw you out on your ear and you could walk away with your conscience clear and your anger directed at me. Well, I'm not going to do that. Mr. Collier—may I call you Clay?"

Clay nodded. Fairfax went on. "Well, Clay, you say you love her, and you've proved that you are a man of honor. That gives me no right to stand between you and Annabel. It is up to you to decide if the life you can offer her is what she deserves."

"She deserves better." The words burst out of Clay before he had time to think. He knew they were the truth. Perhaps he'd known from the beginning. Damn Fairfax for doing the unexpected, for not taking on the role of the enraged guardian.

Clay spoke through gritted teeth. "With me, she might starve and freeze, or come to some harm, but that's not the worst of it. She might survive the hardships, but one day I'll see her looking at me across the breakfast table with hate in her eyes. She deserves better." He lifted his chin and looked at Fairfax, pride stiffening his posture. "I deserve better, too. I can't marry her unless I'm sure we can make it stick."

On the bed, Fairfax stilled. His eyes widened. For an instant, he seemed to consider Clay's words with a strange intensity, and then a rueful smile spread on his face. "You may just have answered a question that has been bothering me for fourteen years." Efficient now, he picked up the stack of telegrams on the bedside table. "The choice is yours, Clay," he said. "But if you decide against it, take a moment to comfort her. I'm no good with a woman's tears."

Chapter Twenty-Two

Clay saddled the buckskin and rode out into the desert, letting the horse run until it grew tired. Emotions seethed within him, seeking a way out. Earlier, when he held Annabel in his arms, the lifeless bodies of the bandits strewn about them, he'd managed to suppress those feelings, but now they demanded to be released, demanded to be recognized.

Annabel had done that to him. She had taught him to accept his grief for Mr. Hicks, and now it felt as if she was doing the same, forcing him to accept the emotions he might have preferred to deny.

He loved her. Truly loved her, without hesitation, without reservation, with a depth of feeling that would last for as long as he lived. In those few terrible hours when he didn't know if Annabel was safe, if he could rescue her, it had become clear to Clay that his happiness was tied to her. Without Annabel, his world would be empty and lacking. Without Annabel, his future would be grim and bleak. Without Annabel, his nights would be lonely and cold, his days too long and without meaning.

And that was why it hurt so much to know that he had to give her up. A bitter groan at the irony of the situation caught in Clay's throat. Before, he'd hesitated to marry

Annabel because he hadn't been certain he loved her with a devotion that would last a lifetime. Now that he knew he did, a union between them had become impossible.

He had nothing to offer her. No home, no money, no secure future. Nothing but the bitter past of an orphan and a few mining skills. How could he take her away from her safe, comfortable life to the precarious existence at the mining camps? He had no right to do it. No right at all. Either she would get hurt or she would lack the stamina to endure the hardships, and her love might turn into bitter resentment, a prospect almost as unbearable as losing her to an illness or some accident.

On his return to the livery stable, Clay rubbed down the buckskin. Then he went to the bathhouse, where he had a wash and shave and a haircut. In the mercantile, he spent five dollars on a silk shirt as soft as a woman's touch. He wanted Annabel's last memory of him to be the best he could be, someone closer to the world she knew.

He waited until darkness fell. Like the night before, he did not knock on the door of the hotel suite but forced the lock open with the blade of his knife. Again, he found Annabel in bed, sitting up against the pillows, but this time a lamp burned on the bedside table.

She flung the covers aside, swung her feet down and hurried out to him. Again, she was wearing the white cotton nightgown that came high at the neck and down to her toes. Did she realize how much more tempting it was to let a man imagine what the garment covered, instead of seeing it all on display?

Clay steeled himself against the temptation.

He had a job to do. The hardest job he'd ever faced.

"Did you see Cousin Gareth?" Annabel asked. "What did he say?"

Clay did not reply. Curling his hands around Annabel's

arms, he halted her before she had a chance to throw herself against him, the way she liked to do. He held her a step away from him and looked down into her expectant face.

"He gave his consent, but despite his permission I can't marry you," he told her. "There are too many dangers in a mining camp. Just yesterday you were abducted, taken hostage, almost raped and sold into slavery."

"But you stopped them."

"What about next time? When we locate a claim, I'll be working in the mine pit. Underground. Out of sight. Out of hearing. You'll be left alone."

"I'll have a gun."

"Annabel." Clay heaved out a sigh. "You might be in possession of a gun, but you'll be inexperienced in the use of it, and it is hard to kill a man. If a stranger rides up to the claim, you won't pull the trigger unless you can be absolutely certain he intends to do you harm, but by the time you know for sure it might be too late."

She took a step toward him. "I could work in the pit with you."

Clay reached out and bundled her into his embrace. He tucked her head in the crook of his neck and breathed in the scent of lavender soap in her hair, felt her slender shape that fitted so well against him.

"There are other dangers," he said, talking to the top of her head. "Cold. Starvation. Landslides. Rockfalls. You saw what happened to Mr. Hicks. Mining is hard work, a hard life. Too hard for you."

He could feel the tension in her. How could he explain why he could not marry her? Clay knew only one way. He had to open up the vault of old pain inside him and let her peek inside.

"Let's sit down." He steered her to the bed, scooped her up in his arms and settled her against the pillows, then removed his muddy boots and climbed in beside her. Leaning against the headboard, he wrapped one arm around her and hauled her against his side. It seemed easier if they were not looking at each other.

"You remember how I told you that when I left the orphanage I took two other boys with me."

"Yes."

"They were called Lee and Billy. They were both twelve. Lee was small, fair-haired. He laughed a lot and liked to tell jokes. Billy had red hair and very pale skin. He was a sickly boy. He struggled to do heavy physical work.

"We traveled north from San Francisco, into the hills, thinking we'd get rich with gold. We got jobs. I was digging. Billy was helping a cook, and Lee was crawling into narrow spaces to set gunpowder charges, just the way you did."

"You said the danger of blasting can be controlled by being careful."

"That's right. But something else happened. One evening two men got hold of Lee. They—" Clay inhaled a sharp breath. "They did to Lee what I thought men could only do to women. They nearly tore him apart. Afterward...afterward his body healed, but I never heard him laugh again. A few weeks later, he was lighting the fuses in a narrow passage. We were waiting down the slope, expecting to see him running out, yelling *fire in the hole* as he hurtled toward us and threw himself down on the ground beside us. But he never came."

"Did he die of his injuries?"

"There was nothing left of him to bury. He trimmed the fuses too short, the mine boss said. Or he might have stumbled on his way out through the mine tunnel and bashed his head. But we knew. He chose to stay inside. He chose to die."

Clay stroked Annabel's hair, leaned in to press a kiss to her forehead. "I can't bear the thought of something similar happening to you. That some act of violence might rob you of all that joy, all that enthusiasm I hold dear."

"And the other boy?"

"Billy had always been sickly. He started coughing all the time. When he held a handkerchief to his mouth, spots of blood appeared on it. He grew weaker and weaker, until he could no longer stay on his feet. He just withered away."

"I'm not sickly."

"I can't take the risk. It was different when I thought you had nowhere else to go. The dangers for a young woman alone are even greater, and you might have been better off with my protection. But now that I know the truth about your background, my conscience will not allow me to take you away from the comfort and protection your cousin can provide."

He bent over Annabel and gave her another gentle kiss. He'd expected her to argue, but instead she wriggled around to kneel in front of him on the bed and looked at him with a new maturity in her expression.

"I understand," she said. "You believe it would be too dangerous for me to join you on a mining claim. And you fear I might not endure the life as a miner's wife. But you are wrong, and one day you'll see it. I shall go to Gold Crossing and join my sisters. I shall wait there until you realize it is better to take risks and be together than to be safe and be alone. One day, you'll come for me, and I'll be waiting."

Clay sighed. "Annabel, don't be foolish."

"No." She shook her head. "I am not dreaming foolish dreams. I am simply stating what I believe, and what I plan to do. I could be wrong, and you'll never come. But I will wait. I will wait forever."

"Forever is a long time, Annabel."

"I know." She leaned forward, lifted her hands to the buttons on his shirt. "And I need something to take with me, another memory to keep me going. If I can't have a wedding night, I shall have tonight."

Clay leaned back against the headboard while Annabel's nimble fingers slipped the buttons free on his new shirt. The rich silk fabric rustled as she pushed the edges apart. He'd bought one in creamy white, like a gentleman would wear, and it made a sharp contrast against his bronzed skin.

Would one more night make it easier or more difficult to leave her? Would it ease the pain of the parting or deepen it? Then Annabel raked her fingers into the sprinkling of dark hairs on his chest, and Clay found the choice was taken away from him.

"Annabel." His voice was hoarse as he said her name. "Annabel."

It might not be a wedding night, but there was something solemn in the way they sat facing each other on the bed, the soft lamplight falling upon Annabel's skin as Clay slowly lifted the nightgown over her head, baring her before his eyes.

For a moment, he merely looked. The room was quiet, except for their rapid breathing and the rustle of bedding. Down the hall, a door banged and someone strode away. Then the footsteps faded and silence ruled again.

Clay lifted his hands and began sliding his palms along Annabel's soft, warm skin. Was it wrong to want someone so much? It felt as if his heart might burst with love and loss and longing.

Annabel fumbled with the buckle of his gun belt. Clay took over the task of unclasping it, then quickly stripped naked. They did not speak at all. Clay let his lips roam over Annabel, seeking to kiss her in places he'd never kissed her before, marking every inch of her as his, tasting the flavor of her skin. He breathed in her smell, lavender soap and woman, and tried to store it in his mind.

When they could no longer wait, he curled his hands around Annabel's waist and guided her to straddle him. Slowly, she sank over him, taking him inside her.

Rising and falling, rising and falling, she moved over him, her eyes holding his. Clay watched her face, memorizing every expression. It seemed to go on forever, that slow rising and falling, as steady and inevitable as the ocean waves.

When the tension inside them crested and broke, neither of them closed their eyes, but their gazes remained locked. Once the ripples of completion had faded away, Annabel slumped against Clay. He wrapped his arms around her and cradled her close. A few moments longer, he wanted to hold on to her. A few moments longer, he wanted to feel that intimate contact, the closest bond a man and woman could share.

He'd never given her a proper declaration of love, and it had bothered him they would part with those words unsaid. He was a private man who found it hard to frame his thoughts, and even harder to open up and let his feelings show, but now he wanted that final step of closeness between them.

He turned his head and spoke into her ear. "I love you."

For an instant, Annabel did not move. Then she lifted her head and gave him a wistful smile. "I know you do," she told him. And it meant more to him than hearing her repeat the words back to him, for knowing something in your heart was more important than having it put into words.

Afterward, they lay in the big brass bed, propped up against the pillows, Clay cradling Annabel in his arms.

Her eyelids fluttered down and she drifted off to sleep. In the dull glow of the lamp by the bedside, Clay watched her, storing her features in his memory.

When the first hint of gray eased the darkness outside, Clay gently untangled himself from the sleeping girl. Standing by the bedside, he paused to look at her one more time. Her face looked soft in sleep, and very young. Her dark hair fanned across the pillow, and the long lashes formed a dark sweep against the pale skin.

I'm doing the right thing, Clay told himself. *She's too delicate.*

He dug in his pocket and pulled out a handful of coins. Two hundred and eighteen dollars remained of the money they had received for their gold. He left a hundred and ten on the table, added the note he'd prepared in advance.

Partnership earnings.
With Mr. Hicks gone, half is yours.
Clay Collier.

He had signed the note with his full name, wanting Annabel to have that little piece of him. The message was too impersonal, he knew, but he could not bring himself to put his emotions down on a piece of paper.

Slowly, he eased across the room to the door. Outside, a rooster crowed, announcing the start of a new day. The start of his life without Annabel. Clay turned the knob, opened the door. He slipped through and closed the door after him, and walked away, as silent and insubstantial as a ghost.

Chapter Twenty-Three

"**P**ick a card. But don't show it to me." Cousin Gareth held the worn deck out to Annabel. She reached across the small table, pulled out a card and glimpsed at it—five of spades—then slid the card back into the deck.

They were in a first-class compartment on a Southern Pacific train, traveling toward Phoenix Junction. After Clay had left, it had taken Cousin Gareth three more days to be up on his feet, and he still lacked the full use of his left arm.

They had bought a horse for her, a small gray mare, and ridden south to Las Cruces, where they had put their mounts in the freight car and boarded the train. Throughout the journey, Cousin Gareth had been polite but laconic, making no special effort to bridge the gulf between them.

He pulled a card from the pack. "Is this it?"

The king of clubs. Annabel frowned. "No."

As a child, when Cousin Gareth had been an adored visitor at Merlin's Leap, she'd seen him perform the trick many times. Were his skills going rusty? Had the blow to his head affected his mind?

"Hmm…" Cousin Gareth studied the card, then laid it face up on the table between them. "Are you sure?" he asked, glancing up at her.

"Positive."

He slid another card out of the pack, laid it next to the first. Annabel craned forward to look. The five of spades. "That's the card I chose," she told him.

"Are you sure?" Cousin Gareth asked. He laid his forefinger on the king of clubs and switched the places of the two cards on the table. "Sometimes things are not what they seem," he went on. "A man who appears to be worthless on the outside might be a prince inside."

Baffled, Annabel contemplated her cousin. She was still getting used to how he looked now. The excess flesh around his waist was gone, and his skin was smooth and tanned. He was a handsome man, even at thirty-two. Why had he never married? It occurred to her she didn't really know much about him.

Cousin Gareth slid the king of clubs toward her. "I didn't refuse my consent to the marriage," he told her. He picked up the five of spades. "Had you really chosen this card, a man who would have been as lacking in moral values as he was lacking in worldly goods, I would have withheld my permission."

"Are you saying...?"

"I'm saying that your young man loves you. But he believes love is not enough to live on, and he is honorable enough to accept the fact. I hope he makes something of himself. I wish him luck, and I am grateful for his decision not to expose you to the dangers and hardships of a mining camp."

Cousin Gareth fell silent, picked up the papers stacked on the bench beside him and began shuffling through his notes. He'd been the same at Merlin's Leap, always shut away in Papa's study, buried in ledgers, a frown on his face. For a moment, Annabel contemplated him, only the rocking of the train filling the quiet.

"What happened to you?" she asked in a low voice, a question she and her sisters had debated endlessly but never dared to ask. "What made you change?"

Cousin Gareth hesitated. He spoke with reluctance, the words dragged out of him. "You and your sisters ruined my life. You stole my birthright, and remained blissfully unaware of it, for your father blackmailed me into silence."

Baffled, Annabel stared at him. "We did nothing of the kind. How could we have? We're young women, wholly without influence."

Cousin Gareth turned his attention to his papers. "I'll tell you when we find your sisters. I do not wish to repeat myself. I will explain once, and once only. Then I wish never to mention the topic again."

As Annabel mulled over the point Cousin Gareth had demonstrated with his card trick, it occurred to her that he might have been talking about himself as much as Clay. Was he suggesting she and her sisters had misjudged him? That in their grief for their parents they had heaped more blame on him than he deserved?

In Phoenix Junction, instead of waiting for the train to Gold Crossing that ran only once a week, on Thursdays, they unloaded their horses and rode north across the rolling hills covered with towering saguaros. When the night fell, they struck camp, talking quietly in the firelight, something of their old friendship rekindling between them. Late in the afternoon on the second day, they came to a wooden sign.

Gold Crossing
Population 8

Cousin Gareth burst into laughter. "What is this? A town of eight people? Why, that would make the staff quarters at Merlin's Leap a greater metropolis than this place."

Curious, they rode on. In the slanting rays of the setting sun they arrived into a town made up of a single dusty street bordered by ramshackle buildings. A general store, with a post office and a telegraph. A hotel with a saloon. Railroad station. A few residential buildings, most of them boarded up.

They had telegraphed ahead, to alert Charlotte and Miranda to their arrival. Annabel felt her heart pounding as she studied the dusty street. A few ragged children were playing around the water trough, and the mournful sound of a trumpet drifted out through an open window above the saloon.

Then two slender figures jumped down from the boardwalk and raced toward them, skirts flapping around their feet. Charlotte's dark curls unraveled to spill down her back. Miranda's blond upsweep was more robustly constructed. Behind them, two men stepped into the evening light but remained in the background.

"Scrappy!" Charlotte called out. "We were so worried!"

Annabel tumbled down from her mare, and then Charlotte was hugging her, and Miranda wrapped her arms around the both of them. For a moment, emotions welled up in Annabel, joy and relief and a fierce surge of love, but the new maturity she had gained in the last few weeks stopped the tears from falling.

"Cousin Gareth has regained his memory," she whispered to her sisters. "But that knock on the head seems to have done him good. He is more like he used to be when we were small. He's even said he is sorry for behaving so beastly toward us."

Charlotte and Miranda turned to dart a suspicious look

at their cousin. Annabel smiled, not letting anything ruin her joy of the reunion. Her sisters would observe Gareth, put him through an interrogation and make up their own minds.

On their first evening together, they congregated in Miranda's house. She and her husband had bought one of the boarded-up homes and were refurbishing it to live in, even though most of the time they were touring the western territories in their private railroad car.

Miranda's husband, James Blackburn, was part Cheyenne Indian. He'd earned his living as a bounty hunter before he inherited a fortune in railroad stocks from his Baltimore grandfather. Charlotte had married Thomas Greenwood, a fair-haired giant who owned a farm out of town.

They trooped into the living room, where a few crudely made wooden chairs provided seating around a low pine table. Surrounded by the smells of sawdust and paint, they sat down and turned their expectant eyes to Cousin Gareth.

"You promised to tell us why you were so beastly to us," Annabel prompted him.

Cousin Gareth shifted in his seat. "So I did."

"Well, go on then," Miranda ordered. "Spit it out."

Cousin Gareth tugged at the collar of his coat, as uncomfortable as a sailor biting into maggot-filled hardtack. "As we all know," he began, "my father was the younger son of Lord Fairfax, and your father was the elder son and the heir. However, as your father did not marry until late in life, for the first few years of my life I was treated as the heir presumptive to the title and the fortune. Then your father married, but only girls were born. I remained the heir."

Annabel glanced at her sisters. Miranda was scowling.

Charlotte looked troubled. Did they guess what would follow with the same clarity as she did?

Cousin Gareth went on. "Your father petitioned to get the patents to the title altered, so females could inherit. Of course, the petition was rejected. Your father renounced the title and stripped away the fortune. It was unlawful, of course, but he said the English crown no longer ruled the colonies and to hell with their rules and regulations."

"Papa said he renounced the title because such things were outdated," Miranda cut in. The tallest of the sisters, and the only one with fair hair, she was the feisty one, a natural leader. "He never mentioned it had any impact on who would inherit the wealth."

"No." Cousin Gareth studied the silver handle on his walking stick. "But I am telling the truth. I was eighteen at the time, and you were too young to understand the implications. Charlotte was ten, Miranda eight and Annabel four."

"Why did you not contest it?" Charlotte asked.

"My father was dying and I did not wish a family dispute to overshadow his final years."

"But later on, after your father died?" Charlotte pressed. "You could have contested it then." Few people understood that, although soft and pliant on the outside, the eldest sister possessed a steely core of determination. She had asked a question, and would not be silenced until she had received a satisfactory answer.

Cousin Gareth looked pained. Annabel's recollection stirred. "You said Papa blackmailed you into not telling us."

Cousin Gareth would not meet their eyes. "Your father said that if I told you, he'd never allow me to see you again, or set foot in Merlin's Leap." A flush rose on his face. "My mother died when I was small, and my father was in ill health. You and your parents were the only living relatives I had, and I did not wish to cut off the family bond."

"But you turned against us." Miranda's tone was cool.

"I was eighteen when your father altered the line of inheritance. I'd grown up filled with pride about my role as his heir, the one to carry on the family name and tradition. When your father did what he did, it felt like a rejection. And I had an understanding with a young woman..."

Cousin Gareth's mouth tipped into a bitter smirk. "But when my prospects altered, the understanding turned out to be a misunderstanding. With one strike of a pen, I had lost my birthright and the girl I loved. In my bitterness, I took to drinking and gambling."

"There was no need to keep us locked up in the house," Charlotte complained.

Miranda scowled. "Why did you never let us have any new clothes?"

Cousin Gareth swore under his breath. His expression darkened. "All right," he said harshly. "You want to know, and I'll tell you. There was no money to pay for new dresses. No money to splash out on parties and balls. Even if I'd found some time to escort you, the fact that your clothes were three seasons out of date would have revealed we were strapped for cash. I did not wish our precarious financial position to be known, and neither did I wish to start selling ships."

Charlotte launched into a protest. "But—"

Cousin Gareth cut her off. "Your father was a sea captain, not a businessman. He lacked the skills to negotiate contracts and administer credit lines. My father took care of that, and when he died, things started sliding downhill."

"But there is money," Charlotte argued. "Lots of it."

"There is. Now." Cousin Gareth's tone was grim. "It took me three years to get the business back to even keel."

He glared at them. "I might have succumbed to drinking and gambling as a young man disappointed in love, but since your father died, the only gambling I've done has been against the benevolence of the ocean. Half the time, I couldn't afford to insure the cargoes. If I drank too much whiskey, it was because every rumble of thunder made my blood run cold with fear."

Miranda held up her hand and spoke slowly, incredulity in her tone. "Are you telling us that Papa had run the shipping line to the ground? And all those hours we thought you were getting whiskey-soaked in his study, you were working hard to restore our fortunes?"

Cousin Gareth gave a reluctant nod.

"Why didn't you tell us?" Charlotte pressed.

"You were mourning for your father. What kind of a man would I have been to sully his memory in your eyes? And in some way, I felt you needed an outlet for your grief. Hating me seemed as good as any, so I made no effort to apologize for my grim moods or to explain that money was scarce."

"You've rebuilt the shipping line, and yet it is not yours," Annabel said quietly.

"But the Fairfax name is. That I still have." Cousin Gareth touched the scar on his forehead. "Although for a while it seemed I had lost even that."

Silence settled over the room, broken only by the sound of the trumpet from the saloon. Annabel cleared her throat. With help and support from Clay, she had found independence for herself. She longed for him to be here now, to witness another great step she was about to take—to act as the leader before her sisters.

She made her point carefully, weighing each word. "When Cousin Gareth coveted Merlin's Leap and the fleet of ships, he may have acted like a brute, but it was not out of greed. It was because his dreams had been smashed, his pride trampled upon, his love rejected, the family bonds of affection seized away from him. When deciding what is right, we should keep that in mind."

Charlotte stared at her through narrowed eyes. "You said *when deciding what is right*. Scrappy, are you suggesting that we do something—change the existing set of circumstances?"

"Yes," Annabel replied. "That is what I am suggesting. That we accept Papa was wrong. Whatever his reasoning, it was faulty, and we have the power to remedy his mistake."

For a moment, the mournful tune of the trumpet seemed to sum up all the misunderstandings, all the past hurts and wasted opportunities. Then whispered voices hushed around the room as Miranda and Charlotte conferred with each other and with their husbands. Annabel suppressed the sting of loneliness. One day, she hoped Clay would sit beside her, the way her sisters had their husbands sitting next to them.

Finally, Miranda looked up. Before she spoke, she reached out to take her husband's hand. "I have no need for Papa's money. Jamie has plenty from his family."

Charlotte craned her neck to look up at her fair-haired giant of a farmer and smiled at him. "I have little use for a shipping line and an East Coast mansion. I never wish to live anywhere but our secluded valley."

"I don't want the Fairfax fortune either," Annabel said. "From what we've just heard it belongs to Cousin Gareth, and since losing it he has earned it again."

Miranda got up, fetched a piece of paper from the packing crates stacked in the corner. "It is settled, then," she said as she sat down again. She gave Cousin Gareth a quick glance not totally void of lingering hostility and started scribbling. "We shall give you a power of attorney, and you can reverse what Papa did."

Cousin Gareth had been sitting ramrod-straight on the rough wooden chair, his features devoid of emotion, except for the muscle that ticked in his jaw. Now he blinked rapidly, as if to hold back tears. "If you are certain… I will of course give both of you your portion…and to Annabel when she marries…but until then I will be her legal guardian and it will be my duty to look after her."

I will be her legal guardian and it will be my duty to look after her.

The words made Annabel's stomach churn. She swallowed down the bile. If the suspicion that had taken root in her mind turned out to be true, Cousin Gareth might once more become the enemy, for he would have the power to issue an ultimatum that might mean she would never have a chance to find happiness with Clay.

Chapter Twenty-Four

After he'd walked away from Annabel, Clay felt empty and aimless. He rode back to the Mimbres mine, thinking he might clear a way into the cave with gold, but he found he could not bring himself to disturb the peace of a tomb. He watered the saplings that hid the mine entrance and replaced the two small spruces that had died.

He rode back to Hillsboro and took a look around the Black Hills mining district. Gold had been found in 1877, more than a decade ago, and all the good claims were taken—Snake Mine, Opportunity, Ready Pan and dozens more.

Back in town, Clay stopped at the assay office. A small, dapper man in his fifties stood behind a counter, studying a piece of ore through a loupe.

"Do you know anything about mining around Gold Crossing over in the Arizona Territory?" Clay asked. The knowledge haunted him that he could ride out to Annabel, and she would be his again. He had no intention of doing so, but being near her might ease the emptiness inside him.

The man gave a prompt reply. "Desperation Hill mining district. Name says it all. Gold discovered eight years ago and since then nothing but blood and sweat and misery."

"Who's the recorder over there?"

"Man called Art Langley. Runs the hotel in town."

Clay rode west. He took a month over the journey, riding slowly, a rifle at the ready. Even though Geronimo had surrendered three years ago, a few renegade Apache braves still roamed the hills. He'd been right to give up Annabel, Clay told himself for the thousandth time. Had she been with him, she would have been exposed to danger.

Gold Crossing was a sorry sight, a single street flanked with dilapidated businesses. Clay tied the buckskin to the hitch rail outside a building with a sign that said Imperial Hotel. Below it a cloth banner spelled out "Vacation Camp for San Francisco Widows and Orphans Association."

In the lobby, a muscular youth stood behind a newspaper stand, selling a newspaper called the *Gold Crossing Informer.* Clay resisted the temptation to buy a copy or ask about Annabel and her sisters. If he saw her, if he spoke to her, he might lack the strength to walk away from her again.

At the reception desk a lanky, brown-haired man around forty, wearing a black vest over a white shirt, was playing solitaire. Clay marched up to him.

"I'm looking for Art Langley."

The man put the cards down. "You've found him."

"I've come to inquire about mining claims."

The man's eyebrows went up. "You want to locate?"

Clay's mood sank. Judging by the recorder's tone of surprise, the district was all played out. "Haven't been to look around yet," Clay explained. "I thought you might be able to steer me to the best prospects."

The man reached down and slapped a stack of documents on the counter. "I don't allow overlapping claims. These have lapsed. Go and take a look, come back to tell me which one you want. Or, if you want to trust Lady Luck, pick one now."

Clay rifled through the pack of location notices. A man staked a claim on the ground, then filled a form to indicate the location of his claim and paid a fee to record it. If a man abandoned the mine, the claim lapsed and was open to others.

Art Langley tossed another folded piece of paper on the counter. "I have also a patented claim, if you prefer owning the land at your diggings. The owner died a few months back, and the deed came to me in payment of debts."

Clay inspected the deed.

High Hopes Mine.
Owner Sam Renner.

"Any gold in the ground?" he asked.

Art Langley shook his shoulders in a gesture that attempted to turn bad news into a promising prospect. "Sam took out a big nugget seven years ago. He got injured and could dig no more. He leased the mine a few times, but those men found nothing and moved on. It's good land, full twenty acres of it. There's a creek running through and enough grazing for a few horses."

Clay put down the mine deed. "How much?"

"I'll give you the government price. Five dollars an acre."

Clay emptied his pockets, counted out ninety-five dollars, including the small change. "Can I owe you five?" he asked.

Langley stirred the pile of money with his forefinger. "What about tools and grub?"

"I have all the tools I need, and I can hunt to eat."

The claims recorder took out a silver fountain pen, uncapped it and lined up the mine deed on the counter. "What's the name?"

"Clay Collier."

Langley added the name to the deed and wrote out a separate bill of sale. "You can owe me fifty," he said. "No interest. A year to pay."

Clay contemplated the lanky businessman. "Why?"

"Because you seem like a hardworking miner, and this town needs good men." Langley gave him a wry smile. "And because I'm curious to find out what brings you here."

The smell of laundry soap hit Annabel's nostrils. She gritted her teeth to hold down the nausea. The smile she gave to the customer may have been more like a grimace, but at least she didn't make gagging sounds. "Anything else, Mrs. Perkins?" Annabel asked.

The pretty blonde widow gave her a curious look. "Are you all right, dear?"

"I stubbed my toe beneath the counter," Annabel blurted out. "It hurts like the blazes."

Mrs. Perkins made comforting noises, and Annabel went on filling the grocery order. It was five weeks since she'd arrived in Gold Crossing. Thanksgiving was over, and soon it would be Christmas. It should have been the season for joy, but loneliness and worry overshadowed Annabel's existence.

Both to have something to do and to demonstrate her independence, she had taken a job at the mercantile. A man named Gus Osborn and his fifteen-year-old son, Gus Junior, ran the business. However, Art Langley, who owned the store, had decided lady customers might be more comfortable with a female clerk when purchasing personal items.

Annabel waved Mrs. Perkins off on her way and hurried to the storage room in the rear of the building. She collapsed on a crate of milk tins and pressed the flat of her palm to her stomach. No longer could she ignore the signs. Every strong smell sent her retching. Cigarette smoke. A dog scurrying by. Cooking. Meat, onions, fish. Everything.

For two weeks, she'd prayed her period was merely late, but now she accepted it would not come at all. For she was going to have a baby. Another wave of nausea hit her as she caught a whiff of Mr. Osborn's boot polish through the open doorway.

"Are you all right, Annabel?"

"I'm fine, fine. Stubbed my toe."

Lies. Clay hated them, and now she would need to keep lying, to protect her secret as long as she could. It must have happened that last night in Hillsboro, when Clay came to say goodbye to her.

If only she knew how to reach him, she could send a message and he would come. But she had no way of knowing where he'd gone. *One day, you'll come for me, and I'll be waiting*, she had told him, defiant with the certainty of her young love. But would he? Would he ever come? And if he did, would it be too late?

With a flash of intuition, Annabel guessed what must have happened between Mr. Hicks and his Sarah. She too must have waited. Waited and waited, counting days, watching her waistline expand beneath her gown. Waited and waited, until she could no longer hide her pregnancy. Until she could no longer wait.

Clay found the site of his mine, inspected the abandoned tunnels. In his mind, a stubborn, crazy hope sparked to life. Annabel had promised to wait for him. If he found gold, the terrible dilemma between keeping her safe and having her beside him would go away.

With a fevered obsession, Clay set to work. Day and

night, he labored, barely pausing to eat or sleep, let alone to cook or hunt for food. His muscles grew lean and wiry. The skin on his hands bled and toughened. His hair turned into a shaggy mane. A thick beard covered his jaw.

He wasted no time on building a cabin but slept in the mine, a rabbit warren of short tunnels in the hillside. Sometimes, when the underground darkness got to him, he slept with the horse and mule under the tarpaulin canopy he'd erected outside.

Bucketful after bucketful of dirt he hauled out, looking for the glint of gold. It was a reef claim, where the forces of nature had broken down the lode but the rains had yet to wash the gold down the mountain into the creeks. If he found nuggets, they might be large and clustered with many more.

Weeks turned into months. Winter added cold to the hardships, for he didn't take the time to collect enough firewood to burn. On his stomach the skin stretched taut over a line of ribs. His clothing wore to rags. On his boots, the toes poked through.

Sometimes, when Clay crawled beneath a blanket for a few hours of rest, despair and loneliness pressed down upon him. Had he been wrong about Annabel? Would she have endured? How much brighter would his days be with her by his side? How much easier his nights? He should have let her decide for herself.

Then he woke again, and certainty filled him that he'd done the right thing. There was no way he could have asked Annabel to join him at the mine. The life was too hard on a woman. Without a cabin, she might not have survived the winter months.

Annabel pulled the fabric of her loose-fitting dress tight to display the rounded bump of her belly and braced herself against Charlotte's reaction. Miranda was away in Wyoming, inspecting some ranching land her husband owned.

"You...you're with child." Charlotte collapsed into a padded wingback chair.

They were in Miranda's house. The rooms were fully furnished now, with heavy pieces in Mexican style, ordered from the craftsmen in Tucson. Cousin Gareth had returned to Merlin's Leap three months ago. On his way through New York, he had promised to visit Colin and Liza and give them enough money to travel out to the West, or to build a more comfortable life in the East, as they chose.

Charlotte recovered from the shock of seeing the evidence of her younger sister's disgrace. "The father is that miner you told us about...?"

"Yes."

"Where is he? Does he know? When...?"

"He doesn't know about the child, and I have no way of contacting him. The baby is due in July." Annabel spoke without emotion. She'd worried so much her fears were all frayed away, like fabric worn through.

"July? That is only four months away." Charlotte pressed her hand to the slight rise of her own stomach. "You'll be the first of us...and not married." She stared at Annabel. "You can't have a baby out of wedlock. Think of the scandal. Think of Papa's reputation."

Annabel hung her head. She had tried to ignore the prospect of public disgrace. "I've managed to keep it hidden until now. Maybe a bit longer..."

Charlotte frowned. "Scrappy, you may be able to hide your pregnancy under loose clothing, but there is no way to hide a baby." She jumped up from the chair and wrapped her arms around Annabel. "Oh, Scrappy, what are we to do?"

The warmth of her sister's embrace eased Annabel's

despair. She'd been taking her independence too far. What are *we* to do? Charlotte had said, making her problem shared. Annabel lifted her chin. "I'm sorry I didn't tell you before."

"Is there any chance your young man might come for you?"

"I thought he would...but time is running out."

"Poor Scrappy," Charlotte said. She cradled Annabel to her chest and stroked her hair in a soothing gesture. When she spoke, her voice was very gentle. "You know what you have to do, don't you, Scrappy?"

"I want to stay here and wait for Clay," Annabel muttered, but she knew the words were those of a petulant child. "I promised."

Charlotte sighed, a deep whoosh out of her chest. "But you know you can't wait forever, don't you? Perhaps another month or two, but no more than that."

Reluctantly, Annabel nodded. She spoke with her voice muffled against the collar of Charlotte's gown. "I know. I must either marry, or go back to Boston and pretend to be a widow. Otherwise I'll besmirch Papa's memory and ruin the reputation of the whole family, including the children yet to be born."

"I am sorry." Charlotte clutched Annabel's shoulders, urging her to look up. "I'm proud of you, Scrappy, for facing the situation like a responsible adult. I wish we could indulge you, but this is too serious, and there really is no other choice. As Papa would say, you've made your berth and now you'll have to roll around in it and feel all the lumps."

"Can't we wait?" Annabel pleaded. "A few more weeks?"

Pity shadowed Charlotte's features. "I'm sorry, Scrappy. Cousin Gareth is your legal guardian now. I must write to him at once. I can't put the information into a telegram for others to see, but he'll be able to telegraph his reply." Charlotte eased out of the embrace and took a step back. "It will be up to him how long you can wait before you make your choice. You said it yourself—your only options are to marry or to return to Boston and pretend to be a widow."

As Clay's strength began to wane through cold and the lack of nourishment, restless dreams disturbed his sleep. He dreamed of his parents, of a burning wagon. He dreamed of Billy and Lee. He dreamed of Mr. Hicks.

"*Women,*" the old man said in his booming voice. "*They promise you paradise, but they give you hell. She won't wait. Just like my Sarah, she won't wait. You'll see.*"

Occasionally, another miner or a prospector passed by.

"You're turning into Sam Renner," Clay heard one mutter.

Sam Renner had been a madman, he'd been told. Clay didn't care. Day after day, week after week, month after month, he kept digging. Exhaustion made his hands unsteady. His eyesight dimmed. Barely able to stand up on his feet, he lifted the pickaxe and struck the rocky ground, again and again, until one cold spring morning the sharp point of the tool glanced from a stone and pierced his leg.

The pain arrowed up his shin. Clay jerked the pickaxe free, lifted the tool high and struck the ground once more. His head swam. His knees buckled, and he fell to the ground, knocking over his coal oil lantern. The glass broke, and the flames flared up in a whoosh, for an instant making the mine tunnel glow like the fires of hell.

Then darkness fell. Dazed, only half-conscious, Clay crawled along the tunnel on his belly, dragging his injured leg against the uneven ground. There'd been no crack of bone, he told himself. It was only a flesh wound, with the sharp point of the pickaxe tearing through the muscle. But he *could* have smashed the bone, and the coal oil *could* have splashed over him, setting him aflame.

What was he doing?

Was he trying to kill himself?

Gritting his teeth against the pain, Clay crawled out into the daylight. His threadbare coat tore from scraping against the ground. The skin on his hands and elbows bled from the effort. When he reached the entrance, he braced up on his arms and inhaled the crisp morning air. In the distance, he could see sunshine glinting on the hilltops, melting away the snow. By the creek, birds were chirping, ready to build their nests.

Slowly, Clay let the truth penetrate his mind. Perhaps subconsciously he *had* been trying to work himself to death. Because life without Annabel was no life at all. A great weight seemed to roll off his shoulders as he admitted how misguided he had been, how wrong. *It is better to take risks and be together than to be safe and be alone*, Annabel had told him, and she had been right.

Gathering his strength, Clay stumbled to his feet and staggered down the hillside to the tarpaulin canopy, where the horse and mule greeted him with a friendly whinny. Clay stroked the flank of the buckskin, relishing the connection to something living.

Annabel.

Annabel.

He said her name out loud, the sound drifting away on the cool mountain breeze. He should have had more faith in her. He should have trusted her love, as she had trusted his, believing he would go and find her.

Limping, Clay left the animals beneath the shelter and made his way to the creek, where he had cleared a site for a bonfire, with a pair of flat stones for seating. He put water on the boil and searched out clean rags to dress the wound in his leg.

While he tended to his injury, emotions welled up in him. He loved Annabel. She loved him. Nothing else mattered. Nothing else should be allowed to matter. As soon as his leg healed and the spring banished the last of the winter, he would go for her. They would be together, as long as they both lived.

Calmer now, feeling at peace, Clay had some breakfast and settled down to sleep. Hours later, he woke up refreshed. As the days went by and his leg healed, he returned into the mine, but his labors were no longer fevered. He was a miner working at his profession, not a man with an obsession, hoping to purchase happiness with riches dug up from the earth.

One evening in early May, just when Clay was about to quit and cook his supper, his pickaxe struck something that gave the clang of metal, a sharper sound than the pounding of the tool against the stony ground. Sinking to his knees, Clay scooped away the loose earth with his bare hands. The dull gleam of gold shone beneath his fingers. He kept brushing the dirt aside until he had uncovered a round nugget the size of a small cannonball.

He scrambled to his feet, dug with a shovel. *Clang.* He fell to his knees again. Another nugget, as big as his fist. The fever Clay had thought already conquered infected him anew. Frantic now, he attacked the ground beneath him, ignoring the pain in his leg, ignoring the strain in his muscles.

By the time exhaustion forced him to halt his labors, he had unearthed six large nuggets buried together in the dirt, like a cluster of eggs in the nest of some huge, long-forgotten, gold-laying bird.

In awe, Clay studied his hoard in the lantern light. He

ran his fingers over the roughly textured surface of the largest nugget. In his mind, he saw a house, with a white picket fence and flowers blooming in the yard. He stroked another nugget, saw a trip to the East, to visit Annabel's home, perhaps a fine wedding with Gareth Fairfax giving her away. Touching each nugget in turn, he imagined the comfort and security they would bring—clothes, furniture, horses and carriages, doctors and medicines.

For an instant, regret filled him that Annabel wasn't there, to share the triumph of the discovery with him, the way a partner should be able to do. He would make it up to her. He would polish up the nuggets and take them to her, like a wedding gift.

As Clay carried his gold out into the evening twilight, euphoria held him in a firm grip. He'd already accepted he needed Annabel in his life, no matter what the hardships, but now he had the means to provide for her. Was this how a man felt when he knew all his dreams were about to come true?

Clay rode down the street in Gold Crossing, the pack mule trailing behind the buckskin. He'd washed and shaved and done his best to tidy up his ragged clothing. The mule carried half a man's weight in gold. Thirty thousand dollars, Clay reckoned. Not enough to buy a mansion by the ocean or employ an army of servants, but enough to keep Annabel safe, and the mine might produce more.

The sun was low in the sky, the air warm and sweet with a spring breeze. In the desert, the flowers were in full bloom. A good time for a wedding, Clay thought. He reined in outside the Imperial Hotel but remained in the saddle. A boy of around ten squatted by the water trough, poking at a lizard with a stick, a cruel smirk of fascination on his freckled face.

"Do you know where I could find a lady called Annabel Fairfax?" Clay asked.

The boy looked up and wiped his runny nose with his sleeve. "She ain't called Fairfax no more. She is married now." The boy pointed with his stick. "They own the mercantile and the house next door to it. Over there."

Married?

Annabel married? There had to be some mistake. Cold fingers of fear closed around Clay. The taunting warnings of Mr. Hicks that had plagued his dreams echoed in his head. Frantic now, his hands fisting on the reins, Clay urged the buckskin toward the mercantile. From the house next to it came the pounding of hammers. The exterior showed signs of renovation, as did the house opposite.

"They own the mercantile and the house next door to it," the boy had said.

Clay gritted his teeth. *I will wait forever*, Annabel had told him, but he had given her no promises in return. Had she given up on him and married some other man? A man who came from her affluent world, a man with education, born to be a gentleman?

Outside the mercantile, Clay jumped down from the saddle and barely paused to tie the horse and mule to the hitching rail. His boots pounded on the boardwalk as he charged in through the open door of the store.

Annabel stood behind a counter, dressed in a loose dress of lavender blue. For an instant, Clay froze at the sight of her. She looked radiant. Her skin glowed and her eyes sparkled, and her breasts seemed fuller than he remembered. She certainly did not appear to have been wilting from loneliness.

A man's voice called from the back of the store. "Annabel, you ought to go home early today. Don't tire yourself out."

The hardships of working at the mine through the winter months buffeted Clay along, as though he had no control over his movements. Dimly he could hear Annabel cry out his name, but he was already storming into the back room.

Two men crouched on their heels, unloading a crate of goods on the floor. Father and son, by the look of it, cut from the same pattern of unruly black hair and bulbous nose and thickly muscled frame. The father seemed too old for Annabel, the son too young. It had to be someone else.

Clay strode back to the store. "Where is he?" It was not the reaction of a reasonable man, but he did not want to be reasonable. "I'll make him regret the day he laid a finger on you."

Annabel stared at him with those big amber eyes. "Clay!" she shouted. "What is the matter with you?"

"What's the matter with me?" He stalked up to her. "*'I will wait,'* you said. *'I will wait forever.'* Barely six months I've been gone, and I come back to find you married. You're no better than that woman who betrayed Mr. Hicks while he was away making his fortune."

"I see." Annabel put on her nose-in-the-air expression. "I am not only a spoiled rich man's daughter. I am a fickle woman, too. Untrustworthy and flighty and unfaithful."

There was something strange about her behavior. The momentary flash of fear was gone, and now she appeared to be taunting him. The hot flare of jealousy that had driven Clay to act like a fool cooled down, leaving behind the smoldering ashes of doubt and misery.

He spoke in a low voice that had an edge of despair to it. "I told you once that I'll forgive you anything, except betraying me with another man." His hands clenched into fists at his sides. "Who is he? I have good mind to kill the bastard."

Annabel craned her neck to call out past him. "Mr. Osborn, could you bring me a coil of rope, please?"

Returning her attention to Clay, she contemplated him with a challenge in her amber eyes. Clay fell silent. His heart was hammering in his chest, his breathing harsh, his body shaking. He fought to conquer his agitation, but the weeks and months of suffering at the mine acted like a gunpowder charge inside him.

The middle-aged man walked in from the back, the thud of his boots ominous in the silence. Annabel took the coil of hemp rope the man held out, spun back to Clay and banged the rope down on the counter. "Here," she said. "Go find a tree. Or a balcony railing might do."

"I need to find the guilty man before I can hang him."

"That's easy," Annabel said. "You just look in the mirror. Then make a noose and stick your neck in it." She reached up to the shelf behind the counter, took down a leather folder, opened it and slipped out a document and shoved it at him. "Read," she ordered. "And apologize."

Clay took the piece of paper, scanned the few lines of text. It was a marriage certificate, dated seven months ago. And the husband was... *Clay Collier*. Baffled, he looked up at Annabel. It appeared she was married to *him*.

"We didn't get married," he pointed out, confusion dulling his mind.

"Oh, yes we did," Annabel told him. "We got married in the light of a bonfire under a rock overhang in the Mimbres Mountains. I have proof of it right here." She pulled her loose dress tight against her body to reveal a rounded belly.

Clay staggered backward. "You're...? A baby?"

Annabel tried to look stern, but a smile was breaking out on her face. "A baby. Yours and mine. A little gold miner. We can call him Aaron, after Mr. Hicks. Or Aria or Arlene if it's a girl."

"A baby." Clay shook his head, but the idea refused to sink in. All he could think about was that she hadn't married someone else. That she had waited. That she was still his, as she should be. Forever. He folded the marriage certificate and put it carefully away in the pocket of his threadbare coat.

"Are you pleased?" Annabel asked, hesitant now.

"Of course I'm pleased," Clay said. "It's just that…" He cast a quick glance toward the open doorway of the storage room, stepped up to Annabel and laid his hand over her rounded belly. He lowered his voice. "I'm sorry for leaving you without any promises to give you comfort. Sorry for making you face the world alone with a baby growing inside you. I know it won't make up for those months, but it eases my conscience that I found gold. I can support you and the child, keep you safe."

Annabel reached out and brushed aside the unruly curls tumbling across his forehead. "I always knew you would come for me," she said softly. "I just didn't know how long it would take, so I had to marry you in advance. I have money, too, from Cousin Gareth. It is something called a portion. I bought us a house and the store, and it has given me great pleasure to prepare a home for us, like an equal partner should." She tugged him toward the exit. "Come and see."

"Wait," Clay said. "Are you sure the marriage is legal?"

"Perfectly so, unless you dispute your signature."

Clay pulled Annabel closer to him, her pregnant belly pressing against his hips. His child, and the memories of how they had brought that child into being, mixed in his mind, filling him with a sense of peace and homecoming. "How did you make it happen?" he said. "I mean the marriage."

"With some forgery, some trickery and a total lack of

shame. My sisters helped. They took some persuading, but I won them over." Annabel gave him a cat-with-the-cream smile. "And I'll tell you nothing more until you come and see the house."

know. My Mary [...]ejoin[...]. The [...]rooms were pressed to[...]
place them over Annabel's eyes, him in a case with the room
smiled. "And I'd lay a hundred mothn't sell you could and
so, the husband.

Chapter Twenty-Five

I n her hurry to show Clay around their new home, Annabel stumbled on the rutted street. Clay scooped her into his arms and carried her through the open doorway next door. The house was two-story, with a fresh coat of white paint on the outside and a tiny front garden with wooden tubs planted full of spring flowers.

The workmen had finished for the day, the pounding of hammers ceased. Clay set her down on her feet, kicked the door to a close and eased her back against the hallway wall. *Check for fresh paint*! Annabel wanted to cry out, but it was too late, for Clay had silenced her with his mouth.

The kiss was warm and gentle, full of regret and longing. Annabel parted her lips, asking for more. Clay made a rough sound. The pressure of his mouth grew hungry. How she'd missed him! Missed his companionship during the day, his warmth at night, his partnership in every aspect of life.

When Clay lifted his head, he searched her face and spoke softly, with a new humility in his tone. "I'd never have left you had I known you were with child, Annabel. Please believe me, I had no idea. I thought…"

"So did I." She lifted one hand to stir his unruly curls,

a familiar gesture that filled her with memories. "It must have happened that last night, when you came to say goodbye. I only discovered a month later."

Clay curled his fingers around her wrist and pressed her hand against his heart, to let her feel how hard it pounded. "I was wrong," he said. "And you were right, about everything. You were even right to lie to me about your background, for when I found out, I did exactly what you feared—I judged you as a rich man's daughter instead of the brave, resourceful miner you were. I didn't treat you as an equal partner. I refused to let you make your own decisions, and for that I am ashamed. Will you forgive me?"

"There is nothing I wouldn't forgive you," Annabel replied. "Except betraying me with another woman." Her tone was fierce, in the name of equality, as well as from true emotion.

Clay settled the flat of his palm on her belly, as he'd already done in the store, the heavy weight of his hand warm and reassuring. "What is it like?" he asked. "Can you feel the baby move yet? How much longer? Have you been well?"

"The baby kicks like an angry mule," Annabel replied. "I was sick to start with, but it's over now. Two and a half more months to go. By the end of July, we'll have a child." She rested her head against his shoulder. "I think this is what might have happened to Mr. Hicks and his Sarah. But he didn't come back in time." She lifted her head to look at Clay. "If Mr. Hicks had gone to confront Sarah, I think he might have found a sturdy little boy with his features playing in her backyard."

"Maybe so." Clay raked a glance over the dust sheets and paint pots that covered the hallway floor. "Does this house have a bed?" He framed her face with his hands. "In all those lonely winter nights, what kept me going was thinking of you, of how it feels to sleep with your body tucked against mine."

Annabel smiled. "There is a big, soft bed, but first I want to show you the house and tell you about how we got married."

A frown drifted across Clay's features, but it vanished in an instant and an indulgent smile took its place. "Of course," he said. "Show me around, and tell me everything."

There were benefits to having a husband contrite and apologetic, Annabel decided. It gave him the patience to trail behind her, inspecting every corner of their new house, studying every piece of furniture, every scrap of curtain, every pot and pan in the kitchen, never letting his frustration show.

When their tour reached the bedroom, Clay's patience came to an end. Gently but firmly, he stripped away her clothing and bundled her into the big four-poster bed, then nearly shredded his threadbare garments in his haste as he undressed and joined her. "Tell me what I can do without harming the baby," he said as he stretched out beside her.

"You can rub my back."

In truth, they could do a lot more, but if she let him get started, he'd never listen to the story of her cleverness and triumph. Curled up on her side, Annabel felt Clay's strong fingers probing at her tired muscles. "Yes," she said, arching her spine like a contented cat. "There. Just there."

She concentrated on the pleasure and talked and talked. She told him about Cousin Gareth, and how the sisters had given the fortune back to him and he was now Lord Fairfax again, living at Merlin's Leap.

She explained about her portion, how in aristocratic families the eldest son inherited, but it was his duty to provide for the unmarried females, and upon marriage to bestow a portion of the fortune on each of the girls.

"Most of the Fairfax fortune is tied up with Merlin's Leap and the shipping line, so my portion is not very big, only thirty thousand dollars, but that is wonderful because that is the value of your gold, which makes us equal again." Annabel craned her neck to look at Clay. "Don't you agree?"

"Yes," he said. "It is very nice that it makes us equal."

Annabel smiled. If Clay ever behaved like a stubborn fool again, she wouldn't mind, provided he would go to the same lengths with his next apology. Her voice breathless with eagerness, she filled him in with the rest of her achievements.

"For almost five months, I managed to hide I was with child, but then I had to tell my sisters. I chose a time when Miranda was away. Big sisters are easier to handle one at a time. I knew I had to marry or return to Boston and pretend to be a widow, but I had been putting it off, in the hope that you would get here in time. Cousin Gareth wasn't as bad as I had expected. He said I could come back to Gold Crossing after the baby was born, and wait for you, pretending to be some other man's widow, but I feared you'd come while I was away. And anyway, I've learned my lesson—that lies don't solve anything but usually lead to even more trouble."

"Uh-huh," Clay said.

It was not much of a response, but it indicated he was listening. Annabel rolled over onto her back. She wanted to see his expression when she told him how terribly clever she'd been. "There's a preacher in Gold Crossing, Reverend Eldridge. He is in his eighties and going senile. He has completely white hair and thick glasses and he forgets things."

"Uh-huh," Clay said. He lifted one hand to her big belly and stroked her pregnant bump, his touch light and dreamy.

For a moment, Annabel was distracted. She raked her gaze over his naked chest and shoulders. "You've gone awfully thin."

"I didn't eat enough. It will pass."

She trailed her fingertips along the ridged pattern of his rib cage. "Your skin feels very hot."

"Uh-huh." Clay bent his head to brush a kiss on her belly.

The tickle of his beard stubble made Annabel giggle. "Listen," she said. "Reverend Eldridge can't tell me and Charlotte apart. Of course, we *do* look very much alike. Miranda is the lucky one with Papa's looks, tall and blonde and blue-eyed."

Clay was kissing the indentation of her waist now, what was left of it, the balloon that she had become. Annabel buried her fingers in his hair, squirmed a little against the onslaught of pleasure, and went on with her tale of triumph.

"The day after I told Charlotte about the baby, I bumped into Reverend Eldridge on the boardwalk. He squints at me through his thick lenses and says, *'I recall marrying a woman who looks exactly like you on the porch of the Imperial Hotel, and another one in my church. Which one are you?'*"

She tugged at Clay's hair to pull his head up so she could see his expression. Once he was looking at her with proper attention, Annabel resumed talking.

"*Boom!*" she said. "It came to me like a gunpowder charge going off. You see, Charlotte had been married twice because the first time Reverend Eldridge forgot to enter it in the church register and they had to do the whole thing again."

Clay lowered his head once more and began nuzzling her neck.

"Listen," Annabel said in a breathless rush. "I hurried back to Charlotte and begged and begged and begged until she agreed to help. We had to wait until Miranda returned because she is the best forger of the three of us."

Clay was edging lower now, his lips skimming toward her breasts, his breath brushing heat against her skin. Annabel arched her back, succumbing to the pleasure. But she wanted to finish telling him how ingenious she had been. "Listen! Listen!"

Clay lifted his head. "I *am* listening. I can listen with my ears…while I touch with my hand…" His fingers did another butterfly dance over her pregnant bump. "I can kiss with my lips…" He dipped his head and closed his mouth over the tip of her breast.

Annabel gasped at the sensation. Fighting to focus on her story, she spoke in a husky murmur. "Charlotte went to Reverend Eldridge and said she wanted a copy of her marriage certificate. While he wrote it out, Charlotte stole a blank form. We all learned sleight of hand from Cousin Gareth when we were small."

Clay was cupping her breast now, studying the shape. "These are bigger now than they used to be. Is it because of the baby?"

"Yes…" Annabel was trembling now. "Listen!"

"I am listening." Clay's mouth went to work on her breast again, kissing and teasing and tempting.

"So," Annabel said, fighting to suppress the tiny moans of pleasure. "We had the blank form, and we filled in your details and mine, and then Miranda forged the signatures. We got your signature from the note you left for me with the partnership money in Hillsboro, and, of course, the reverend had signed Charlotte's marriage certificate."

"Uh-huh."

"Are you listening?"

"Uh-huh."

"And then I took the marriage certificate and went to see Reverend Eldridge and I told him I just wanted to check that he had remembered to enter our marriage into the church register. He took out the register and looked terribly crestfallen—I felt so guilty for tricking him—and then he entered our marriage in the church register, and because no one had been married since Charlotte, the entry is in the right sequence, too."

She tugged at Clay's hair to indicate she wanted him to lift his head, but she did not tug very hard because what he was doing to her breast felt so wonderful. "Are you listening?" she said.

"Yes," Clay muttered against her skin. "Go on."

"This is the best part. I asked Reverend Eldridge for a copy of our marriage certificate, so he wrote one out and signed it and gave it to me. There is a blank space for your signature. I've already signed. If you sign, too, all the signatures will be genuine and it is no longer a forgery at all. Are you listening?"

Clay raised his head. His eyes were dark and burning, his expression hungry and intent. "Yes," he said. "I listened to every damn word you spoke. Are you finished now so I can kiss you properly?"

"Uh-huh," Annabel said.

Clay lowered his head and kissed her, long and hard. Annabel kissed him back, the deep, desperate kisses of lovers too long apart. And then, as the night fell around them, they did all the other things Dottie Timmerman—the dainty silver-haired wife of the ancient Doc Timmerman—had explained in scandalized detail it was possible for a pregnant woman to do with her husband in bed.

* * *

The wail of a newborn infant pierced the late-afternoon shadows in the upstairs corridor. Clay ceased his nervous pacing. The door to the bedroom flung open and the tall, fair-haired middle sister, Miranda, stuck her head through.

"You can come in now."

Clay hurried past her. Annabel lay in bed, propped up with pillows. Beads of perspiration glistened on her forehead. Her dark hair hung in limp strands. The room smelled of disinfectant, a scent Clay had learned to associate with disaster and death.

On the table by the wall, Doc Timmerman was finishing his ministrations to the baby. In the corner, the small, dark-haired Charlotte was stacking away blood-soaked towels. Clay turned his head away, not brave enough to ask about the blood, not brave enough to see the evidence of Annabel's suffering. He never wanted to feel such helplessness, such terror again. "Is she all right?" he asked the doctor.

"It's a he. You have a healthy son. Three weeks premature, but it should cause him no harm."

"I meant…" Clay took a deep breath. "I meant my wife."

Two months wasn't long enough for a man to get used to calling a woman his wife, not when she was about to became the mother of his child.

"Oh, her?" The doc glanced over to the bed and feigned indifference. "She is fine. It beats me how some of these small-boned women have such an easy time over it. They push out their babies like shooting bullets from a gun."

Like shooting bullets from a gun? Clay winced. It had sounded more like a prolonged artillery attack. He halted by the bedside. "Can I kiss you?"

"Yes," Annabel replied. "I am still alive and breathing. Barely."

Clay bent to her and pressed his lips to hers for a fleeting kiss. "I love you," he said, his lips moving against hers, a faint rustle of sound no one else could hear. Since the day he came to find Annabel in Gold Crossing he'd given her those words several times. He'd assumed practice would make them come more easily, but he'd been wrong. Every time he spoke them it felt as if he tore a hole in his chest, letting Annabel see right into his heart.

"I love you, too," Annabel whispered, keeping the exchange private between them.

The doc snapped the jaws of his medical bag shut. "I have a broken leg and a knife wound to attend to at Desperation Hill." He turned to address his words to Annabel. "I'll check on you tomorrow. If you're worried about anything, send for my wife. She knows as much about childbirth as I do."

With a soft thud of his boots, Doc Timmerman hurried out of the room. When he was gone, Miranda carried over to Clay the infant swathed in a square of white cotton and a small wool blanket. She held out the bundle. "Say hello to your son."

Clay touched the tip of his forefinger to the soft skin, then eased the baby into his arms and turned toward Annabel, intending to lower the child beside the mother on the bed.

"You hold him for a moment," Annabel said, watching him with wonder in her eyes. "I've done all the work up to now. From now on I expect you to do your share. And I like looking at you holding our baby."

Fascinated and a little frightened, but with a deep sense of happiness, Clay sat on the edge of the bed, his wife beside him, their child in his arms. In silence they waited while Miranda and Charlotte tiptoed out of the room, their pregnant bellies evident beneath their gowns.

Leaning forward, Annabel studied the wrinkled features of the infant and then directed a questioning glance at Clay. "Aaron Gareth Collier? Does that suit you?"

Clay nodded, too moved to speak. Adjusting his position on the edge of the bed, he held the infant out to Annabel. "Can you take him? I need to reach into my pocket for something."

When Clay had his hands free, he pulled a small velvet pouch from his pocket and shook the contents onto his palm. He lifted a necklace of gemstones set in gold in the air and dangled it in front of Annabel. The last rays of the setting sun through the window struck the necklace, making the stones glitter in deep emerald hues.

"Do you remember how I told you that my parents perished in a fire, and I was found holding a clay cup? And that later a necklace of green stones was found hidden in my clothing?"

Annabel nodded, her eyes riveted on the sparkling gemstones.

Amused by her fascination, Clay told her the rest. "The nuns took the necklace. They said it would be stolen if they let me keep it. They gave me a ticket with a code on it to send to them if I ever wanted the necklace returned to me. Two months ago, I mailed the ticket off to the convent, never expecting to hear back. But a week ago this arrived by express messenger."

He twisted his wrist to make the necklace ripple in the sunlight. Holding the baby snug beside her with one arm, Annabel touched the string of stones that glittered like a green waterfall. "Are they real emeralds?" she asked, awe in her tone.

"The very best," Clay replied. "The necklace used to belong to a princess."

"Oh, Clay! I was right. You're the long-lost son of some noble lady who ran off with a poor soldier or a—"

Clay shook his head to silence her. "Annabel, I told you not to make up foolish dreams. Sister Mary Magdalene also sent me this. She said she was curious, and when she had an opportunity to visit San Francisco on some convent business she arranged to study the newspaper archives."

He handed Annabel a clipping from the *San Francisco Chronicle*.

She ran her eyes over the short article, read out snatches of the text. *"'The Princess Sofia...priceless emeralds... stolen...actress masquerading as a ladies maid...'"*

"I told you my parents were low-class people. Drifters and thieves."

Annabel admired the necklace with a glint of feminine covetousness in her eyes. "If it is stolen, can we keep it?"

"Sister Mary Magdalene thinks we can. It was a long time ago. My parents suffered for their crime, and the princess who owned the necklace no longer lives." Clay paused. "But might be best not to wear it in public." He slipped the necklace back inside the velvet pouch and set it down on the bedside cabinet. "I hope you didn't dream you were marrying a prince."

Annabel met his gaze. "I wanted no nobleman. No great fortune. Only you. All I want is to work alongside with you. In partnership."

"In sickness and in heath." Clay's tone was solemn.

"For richer and poorer."

"Until death do us part."

They had never had the opportunity to say their wedding vows in front of the preacher. Now they spoke them to each other, in the untidy delivery room filled with the smells of carbolic and laundry soap and the aftermath of childbirth. And yet, they both knew that to them those promises meant as much as if they had been given in a cathedral in front of a bishop and a thousand witnesses.

"I love you," Clay said.

"I love you, too," Annabel replied.

Epilogue

At sunrise on the fourth of July in 1890 a lanky man in
a white shirt and black waistcoat walked down the street
in Gold Crossing. In one hand he carried a sanding block,
in the other a tin of white paint and a small paintbrush.

Later in the day he would wear a frock coat and a top
hat and the mayor's sash, but for his early-morning chore
he preferred less formal clothing. Every year he performed
the same task, but this was the first time it had brought
him pleasure.

He knelt by a wooden sign just outside the town and
used the sanding block to rub out the number *eight*. Deep
contentment filled him—as deep as was possible for a
lonely man whose young wife had died years ago, too soon
after their wedding to have given him a child.

A town could be almost like a child, the man mused as
he put down the sanding block and snapped the tin of paint
open. You gave birth to it, you nurtured and nourished
it, and you hoped it would grow up to enjoy a happy life.

The man dipped the brush into the pot, painted the number *two* on the board and then the number *nine*. He leaned
back on his heels to inspect the result. Around him, birds
sang their dawn chorus. The sun was climbing in the sky,

dissipating the night cool, but the gentle breeze kept the heat at bay, promising a perfect day.

Satisfied, Art Langley closed the paint pot and wiped the brush clean with a rag he had pulled out of his pocket. Then he straightened on his feet and walked away from the sign with the fresh paint that shone white in the sun.

Gold Crossing
Population 29

* * * * *

If you enjoyed this story you won't want to miss the other great reads in Tatiana March's
THE FAIRFAX BRIDES *trilogy*

HIS MAIL-ORDER BRIDE
THE BRIDE LOTTERY

Get 2 Free Books,

Plus 2 Free Gifts—

just for trying the Reader Service!

✦ HARLEQUIN®
Western Romance

Get 2 Free Books,
Plus 2 Free Gifts—
just for trying the Reader Service!

HARLEQUIN *Presents*

HP17R2

Get 2 Free Books,
Plus 2 Free Gifts—

just for trying the
Reader Service!